ESCAPE FROM
AURORA

ESCAPE FROM
AUR⊛RA

• • • •

JAMIE LITTLER

VIKING

VIKING

An imprint of Penguin Random House LLC, New York

First published in the United States of America by Viking,
an imprint of Penguin Random House LLC, 2020
Published simultaneously in the UK by Penguin Books Ltd.

Text and illustrations copyright © 2020 by Skrawl Limited

Viking & colophon are registered trademarks of Penguin Random House LLC.

Visit us online at penguinrandomhouse.com.

Library of Congress Cataloging-in-Publication Data is available.

Printed in the United States of America

ISBN 9780451481375

1 3 5 7 9 10 8 6 4 2

Design by Opal Roengchai
Text set in Bohemia LT Std

For Mum and Dad,
who helped me to hear the Song.

Prologue

The sleigh lay in ruins dead ahead.

A navigator's map was the only thing that moved, fluttering in the wind above the shattered deck. Splintered wood and shredded metal littered the desolate valley, and to Captain Norrow's well-trained eye there was no other sign of immediate danger. But he was still unconvinced. "Stay sharp, lads," he said to his crew, as if they needed any warning. Cautiously he steered the *Ice Runner* forward to look for any survivors.

It was a sorry sight indeed.

This carnage had clearly been the work of Leviathans—the terrible fang and claw marks that had torn through the sleigh's hull told Norrow as much. But there was a small chance survivors could've run to the steep hillsides that bordered the valley, away from the menace that lurked beneath the snows. If that was the case, they would need the *Ice Runner*'s help. Norrow prayed to the spirits that it was.

"Looks like it was the *Morning Star!*" his lookout called down from the crow's nest, studying the icon painted upon the wrecked sleigh's sail as it shivered helplessly in the breeze. Norrow cursed under his breath. He knew the *Morning Star.* They were a good crew.

Another Pathfinder sleigh lost.

Not for the first time, Norrow questioned his life as a Pathfinder. He'd always known the dangers and had accepted them gladly if it meant he could bring Aurora's aid to the outer Strongholds. But the world was changing, and Norrow wasn't sure it was a world he could survive in any longer. *I'm getting too old for this*, he thought with a bitter smile.

The *Ice Runner* drew alongside the ruin of the *Morning Star.* "Any survivors?" Norrow called out to his crew. The wind whispered through the valley, snow flurrying white against the slate-gray sky.

They were alone.

But Norrow couldn't shake the feeling that they were being watched. He knew his crew well enough to know that they felt it too; their movements were tense and alert. And Norrow's nerves weren't helped by the headache he'd had since they'd spotted the wreckage. It had started as a niggling buzz in the back of his skull, but it was growing into a distracting drone, slurring through his head. He put it down to stress. *I'm gonna retire after this run*, he thought. *Shoulda done it long ago.*

"Can't see anyone," the lookout called. "Not even—" His voice was cut short.

Norrow looked up just in time to see the man fall over the side of the crow's nest, a black arrow in his chest. Shadows began darting among the *Morning Star*'s wreckage. Skeletal figures with ghostly white faces and twisted horns, clad in tattered black rags, spears and bows in hand.

"WRAITHS!" he heard a crewman shout. "WE'RE UNDER ATTACK!"

And then, striding from the shadows like a specter, was a Wraith that reeked of pure menace. Its horns were larger and more gnarled than the others, its black eyes more pitiless and dead. Norrow's blood went cold.

The Great Horned One.

Everyone knew Wraiths were despicable demons that had crawled from the darkest depths of the underworld, but the Great Horned One was the worst of them. Their *leader*, if such evil could be led.

"ENJIN TO FULL POWER!" Norrow ordered as he pulled hard on the tiller, desperate to be away, his nerves fizzling with fear. But before the enjineer could react, a huge shape swooped down from above, all tail and fangs, and snatched the Pathfinder off the deck. The enjin stalled, and the *Ice Runner* was suddenly dead on the snow. Norrow watched in horror as grappling hooks snagged the sides of his sleigh, his men falling to poisoned arrows all around him.

He was a fool. They'd been lured into a trap. Norrow's aged mind was racing. But he knew he couldn't let his crew end up like that of the *Morning Star*—he had to get them out of there.

Scrambling down from the bridge, he rushed to the sunstone enjin to restore power to the sleigh. But as he reached the controls a shadow passed over him. Another dark shape in the sky, a winged thing hurtling toward him like some awful nightmare, its talons splayed.

"No . . ." Norrow whispered, his heart gripped by ice.

He had failed his crew. The creature let out a terrible scream as it closed in on him.

I should've retired long ago, Captain Norrow thought again for the very last time.

The Center of the World

The *Frostheart* tore across the snow plain, its ragged red sails swelling in the wind.

It was a large Pathfinder sleigh, but even so, it was dwarfed by the immense mountain that loomed before it.

Ash gripped on to the side rail, his black messy hair thrashing about in front of his eyes, which stared in wonder as they drew under the mountain's colossal shadow. Towers jutted out of the mountainside like a forest of ornate trees, warm light glowing from within. Ash could just make out a large domed spire sitting atop the mountain's summit, faint and shrouded, as though the clouds wanted to keep it a secret.

"It's incredible . . ."

The roof of Alderman Kindil's lodge had been the tallest thing he had ever seen before he left his old home a moon ago, but the entire Fira Stronghold would've only risen to the lowest stones of this gargantuan peak. Ash's excitement had grown each day they'd drawn closer to the mountain, and now he couldn't help but whoop and laugh.

"Pretty cool, eh . . . ?" Ash's best friend, Lunah, said from beside him, her constellation-embroidered cloak flowing behind her.

The *Frostheart* approached a second great wall that encircled the mountain, having passed through the first several leagues back. It stood as tall as a cliff, and was lined with watchtowers and windmills high above, whose turning vanes seemed to be waving at the sleigh, beckoning them through. "The walls go as far under the snow as they do above it," said Lunah, as proud as if she'd built it herself. "Keeps any snoopin' Leviathans out, y'see?"

Ash could see other Pathfinder sleighs in the distance, drifting toward different gateways in the wall's enormous circumference, leagues upon leagues in length. Ash wondered who crewed them, and the kind of adventures they were returning from. Whether they too had feared they'd never make it back at all, like the

Frostheart had. A warmth filled Ash's cold bones as he looked back at the crew who had taken him under their wing. He knew there was no other group in the whole Snow Sea he'd rather be with.

"CHECKPOINT AHOY!" the sleigh's lookout, Teya, called down.

"Signal flags!" ordered Captain Nuk from the bridge.

"Aye aye!" Kailen answered, releasing a line of colored flags at the sleigh's prow up into the air, alerting the guards atop the wall as to who was approaching. Her short flaxen hair swept in front of her scarred blind eye as she watched the gatekeepers pull on large wheels, the massive gateway creaking open to allow the *Frostheart* in. Passing through, Ash finally got his first view of the mountain's base, which was surrounded by bubbling pools that breathed steam into the cold air. To Ash's surprise he saw that large patches of green vegetation clung to the mountain's sides, with workers tending to them with tools he didn't recognize. "What—" Ash began.

"Farms," Lunah answered before he could finish.

"Farms?"

"*Farms.* This mountain used to be a mega-volcano, an' what with the heat still comin' from below, an' all the water channeled out here, s'one of the few places in the

Snow Sea you can grow things. Saves hunters havin' to go out for food all the time. Pretty clever stuff."

Ash had to agree.

He grinned as he saw his large yeti guardian, Tobu, approaching from the healing tent. Tobu had been wounded during the *Frostheart*'s daring escape from a Wraith attack a few weeks ago, and, after lots of rest (thanks only to the sleigh's old healer, Arla, begging the yeti not to train with his spear), Tobu had quickly recovered and was now almost standing up to his full, imposing height.

"Food grown right on your doorstep, Tobu!" Ash said to him as he came to stand beside them. "Imagine not having to worry about hunting!"

Tobu grunted, which was about as impressed as Tobu was ever likely to sound.

"Trust me: you ent seen nothin' yet, fire-boy . . ." Lunah said, clearly enjoying being Ash's unofficial guide.

The enormous gateway that allowed entrance into the mountain—and the Stronghold of Aurora itself—drew close. Ash could make out intricate designs on the mighty wooden doors, carvings that appeared to tell the history of the Pathfinders. He didn't have long to take them in, however; ice rained down on the *Frostheart*'s deck as it passed through the gateway and into the mountain itself. Yallah, the sleigh's enjineer, cut the power to the sunstone enjin, and the *Frostheart* drifted to a stop inside a deep cavern just large enough for the vessel to sit in.

Doors thudded shut behind them, plunging the cavern into darkness.

After the blinding white of the snow outside, it took a few beats of Ash's thrumming heart for him to become accustomed to the gloom. He craned his neck to look up at the cavern's ceiling, and was surprised to make out a light at the top, illuminating what looked like large hollowed-out tree trunks protruding from the walls. Was it the way in? In which case, how on earth were they meant to get up there? The rest of the crew didn't seem concerned, though. Teya climbed down from the crow's nest to help Kob, Twinge, and Kailen lower the sails.

"So . . . how're we going to get up there?" Ash asked.

"We're gonna take the sleigh for a little swim . . ." Lunah grinned in reply, just as Ash heard a rushing sound from above. Water gushed out of the tree trunks and thundered down into the cavern like waterfalls. "Here we go . . . !" Lunah whooped. To Ash's amazement the cavern began to fill with water and the *Frostheart* rose with it. Up, up, up it went.

Lunah giggled, spreading her arms wide and running about as though she were flying. Unable to contain himself, Ash joined her, laughing with joy as they leaped and danced through the mist the torrents created around the sleigh.

"You kids gonna do some work around here or

what?" Kailen called over, holding out a line of rigging for them to take, an eyebrow raised.

Captain Nuk chuckled. "Oh, leave the tykes alone, Kailen. Even you must remember the thrill you felt when you first rode Aurora's aqualifts!"

Kailen didn't answer, but Ash noticed she allowed herself a little smile.

"Now, crew," Nuk declared. "As always, Master Podd and I would like to thank you all for your valiant service aboard the *Frostheart* and your continued bravery toward the Pathfinder cause."

"Indeed," confirmed Master Podd in his deep voice. The small vulpis stood at Nuk's side, his arms behind his back and head held high.

"We did it, my dearest fellows. We made it back home!"

The crew cheered, and as they did the sleigh rose above the aqualift's rim. Light washed over the deck as the true grandeur of Aurora came into view.

Ash's jaw dropped.

Never mind the cave they'd just left—the whole *mountain* was hollow, and filling the immense space was the largest, most *awesome* Stronghold Ash could ever have dreamed of. A mighty tiered city rose up all the way to the top of the dizzying heights of the dormant volcano, lava thankfully nowhere to be seen. The stone buildings, palaces, and spires were bigger than Ash could ever have imagined, each one intricately decorated with carvings, tiles, and moss-covered pillars. Dazzling curtains of light poured down from large openings in the mountain wall, illuminating the dense crowds that roamed the lofty streets. Bridges and aqueducts crisscrossed the vast space, canoes and sleighs traversing canals that weaved their way about the city, which also seemed to power huge waterwheels and other strange wooden machinery.

Compared to the Fira, the other Strongholds Ash had seen over the last few weeks had been impressive, each one mightier than the last. But this was different. They all paled in comparison.

This was so vast Ash's eyes could barely comprehend what they were seeing.

This was awe-inspiring.

This was *beautiful*.

"Might wanna pick your jaw off the floor, there, Ash," Lunah said, nudging him in the side. "They have a strict *no-drool* policy here, y'know."

Ash barely even heard her. He gasped. "We've made it, I can't believe we've made it . . ."

After all the stories he'd heard from traveling Pathfinders—from the Fira themselves. After traveling halfway across the Snow Sea with only a lullaby as a guide. After battling Wraiths and Leviathans . . . after nearly losing everything he'd come to hold dear. After all that, he'd finally arrived. He knew that the lullaby his parents had left him had been leading him here, that the next clue was hidden somewhere in the Stronghold's depths . . . but what if his parents were here themselves? Ash's belly leaped at the thought. He might finally find them, be able to speak to them, to touch them, to at last be pulled into the safety of their arms.

Ash knew one thing for sure. Whatever he discovered here, he knew it would be big.

For at last he was in Aurora: the center of the world.

2
Where to Start?

The *Frostheart* sailed lazily down a large canal that circled the entire base of the monumental city. Hundreds of wooden jetties jutted from docks and Pathfinder sleighs of all shapes and sizes were moored at them, bobbing up and down on the small waves that rose in the *Frostheart's* wake.

"Strange . . ." Kob said. "Looks like the entire Pathfinder fleet is docked here."

"Never known that to be a good thing," Arla mumbled, looking out at the forest of masts with her old eyes. Ash wondered if one of them might be the *Trailblazer*, the sleigh his mother had captained. His nerves fizzled at the idea.

Eventually the *Frostheart* managed to find a space to dock, and the crew threw down thick ropes for the swarming dockhands to tether the sleigh with. Ash wobbled after the others down the gangplank, discovering that his legs were rather unsteady upon solid ground after weeks speeding across the Snow Sea. The inside of the mountain was surprisingly warm, the air thick and humid and a far cry from the frigid temperatures outside. Sweat beaded down Ash's back.

"Welcome back, *Frostheart!*" One of the dockhands, who wore simple scruffy clothing, greeted the crew with a smile. "We were beginning to worry we'd seen the last of you . . ."

"You aren't going to be rid of us that easy!" Captain Nuk laughed. "Though it was a bit touch-and-go out there, I cannot lie."

"Had a rough run, eh?" the dockhand asked,

eyeing the damaged *Frostheart*, which was barely holding itself together.

Nuk sighed. "You don't know the half of it . . ." she said just as the mainmast's crossbeam came crashing down onto the deck.

"Unfortunately, I do." The dockhand winced. "Somethin' has the 'viathans actin' up; they're getting more an' more aggressive. All too familiar a sight, sleighs coming back like this, if at all. And each time the crews return a bit smaller." The crew cast their eyes down as one, sparing a thought for their own fallen comrade Yorri. "Anyway, glad to have you back," the dockhand said hurriedly, sensing he'd touched a nerve. "I'll see to it the *Frostheart* gets the repairs it needs; it'll be good as new soon enough."

"You have our thanks," Nuk said. "I couldn't help but notice the number of sleighs that are docked. Is there something we've missed?"

"Matter of fact, there is! You've been gone so long; word must've missed you. All sleighs have been grounded. The Wurmslayer has declared a Council Moot, an' all Pathfinder captains must attend, you included, course."

"*Wurmslayer?*" Nuk laughed. "Is that what Captain Stormbreaker calls herself these days?"

Wurmslayer. Stormbreaker. Ash thought this sounded like a captain you did not want to mess with.

"Not at all," sniffed the dockhand. "She's far too modest, as well you know. It's what the people have taken to callin' her, an' from the number of Leviathans she an' her crew 'ave slain, I'd say she's more'n earned the title."

Nuk's brow furrowed at this. "That I cannot deny. Her sleigh has more bolt-throwers than cargo."

The dockhand frowned back. "The people love her here, Captain Nuk. They see her as a hero, and you'd do well not to rock the boat."

"I wouldn't dream of it." Nuk grinned, her tusks gleaming.

The dockhand didn't look convinced but nodded and, with a wave, left.

"Right, dear fellows," Nuk said, addressing her crew, "I need to go and make my reports to the Council. But I believe a little celebration is in order tonight, don't you?" The crew cheered their approval. "Until then, you're all on leave. Rest up and have a break. Valkyries know you deserve it." The crew sighed with relief as their captain headed off into the city, Master Podd following close behind.

Clearly it was good to be back.

"Thiiiink I'm gonna hit a proper bed and not get up till our next run," Teya said, groaning.

"Not me!" Lunah said, standing on tiptoes and stretching her arms high. "Been stuck in a cramped space for *way* too long, thanks. Wanna get your explore on, Ash?"

Ash nodded eagerly. He felt as though every second not spent investigating the great city would be a second wasted—and a second he could be spending with his parents, once he found them. Who could rest at a time like this?

Ash beamed. "Where do we even *start*? There's so much to see!"

"Luckily fer you, you got yourself the perfect guide . . ." Lunah raised two thumbs and pointed them at herself. "And I ent forgotten you got a meetin' with the wayfinder to get to either."

Ash's heart skipped a beat as he thought about the new lullaby verse he and Lunah had recently solved:

Where spirits dance behind walls so great,
the wayfinder's song will reveal your fate.

It seemed the wayfinder—whoever they were—

would hold the next clue in the breadcrumb trail that was leading him to his parents. And although Ash hoped they might be in Aurora, he suspected his parents had been forced to hide somewhere much more secret—the hidden Song Weaver Stronghold of Solstice. But either way, the lullaby was suggesting that the end was in sight—it *had* to be, after all he'd gone through.

Ash had once wondered why his father had left such an elaborate trail for him to follow, but his terrible experiences with a traveler known as Shaard had proven there was good reason for Ferno's caution. Ferno was a native of Solstice, and Shaard had been hunting for any sign of him, hoping to find the hidden Stronghold for himself. Ash wasn't sure what Shaard wanted there, but he did know he was a vicious, hateful man, and that it was in the best interests of everyone if Shaard never found his way there. Ash had escaped Shaard once, and wasn't planning on crossing paths with him ever again.

Ash turned his mind back to the latest clue. Who *was* the wayfinder? Were they a Song Weaver? Lunah seemed to have an idea, but she was enjoying keeping Ash in suspense too much to tell him.

Then Kailen's angry voice snatched Ash from his thoughts. "D'ya think you could make any *more* mess?"

Lunah and Ash exchanged a glance, and went to investigate. There on the *Frostheart*'s deck stood Kailen, gesturing furiously at Rook, who was barely visible amid the shadows of an awning in the corner of the main deck. It looked like she was rummaging through the belongings Shaard had left behind—ancient relics, elder texts, and strange machines—discarding the bits that didn't interest her over her shoulder. It seemed that the *Frostheart* wasn't complete without a dark, mysterious stranger residing in that corner.

Kailen went on. "It's bad enough havin' your stupid crows molt feathers all over the place, now we need to be trippin' over that traitor's junk too?" The crow that

perched upon Rook's shoulder cawed as Rook hissed in response. Kailen flinched. *"Urgh!"*

The crew were still wary of the strange Song Weaver who had so recently joined them, which was not helped by the fact that Rook could only communicate in a harsh broken Song only Ash understood.

And "understood" was being generous.

Rook was the only other Song Weaver Ash had ever met, besides Shaard (who had not exactly been a great Song Weaver ambassador), and he'd been over the moon to discover that she had once known his missing father. He'd hoped to have at least some of his many questions answered, like how they'd come to know each other, what Ferno had been like, and why he'd needed to leave Ash behind. But it was as difficult to get answers from Rook as it was to get a laugh from Tobu. The main problem was that Ash could barely make sense of what she Sang. Something seemed to have happened to her in the past, something bad, and it had affected her Song. So, after all was said and done, Ash still knew nothing about Rook. Spirits, he didn't even know what she *looked* like under that deep hood of hers!

None of this had stopped Lunah from trying to get to the bottom of Rook's mysteries, however.

"So, where d'ya come from?" she'd ask any opportunity she got. "Who are you, who's the *real* Rook behind the hood?" Rook never gave an answer. "Come ooooon, I wanna get to know our newest crew member! D'ya have, like, no face under there? Or maybe two?"

"*SILENCE, PEST*," Rook had once hissed, irritated at the constant grilling.

"Oooh, what'd she say?" Lunah had eagerly asked Ash, thinking she'd finally received an answer.

"She, er, she said it's a secret . . ."

"I see." Lunah had paused. "*Three* faces then? OW!" Lunah had then cried out as the crow on Rook's shoulder nipped her ear.

"Would you like to come exploring with us, Rook?" Ash asked her now. It might be an opportunity to get to know her better, and also prevent Kailen from throwing her overboard . . .

"*NO. Searching.*" Rook paused in her rummaging only to point accusingly at Ash. "*Protect. HEART.*" Ash instinctively reached for the archeomek device that hung from his belt. As always it was cold to the touch, but comforting all the same. The frost-heart encased within it was supposedly the heart of some long-dead Leviathan, passed down through generations before finding a home as the *Frostheart*'s lucky charm and namesake. Captain Nuk had gifted it to Ash as thanks for saving their lives a few weeks past at the Isolai Stronghold, and after Shaard had tried his very best to steal it for his mysterious plans.

"Besides," Nuk had explained, "I've often found that when an ancient stone starts chatting away and making friends with someone else, the time has come to let it go . . ."

All Ash knew was that the lullaby had told him to protect it at all costs. And, whatever Rook's story was, she seemed to agree—and to be almost obsessed with the frost-heart, though Ash was still struggling to discover *why*. To be fair, Shaard had seemed as fixated with it as Rook, so there must be *something* special about it. As if it could hear his thoughts, the frost-heart gave a gentle chime of Song, immediately soothing his troubled mind as it so often did nowadays.

"Oh, o-okay. Well, let us know if you change your mind," Ash said to Rook, but she was already delving back into Shaard's things.

"*Welp*, that was as strange as ever," Lunah said. "You ready, Ash?"

"I've been ready all my life." He grinned, impressed with how cool he'd managed to sound. He looked around for Tobu, and was surprised to see him standing alone on a barrel at the opposite side of the deck, eyes lost in thought.

"You ready, Tobu?" Ash asked as he got close.

Tobu snapped out of his contemplations and gave the children his usual hard look.

"This place is unlike anywhere we have ever been, boy. Danger could lie in wait in every shadow, round every corner. We must be vigilant. Survey our surroundings and the people. Make certain this is a safe place to continue your Song Weaver training."

"Relax, furball!" Lunah laughed. "You're both gonna love it here!"

Tobu grunted, unconvinced. "I insist we keep a low profile, and do not attract attention to ourselves."

"Yeeeeah . . . that's gonna prove kinda difficult with you guys, no offense."

"What do you mean?" Tobu growled.

"Look, *we* all know that yer nothin' but sunshine 'n' smiles, but Aurora doesn't. It's not normal to see yeti wanderin' about the place, 'n' it can make people . . . well . . . *skittish*."

"*Skittish?*" Tobu said, baring his massive fangs.

"Yer not exactly hard to spot in a crowd, is what I'm sayin'. Nor's a kid from the Fira, a Stronghold so far away most people doubt it even exists! But not to worry— I have the perfect disguises . . ."

"*Disguises?*" Ash and Tobu said together.

"I got ya both covered," Lunah said, a grin on her face and a glint in her eye.

3

On the Trail

Aurora had certainly already made an impression on Ash, but not much could've prepared him for the people.

There were just *so many of them.*

As the crew navigated the steep stone lanes that led from the docks into Aurora proper, Ash struggled against the bustling masses as though he were fighting the current of a raging river. The entire Fira Stronghold consisted of a few hundred people, but there must've been *thousands* of Aurorans just on these lowest levels alone!

How does anyone get anywhere? How does anyone think, with so many voices talking at once?

Ash spotted people from all over the known map, but you could tell the Aurorans from a mile off. Unlike other Stronghold dwellers, who mostly lived in skins and furs, they dressed in flamboyant embroidered cloth, and stood in stark contrast to the rough-looking Pathfinders and travelers who strode among them. They were also covered head to toe in as many jewels, accessories, and attractive knickknacks as would fit on their person. Then, standing apart from all others, were the imposing armored Stronghold Guard who stood watch among the crowds. Their dark eyes were ever watchful from beneath fur-lined helmets, their gloved hands gripping tall decorative spears that looked every bit as capable of piercing flesh as Tobu's basic flint one.

Ash followed Lunah and the others as they pushed through the dense press but sensed that he would be better off walking behind Tobu, for whom the crowds were parting like water round a boulder.

"Stars above, Tobu, you look *proper* charmin'," Lunah said, looking back over her shoulder.

"I shame myself, dressed like this."

"Rubbish. You look graceful an' enchantin', an' there's no shame in that, ent that right, Ash?"

"Yeah . . . you look great, Tobu," Ash lied.

Lunah had disguised Tobu all right, but as what was anyone's guess.

She'd used one of Twinge's spare bobble hats to cover Tobu's horns, and had tied a pelt of fur round his chin so that it looked like he had a wild, tumultuous beard.

That, or like a strange creature had taken up residence under his nose. She'd then wrapped bundles and bundles of cloth and rope round his body to hide his yeti appearance—but the effect was more like a giant who had got tangled up in a sleigh's main sail. Tobu was threatening to burst out of every seam. He looked utterly, positively ridiculous.

Ash had required a lot less of Lunah's creativity to disguise, and wore an old fur Pathfinder outfit that wouldn't stand out as much as his Fira clothes. But she'd still drawn a curly mustache on his face with dye just to be sure.

"Hi!" Ash said to a passerby who had been giving Ash and Tobu a very strange look, trying his best to sound confident. The person looked horrified and pushed past without a word.

"See?" Lunah said in triumph. "No one suspects a thing."

"Maybe. But you can't just *talk* to people here, boy," Kailen said. "City folk're *busy*." Ash went red. He still had so much to learn.

"I am not comfortable with this," growled Tobu, and his heavy brows narrowed over his small eyes, the only part of him still visible under his layers.

A lady gasped, and moved her children out of Tobu's path.

"At least this way you get to come with us!" Ash said. "I mean, would you want to miss seeing a place like this?"

The sights and sounds of Aurora tumbled over Ash like an avalanche. He felt like he'd stepped into an old Fira legend, with all its impossible magic and color brought to life before his very eyes. There was a *density* to the place—something to look at in every nook and cranny. Winding streets and stairways snaked in between clustered stone buildings. Robed figures with painted faces prayed and left offerings at shrines to spirits and gods unknown to Ash. Intricately carved wooden posts held porch covers aloft above doorways painted in bright vivid hues. Pots, pans, bells, and charms dangled from shuttered windows and rooftop beams. Ash wanted to look round every corner to see what other wonders he might see, but he was also scared he might do something wrong, something to offend these fast-paced, no-nonsense people. The locals went about their daily tasks, cooking, cleaning, working, but it was all a spectacle to Ash. The only thing that reminded him even slightly of his old home were the lanterns hanging from cords that stretched from rooftop to rooftop. A surprising, slight pang of homesickness niggled at him, adding to his mounting feeling of being rather tiny and insignificant. He was used to the Fira way of things, where they survived by the skin of their teeth and made what they needed with what little they had. Aurora, in comparison, was overflowing with culture and art, and everything seemed to have been made with beauty in mind.

"You all right there, fire-boy?" Lunah asked, as if reading his thoughts.

"Y-yes," he responded. "The stories I heard always said how massive and amazing Aurora was, but I just never imagined . . . I never thought it could be . . . so . . . well, *massive*! And amazing! It feels like giants should live here, not people . . ."

"An' this is only a *teensy* bit of the whole thing. You just wait till we get higher!"

"It is certainly . . . *big*," Tobu grunted, ruffling his fake beard. Ash rolled his eyes, and not for the first time pondered if Tobu had any space left for awe and astonishment among all his cantankerous scowls and grouchy frowns.

After much walking (and gawking from Ash), the crew passed a large hall that was absolutely overflowing with rowdy Pathfinders, most drinking deeply from cups or eating hearty-looking meals that made Ash's mouth water. *The Pathfinder's Rest*, Ash read from the salvaged prow of a sleigh that acted as the hall's sign.

"Here's where I leave you all till tonight," Kob announced.

"And me!" Arla was quick to add, her wrinkled face smiling with glee. "I'm going to eat my body weight in *real* food! If I have to eat another ration, I swear I'll scream!"

"Oh, I'll join you!" Twinge said. "I have so many tales to tell the others!"

"Oh. I . . . er . . . I just remembered that I . . . um, that I have someone to meet in the Guzzling Gargant . . ." Kob said, pointing to a drinks-hall across the square, as Arla swiftly nodded in agreement. Everyone knew how long and agonizingly pointless Twinge's stories could be once he got going.

"Oh, even better!" Twinge smiled. "The Gargant loves a good story even more than the Rest!" Sighing with resignation, Kob and Arla left the group, Twinge close behind, already listing the tales he intended to tell. "Wait until they hear about that rock I saw that looked like a stone! Or what about that time I stirred the cooking pot?"

"Poor fools," Kailen said, shaking her head in sympathy.

"Kailen and I are heading to the Stronghold Keeps, up top," Yallah said to Tobu. "You'll look after the children?"

"Of course."

"Keep yer noses clean," Kailen said.

"Always," Lunah said, hawking up a load of snot. Ash cuffed at his nose, just to be sure, realizing too late that he'd only succeeded in wiping away his fake mustache.

As they spoke, Ash carefully eyed the crews gathered at the Pathfinder's Rest.

My parents must've come here—they were Pathfinders, after all, Ash thought, reaching out to touch the corner of the building. *Maybe they even touched this wall too?* There was warm reassurance in the thought that he was probably following in their footsteps. *Mum . . . Dad . . . I'll catch up with you soon . . .*

Lunah led the rest of the shrinking crew into a market space alive with merchants and traders and patrons perusing the strange and wonderful wares on display. Smells of alluring spices and incense invited the crew into the noisy crowd, and a jolly-looking mursu merchant with a golden tusk waved a pendant in Ash's face. "Come gaze in wonder, my friend, at this ancient relic said to come from the scarred lands of the Rend itself! Is it cursed? Are you brave enough to find out? And are you brave enough to risk missing out on this great, great deal?!"

"He ent gonna fall for that, get outta his face!" Lunah said to the merchant, pushing Ash past, who hoped she hadn't noticed how eagerly he'd reached for the pendant.

Ash spotted a Pathfinder captain bartering with a trader whose face was hidden by folds of scarves, and who stood a head higher than the crowd thanks to the stilts that were attached to their legs.

"He's from the Tekko Stronghold, out in the salt lakes 'n' marshes of the Dancing Waters," Lunah explained. "An' those guys there?" she said, pointing at a group riding great shaggy beasts (and the disgruntled shoppers trying their best not to tread in the droppings that marked their path). "They're Oso beast-tamers."

"They ride *bovores*?" Tobu asked, surprised.

"An' more besides. They ride across the Snow Sea on anythin' they can train, no sleighs in sight at Oso, 's a point of pride. Not many of 'em left, though, on account of how much quicker the Leviathans are than some lumberin' beast."

Ash watched them stomp past in awe, the animals bellowing as a pack of chittering vulpis flocked under their furry legs, carrying large sacks of archeomek slung over their shoulders.

The world is bigger than I ever thought possible, Ash mused in wonder. *There's so many Strongholds I've still not even heard of, let alone seen.*

He smiled as he watched Lunah wade confidently through the crowd, not for the first time thinking how lucky he was to have found her, and how hopelessly lost he'd be without her to guide him.

"So where is this wayfinder person?" Ash asked Lunah as they crossed a canal bridge out of the market.

"Patience, young Ash. We're nearly there," she said, a big grin plastered across her face. She then walked them into a relatively quiet square that felt like a breath of fresh air after the clogged lanes and marketplace.

"It seems a huge risk for your father to have taken, to hope you will find his contact in a Stronghold as busy as this . . ." Tobu remarked.

Ash had learned that sometimes, secrets become too big to keep.

He'd originally only shared the lullaby, and the fact that he saw stars light up in the night sky every time he Sang it, with Lunah. He'd been afraid of what the crew members might've thought of him, and whether he'd be putting himself and Solstice in danger by revealing it. But when Shaard had shown his true colors, Ash had known exactly who he had to keep it a secret from— and who not to. And so he'd confided in Tobu and the rest of the *Frostheart*'s crew. The crew hadn't known what to make of it. Some laughed, some questioned it, but most just left Ash to it, happy not to really under- stand the strange powers of Song Weavers. Ash had been most worried about what Tobu would think, however. It wouldn't be an exaggeration to say that Tobu could be, on occasion, a bit . . . *difficult*. He'd known Ash had climbed aboard the *Frostheart* to find his parents, but he'd had no clue Ash had secretly been following a lullaby toward them and the hidden Stronghold of Solstice.

"You . . . know where your parents are?" Tobu had responded, his darting pupils the only sign that betrayed his clearly racing mind.

"I think so. And I'm getting close now, I hope . . ."

Tobu had seemed at a loss for words. "So the World Weave . . . was guiding you all along . . ."

"I . . . I guess?" Ash still didn't really get the "World Weave." It was a mystical yeti thing; supposedly, the world's Song that connected everything and everyone— and it mattered a lot to Tobu. In fact, he had become entirely preoccupied with this revelation about the lullaby, and Ash couldn't understand why.

But now they were mere steps away from finding out more. "Lunah seems positive she knows who the way finder is," Ash assured Tobu as they walked across the square. "And my dad won't let us down; he hasn't before . . ."

Lunah led them toward a statue of a woman standing proudly in the center of the square. She'd been captured in a heroic pose, her hair billowing in the nonexistent wind, a seeing-glass held to her eye as she gazed grimly out onto the horizon. In her other hand she held a scroll, and she was flanked by two Lurkers who were made to look minuscule in comparison. Lunah stopped in front of the statue and spun round, her hands on her hips.

"Ash. Tobu. It is with great pleasure that I introduce you to . . . the *Wayfinder.*"

4

The Wayfinder

"*This* is the Wayfinder?"

"*This* happens to be the very first Pathfinder there ever was!" Lunah explained, looking up at the imposing statue with genuine reverence. "She was a Drifter, *naturally*, an' I woulda brought you here to pay your respects, lullaby or not! She started it all. Hundreds an' hundreds of years ago, she knew that the Strongholds' survival depended on stickin' together, which gets pretty hard when yer separated by countless leagues of monster-infested snow. So, she had the bright idea of workin' with the vulpis to stick a sunstone enjin on a snow-farin' vessel and BAM! The first Pathfinder sleigh was born. Pathfinders 'ave been doin' her good work ever since."

"A thoughtful, peaceful human," Tobu said. "How rare."

"I mean, she's very impressive," Ash admitted, "but what does she have to do with finding my parents?" His voice was tinged with disappointment. He'd been hoping the Wayfinder was a real person, or at least one that was still *living*. One that could give him some answers.

"No idea, mate." Lunah shrugged. "Guess we gotta figure that bit out. Sorry."

"Are you sure you understood the riddle?" Tobu asked Ash.

"The wayfinder's song will reveal your fate." Ash repeated the line from the lullaby. "Does the statue . . . erm, *talk*, by any chance?"

Lunah gave him a look. "No, the statue does not talk, Ash."

"R-right. No. Well, maybe if we have a look around, something'll jump out at us?" The trio circled the statue, searching for anything out of the ordinary that might offer a clue. Lunah knocked on it a few times with her hand. Ash took a closer look at what had been sculpted hanging from her belt. Pouches. A coil of rope. A sheathed dagger. A sunstone. It was all standard Pathfinder stuff, except for one item that caught Ash's attention. It was a cylindrical tube, decorative toppers on either end, with small depressions running along its length etched with runes from the World Before.

"What's this?" Ash asked Lunah. "Some kind of archeomek?"

"No one really knows, truth be told. None of the beardy scholars can agree on what it is. Some say it represents the Wayfinder's bond to the World Before, an' the sleigh enjins she an' the vulpis found. Others think it's a magic wand that could clear the paths of any Leviathans in her way . . ."

Ash drew closer to the object. Reaching out, he pressed one of the rune-etched depressions. To his surprise it clicked under his touch. He pulled his finger away, ready for something to happen, but nothing did.

"Buttons . . . ?" he whispered. "What do *you* think it is, Lunah?"

"Me? It's pretty obvious, ent it?"

"It is?" Tobu asked.

Ash was glad he wasn't the only one who hadn't guessed.

"It's a fancy water bottle, obviously!"

"Is it?" Ash said.

"Yeah! Course the Wayfinder would have a cooler bottle than the rest of us; she's the blimmin' Wayfinder!

Those clicky buttons are, like, comfortable finger-groove thingies so the bottle fit the shape of her hand." She looked from Ash's skeptical face to Tobu's, and back again. "C'mon, it's not sleigh enjineering, guys!"

"Maybe . . ." Ash said, keen to move the conversation on. "I was wondering . . . maybe I should Sing to the statue? The lullaby clue talks about the Wayfinder's song, after all . . ."

Tobu frowned, looking about at the people in the square. "Careful, boy. Remember how people react to Song Weavers. We do not want a repeat of Skybridge . . ."

"But we're in Aurora now! I'm sure they're more understanding in an awesome Stronghold like this." He looked to Lunah for support, but for once she seemed to have nothing to say, and shifted uncomfortably. Tobu gave a low grumble of worry but nodded for Ash to give it a go.

Ash was sure he was safe, but he still shielded his mouth with his hands as a precaution. Then, no louder than a whisper, he Sang to the statue—specifically to the strange object at its belt. He'd be a mursu's uncle if that thing was a water bottle—it was important, he just knew it. He Sang his lullaby, of course. It had gotten him this far, and if his father had left a clue at this statue, the lullaby would lead him to it. The familiar Song flowed

through him, warming his insides, the hairs on the back of his neck standing up as the frost-heart chimed happily at his side, encouraging him on. Ash stepped back to see if the lullaby had affected the statue.

As far as Ash could see, it had not.

"Nothing . . ." Disappointment darkened his mood. Whatever secrets the Wayfinder guarded, she was keeping them for now.

"Feelin' pretty quiet today, ent ya?" Lunah said to the Wayfinder.

Ash had also become painfully aware of the looks people in the square were giving them, prodding and poking the cherished statue as they were.

"Well, I bet you'll've figured it out by the time I'm back," Lunah said.

"Wait, you're *going*?" Ash asked.

"Jus' borin' Drifter business I need to take care of, up at the Drifter Keep. Gotta fill 'em in about where I've been on my Proving an' all that stuff."

"You don't want us to come with you?"

"*No!*" she said a bit too quickly. "No, no. Don't worry, I'll come back fer you both!"

"Okay . . ."

"Be safe," Tobu added.

"Yeah, yeah." Lunah waved her hand dismissively. "Keep at the riddle, guys. You'll find the answer!"

Ash nodded. "I'm sure you're right."

"There is no answer to this riddle; it's literally, absolutely *unsolvable*!" Ash cried, throwing his arms up in exasperation.

"The puzzle is perplexing indeed," Tobu confirmed.

They'd spent the last few hours investigating the statue further and were no closer to discovering why Ash had been led to it.

"Nothing's ever easy, is it?" A twinge of frustration bloomed deep within Ash, small and biting.

Tobu gave him a sidelong glance.

"Patience, boy. It is better to take one's time and do something right than to rush headlong into careless mistakes."

If there were a surefire way *not* to help Ash calm down, it was by telling him to calm down.

As if I haven't spent long enough on these riddles!

"Nothing worthwhile is ever easy. Especially if . . ." Tobu began, then apparently reconsidered.

"If . . . ?" Ash pushed.

Tobu breathed deeply. "If you truly think chasing after a mythical Stronghold is worthwhile?" He did not look at Ash as he spoke. "Aurora could be a safe home for you. Nowhere is better protected."

"I—I can't stay here!" Ash said, as if it were obvious, which it was. "My parents are out there, Tobu, and they're waiting for me!" Why would Tobu even *suggest* staying put?

"I could train you here, grow your strength and skill until you were older, and truly ready . . ."

"No. I *can't wait*." There was the faintest hint of sorrow in Tobu's intense eyes, a reluctance to agree. But he relented, and with a deep sigh gave a nod. Ash supposed Tobu was right: finding Solstice *would* be hard. He wasn't about to admit it, though.

He forgot his frustration for a moment as something

caught his eye. A short distance away a cloaked figure crouched at the edge of the square, hidden by shadow. Such a sight would've normally passed by unseen, but there was something in the figure's tense movements, as if they had something to hide, that attracted Ash's gaze. The figure was placing a loose brick into what had been a hole in a wall. It fit snug and secure. The figure then looked about the square, eyes barely visible from beneath the shadow of a hood. A jolt ran down Ash's spine as the figure made eye contact with him, holding his gaze for just a second, before disappearing down an alley with a sweep of their cloak.

"*Odd . . .*" Ash started to say, before another commotion at the far end of the square snatched his attention. A large group of people had marched in, chanting and shouting with heated voices.

"NO MORE COWERING BEHIND OUR WALLS!" the leader of the group yelled, the others echoing him. "NO MORE STRUGGLING FOR SURVIVAL!" All eyes in the square were on the protesters. "IT'S TIME TO TAKE UP ARMS AND FIGHT! AURORA SUPPORTS CAPTAIN STORMBREAKER!"

"STORMBREAKER! STORMBREAKER! STORM- BREAKER!" the group chanted, bystanders in the square joining their voices and cheers to the clamor.

"This captain seems to be stirring up quite a fuss . . ." Ash said to Tobu. "I wonder who she is?" Three guards advanced toward the hubbub, looking at first as though they were going to try to restore the peace, but to Ash's surprise they joined in with the chant, throwing their spears up with every shout.

"STORMBREAKER! STORMBREAKER!"

"Trouble," Tobu growled, his brow knitted with a frown.

The march grew in size, the people supporting

Stormbreaker far outvoicing the few that tried to shout a different opinion.

"Perhaps Aurora is not as safe as I'd hoped." Tobu rose to his full towering height. "Up, boy. It is time to collect Lunah. The riddle can wait."

As the angry roar of the crowd grew ever more intense, Ash found himself happy to agree.

5

Race to the End

They'd had to ask for directions five times (they'd actually asked many more times than that, but most people had taken one look at Tobu and rushed by as though they hadn't heard), but Ash and Tobu had finally made it to the Stronghold Keeps at the upper levels of Aurora. After ascending more steps than Ash had ever climbed in his life, a large circular plaza opened up before them, numerous decorated stone buildings, or keeps, lining its circumference. Each keep represented a major Stronghold under the protection of Aurora's Embrace and were decorated in the styles of the people they symbolized. Some were loud and striking, belching out smoke or strange smells, while others were small, subtle, and easy to miss. The large shells of some animal unknown to Ash adorned the entrance to one of them—the same type of shell Kob wore as armor, Ash realized. Another keep had long flowing banners hanging from its veranda, its tree-like patterns reminding Ash of the designs on Kailen's clothing. Gigantic rune-etched bones of a sea creature festooned the gateway to its neighbor.

"The Rus clan, from where Captain Nuk hails," Tobu said, following Ash's eyes.

Ash found it fascinating. This was probably as close to some of these Strongholds as he would ever get.

I wonder if Mum and Dad ever wanted to set up a Fira Keep here. Maybe we could start one in Solstice!

It was quiet in the plaza, a place reserved for outer-Stronghold business. The only people gathered were small groups of Pathfinders sharing news and the odd figure darting about on official business.

"The Drifter Keep," Tobu said, pointing to a building whose walls were decorated with paintings of constellations. Ash and Tobu entered the building, star-shaped charms tinkling above their heads as they passed through the doorway.

It was dark inside, with only a few flickering lanterns lighting the interior. The walls were lined with racks of rolled-up scrolls and navigational tools, their long shadows dancing in the dim light, and the ceiling had been painted to look like the night sky. The few Drifters within were dressed much like Lunah: cloaks draped over one shoulder with beautiful constellations sewn into the fabric, their hair half shaved and adorned with star trinkets.

Ash passed a group of children not much older than himself who were busy chatting away, and approached a smiling middle-aged man who sat behind a large table at the back of the keep. The man's welcoming smile faltered slightly as he caught sight of Tobu, who had to stoop low to fit inside. Behind the man Ash spotted a huge map of the Snow Sea. He studied it in wonder. He'd never seen the world drawn up like this.

"It's massive . . ." he whispered breathlessly.

So many places he had never seen, had not even *heard* of. Mountain ranges, coastlines, forests, Strongholds, the ancient ruined settlements of the World Before, and stranger features besides. He almost laughed at how ridiculous his disappointment was when he saw that Solstice was not marked down. As if the famously hidden Stronghold was going to be displayed clear as day on a Drifter map . . .

Looking hard, Ash managed to find the Fira Stronghold, way up on its own at the highest reaches of the map. How lonely it looked, so isolated amid all the endless white. He wondered what the people he knew there were doing right now, so very far away.

"Can I help you, lads?" the Drifter behind the desk asked, leaning toward Ash and Tobu. "Lookin' for some Drifter maps?"

"Hi! Um, no, we're actually looking for Lunah," Ash said.

"Lunah? The *Frostheart*'s back into Aurora, then?" The man seemed pleased by the news.

"You mean she's not come by here?" Worry began to niggle in Ash's gut.

"'Fraid not, lad. I ent seen Lunah for a good many moons now . . ."

"Oh." Ash looked to Tobu. "You don't think something bad's happened to her?"

Tobu grunted with concern, and the two of them rushed back out into the plaza.

It didn't take long to spot her.

"There," Tobu said, pointing at a small figure sitting alone on a wall across the circle.

"Lunah? Are you okay?" Ash asked as they approached, relieved to have found her.

Lunah looked up in surprise. "Thought I said I'd come get *you*?" She didn't sound happy.

"We had no luck with the Wayfinder statue, so thought we'd come find you. And look—we found you!" Ash gave Lunah a big smile, but she didn't return it.

"You didn't need to. You coulda got lost." Her usual cheer and energy were nowhere to be seen.

"They said they hadn't seen you inside the Drifter Keep . . . Are you . . . Have you not gone in yet?"

"'S too busy in there. Thought it'd be quieter, but with all the sleighs gettin' held fer the Council Moot, well. Best to come back another day."

Ash and Tobu shared a glance. Something was definitely wrong.

"Never put off till tomorrow what you can do today,"

Tobu said wisely. "You stand before the keep, and it was not busy when we left it."

"I'm sure they'd be happy to see you!" Ash said. "C'mon, we'll come with you!" Lunah looked reluctant. She didn't budge. "Lunah . . . are you sure everything's all right?"

"Yeah, course, why wouldn't it be?" she snapped. "Stars above, if you wanna go in so bad, then *fine*." She leaped off the wall, and after briefly hesitating led them back into the Drifter Keep.

Ash knew Lunah to be bold and brave, perhaps the most confident person he knew. But where that person had gone Ash did not know. This Lunah skulked across the room. Her chin was dipped, her hair hiding more of her face than usual. She stepped in front of the man behind the table, and in a voice as quiet as a squink said: "I'm here to chart the progress of my Provin'."

"Lunah! It's so good to see you doing well!" the man boomed. "So you found 'er then?" He smiled toward Ash and Tobu.

Lunah grimaced at the volume of his voice, and the group of Drifter children who had been so busy talking and laughing looked over at the mention of Lunah's name.

"Lunah!" one of the boys said. "Moon in shadow, we didn't know the *Frostheart* was back!"

"Rumors were the *Frostheart* was *lost*, out in the wilds . . ." a girl with a wavy black side-cut said, her mouth creeping into a smile.

"You heard wrong, Astra," Lunah replied bluntly. "We went far north, tha's all. Made it back this mornin'."

"Course." The girl nodded. "An' who're these? Yer friends?"

"'S Ash an' Tobu, my crewmates," Lunah said.

Ash smiled and waved, while Tobu simply nodded. The children smiled warily back, eyes lingering on Tobu.

"How nice. You know you boys're travelin' with an actual, livin' legend?" Astra asked them. "Well, the *daughter* of one anyway. Lunah's ma is one of the greatest explorers in the Convoy!"

"That's so cool! Lunah told us about her," Ash said, smiling, but Lunah didn't seem happy with where the conversation was headed.

"Shame it doesn't run in the family," sniggered one of the other girls. The kids laughed.

"Oi! Watch it, you lot," the man behind the desk warned.

Lunah kept her head held high, but Ash saw her eyes twitch, her cheeks redden.

"I'm pretty busy, guys, so if we're done here—"

"Oh yeah, don't let us get in your way! Can't wait to

see what uncharted land you've mapped. We've all just finished our Provin's too. Maybe we could have a race, first one back to the Convoy?"

"I . . . I won't be racing," Lunah said. Was Ash imagining it, or was her voice shaking slightly?

"Aww, don't be such a spoilsport . . ."

"I won't be racin' cause I ent finished my Provin'. I ent discovered anyplace new." Lunah spoke as if she didn't care, but Ash knew that she cared deeply—as did Astra, apparently, whose grin couldn't have grown any wider.

"Oh *no!*" she said in sympathy as believable as Tobu's disguise.

"That's not true, Lunah!" Ash said, hoping to back

up his friend. "You mapped a trail to the long-lost Isolai Stronghold!"

This silenced the children, Ash noticed with satisfaction, their smiles disappearing. Who did these kids think they were? *Lunah's the best navigator there is.*

"No, I didn't," Lunah said, her face stern.

"But . . . but you did . . . ?" Ash stuttered. Why was she denying it?

"I *didn't*. Shaard took us there. I did nothin'. If I'm gonna do the Provin', I'm gonna do it properly. *I'm* going to navigate the sleigh there, *not*   someone else."

"Good on you, Lunah." Astra nodded. "Imagine—a Drifter havin' to follow someone else's navigatin'. Imagine the *shame* that would bring to yer ma . . ."

"Yeah, imagine," Lunah said, before storming off without another word.

"Hope to see you back at the Convoy someday, Lunah!" Astra called after her, the other children erupting with laughter.

Ash and Tobu followed her outside, Ash's heart hurting for his friend.

"Lunah!" Ash called out, but she didn't turn back.

Tobu placed a hand on Ash's shoulder. "Leave her, boy. These are Drifter customs, and we need to respect their ways. This is something Lunah must do on her own." Ash watched her disappear down the lane, feeling utterly helpless. All the thrill and excitement of the morning came crashing down around him. "Do you remember the way back?" Tobu asked.

"I don't."

"Then I believe this will be a good opportunity to test your own navigational skills, vital for surviving the wilds. Lead the way, boy."

Ash's shoulders slumped even lower than before.

6
Uncharted

The *Frostheart* crew cheered and clinked their cups together as Ash finished playing another song on his ocarina. "You're getting good at that thing!" Yallah laughed. They'd gathered on the dock beside their sleigh, repairs on the vessel already well under way. Even Tobu was joining in, quietly sipping from a cup of water.

"If the captain steered as well as you played, Ash, I imagine the *Frostheart* wouldn't ever need repairs!" Arla joked.

"I beg your pardon. My steering's not all that bad, is it?" Nuk said.

"You literally steered the *Frostheart* along a vertical cliff face!"

"Aye, an' we all live to tell the tale because of it!" said

Kailen, her pale cheeks flushed from the drink. "To the captain—the best there is!"

"To the captain!" everyone cheered, spilled drink raining down from their cups.

"And to our newest crew members, without whom I suspect we'd have never made it back!" Nuk added, dipping her cup toward Ash, Tobu, and then Rook, who was perched on the *Frostheart*'s side rail, ominously peering down at the rest of them. Crows surrounded her, ruffling their feathers and staring at the crew with their black beady eyes. The crew cheered—though a bit more quietly—and drank again.

"Care to join us, Rook?" Captain Nuk shouted up to the hunched figure.

Rook gave a hiss in answer.

"Righto," Nuk commented.

"Well, she's better than that Shaard at least. *She* hasn't tried to kill us!" Twinge said with a smile.

"*Yet*," Kob finished to nervous laughter from all.

Ash loved moments like these, when the crew would come together just to talk and laugh, but he still couldn't quite shake his dampened mood from earlier. Sure, Lunah seemed to be laughing and smiling with the rest of them, but Ash could tell her heart wasn't in it. He wished he could help his friend, but he didn't know how. He watched Lunah slink away from the group, hop onto a crate, and unroll her map. She was gazing at it intently when Ash arrived at her side a few minutes later, rolling it up with haste when she noticed him. "Mind if I join you?" Ash asked carefully. Lunah gave him a look that suggested she did, but she scooted over to make some space for him anyway.

They sat in silence for a while, Lunah not lifting her eyes from her rolled-up map.

"Look, I—" Ash began, but Lunah interrupted him with a punch to the shoulder. "OW!"

"Sorry!" Lunah blurted.

"What was that for?!" Ash cried out.

"I'm not very good at these things, an' it was the only way I could think to say it."

"Say what?" Ash asked, rubbing his sore arm.

"I've already said it!"

"I have no idea what's going on . . ."

"Look . . ." She squeezed her eyes shut. "I'm sorry, okay? I'm sorry for snappin' at you earlier, I didn't mean it." Ash wondered if the apology was worse than what she was apologizing for, but he accepted it nonetheless. "It's just . . . the Provin's *really* important to me. Really, *really* important. You know your lullaby riddle? Well, this is my version of that. An' to see Astra an' the others bein' so smug that they'd all finished theirs, I just . . . It made me . . . y'know, I just . . . I *really* want to punch her in the face."

Ash burst out laughing. "No one knows that feeling better than me. I was bullied back at the Fira. I never understood how they could enjoy being so horrible to me, or why no one would stand up to them. But then this brave girl arrived and did what no one else would. She stood right up to their faces without a bit of fear and told them where to go." Ash turned to Lunah, who still looked so sad it hurt. "That girl was you, Lunah."

"Yeah, thanks, I think I got that, Ash."

"What I mean is, if anyone can prove Astra and those bullies wrong, it's you."

She let out a humorless laugh. "I know I can do this Provin'," she said with no confidence at all. "S'in my blood, s'what my family do. Wouldn't be much of a daughter if I failed, would I?" She studied her boots, looking very troubled indeed. "Not much of a daughter at all."

"C-can I help somehow?" Ash tried.

Lunah raised an eyebrow. With a sigh she unfurled her map.

"Can't hurt to get another eye on things. Even if you couldn't find yer way through an ice tunnel." Ash gasped. Lunah's map was incredible. She'd drawn it with such intricate, loving detail, right down to tiny trees within the forests and individual peaks in mountain ranges. It looked much like the map hanging in the Drifter Keep, just painted in Lunah's unique style. And with a few more ink splotches and dog-eared corners, but Ash thought it all added to the effect.

"Lunah . . . this is *amazing!*"

"An' there's not a dot on it not already mapped by someone in the Drifter Convoy." She sighed.

Ash looked closer. Aurora and the surrounding Strongholds predictably took center stage, making up most of the detail, but there was less and less detail the farther to the edges you went. To Ash's untrained eyes there looked to be a lot of unmapped land.

"What about over here?" Ash asked, pointing to a large area to the southeast. Only a word sat in the huge empty expanse of unmarked space. *Everstorm.*

"Oh, that would be a *great* place to map. It's completely uncharted."

"Well, why don't you—"

"Mostly because it's completely impossible. The Everstorm is a tooth-crackin' blizzard thousands of leagues across that's been ragin' since the fall of the World Before. Compasses go mental in there—you can barely see yer hand wavin' in front of yer face, let alone land-

marks or stars to guide yer way. The place is impossible to navigate."

"Oh," Ash said. "I guess you're right. Maybe I can't help." Ash continued to gaze at the map, then had an idea. "Somewhere on here is the Solstice Stronghold. It may be hidden, but it's there all right, and we're *so close* to finding it. If . . . if we keep on following the lullaby's clues, I know we'll do it. *You'll* do it. The lullaby led me to you, after all, and that's because you're the only navigator who can do this! You'll be the first person to have ever mapped the route to Solstice!"

A small smile crept onto Lunah's face as she thought

about it. "A place of legend . . . finally put on the map . . ." Her eyes widened at the idea, a spark lighting up within. "I guess we'd better get on with makin' the Wayfinder Sing, eh?"

"I reckon it'll be as easy as that." Ash smiled, and Lunah returned it.

"Thanks, Ash." She then dipped her head toward the others, who were enduring one of Twinge's famously terrible stories with good humor. "We should get back, I think the others might need our help . . ." And with that she leaped off the crate and ran to the others, Ash following in her footsteps, pleased to have his old friend back.

7

Memories in Shadow

Nuk had told Ash that whenever Pathfinders normally docked at Aurora, they were welcome to food and bedding at the Pathfinder's Rest. But because of the Moot there were *a lot* of Pathfinders in town, and there hadn't been any hammocks left for the crew of the *Frostheart*.

Ash didn't mind. The snug familiarity of the tent he shared with Tobu aboard the *Frostheart* was just what he needed after the day of culture shock he'd had.

He was too exhausted to dream that night. But something disturbed him nonetheless. He sensed shifting shadows and had the creeping sensation he was being watched. As his eyes squinted open he found himself face-to-face with pitiless black eyes. Ash screamed, shuffling away to the far end of the tent. As the sleep cleared from his head, his heart pounding in his throat,

Ash saw that it was a crow.

CAW, it said, before hopping out of the tent.

Spirits, Rook, we have to find a way for you to communicate without scaring people to death, Ash thought.

"*She* wants to speak with you," came Tobu's voice, causing Ash to jump again. "Make it quick. It is important we start your training again, early in the morning."

"Mm. Great," Ash mumbled, sliding from his bed furs and out of the tent.

There, waiting on the main deck, oblivious to the snores of the crew and the darkness of the sleeping Stronghold, stood Rook. Crows were perched all around, watching Ash with their dark emotionless eyes.

Rook began to Sing in her harsh whisper. "*Look.*"

As Ash walked down the stairs and joined her, she held out an old ceramic tablet, which Ash guessed she'd found in Shaard's belongings. He studied it carefully. Ancient letters had been carved onto its surface in the language of the World Before, words that Ash could not begin to understand. The same could not be said, however, of the etching in the tablet's center. It showed a monstrously large Leviathan laying waste to a giant settlement of the World Before, all under a storm-wracked sky. With a shiver Ash recognized how similar it was to the mural Shaard had shown him within the depths of Skybridge. "*Found. Outcast. Belongings,*" Rook Sang.

"What . . . what is it?"

"*HATRED. Horror. Devourer. DEATH,*" Rook said, her crows cawing.

Ash nodded, not needing Rook's help to understand that. "It's bad . . ."

"*STOP. AVERT.*" Rook tapped the tablet harder and harder with her long white finger.

"Rook, I'm sorry—" Ash said, trying his hardest. "I don't—I don't understand . . ." The crows called out, echoing Rook's frustration as she hissed.

Lights from the Stronghold glinted from the tiers high above them, piercing the darkness of the mountain's interior like stars. Rook paced and scratched at the tablet, perhaps thinking of a way she could better communicate with Ash. The cold silence drew on, and Ash found himself longing for his tent. He glanced back, only to catch sight of Tobu, who was watching from a distance with intense focus. Ash mouthed that it was okay. Tobu gave a small nod but did not take his eyes off Rook. Ash was actually glad for this. He had begun to feel unsafe all alone with this stranger in the dead of night.

"*Sing,*" Rook rasped.

Ash blinked, taken by surprise, but he understood what she meant. And so he took a deep breath and began to Song Weave. He Sang a Song that came to him naturally, his Song-aura whirling around him like a blizzard of starlight, bright in the darkness of the sleeping sleigh. To Ash's surprise Rook started to Sing with him, her broken, disjointed Song-aura reaching toward his. "*Weave.*" Her voice echoed in his head. He guided his Song round hers, their auras diving and swirling round each other as if in a dance.

Ash suddenly felt weightless, like his feet were leaving the deck, away from Aurora, to a place both distant and familiar. Visions flashed before his mind's eye, though they weren't his. It was like thoughts that weren't his own were being poured directly into his head. As Ash's Song-aura weaved its way about the erratic gloom of Rook's, his heart skipped as he realized it was *her* thoughts he was experiencing.

"I didn't know Song Weaving could do this!" Ash's Song Sang in wonder, but Rook was busy concentrating. She was trying to communicate with Ash in a way only possible with Song—he could feel her emotions as though they were his, see her memories as though he were living them.

Sadness suddenly enveloped him. A feeling of being lost, of being pulled in two directions and not knowing which way to go. But one thing shone bright in the confusion. It was the quest Ash's father had given Rook. It was a burning flame in a sea of cold, a raging sense of meaning and purpose. He saw Rook all alone atop the tower at Skybridge. All alone for so very long. Watching. Waiting for the moment Ash would show himself to her, his Song echoing through the World Weave. She couldn't leave for fear of missing him, and for fear of being found.

But found by who? Or what?

The loneliness was terrible. The vulpis that mined the ruins below were scared of her. But not the crows. The precious, beautiful crows. They welcomed her, high up on their perch above the world.

"My eyes. My friends," came Rook's voice, and although Ash could not see her, he knew she was smiling.

The vision changed. There was a chaos of black-feathered wings flocking around Ash the day he had found her amid the ruins. Rook was *happy*. They'd met at last. Ferno's child. But the happiness was short-lived. The boy, like everyone else, was scared of her. Pain shot through Rook like a blade of ice. Ash could feel shame and guilt within his own body, but that body felt very far away.

The vision changed again, this time of Rook stowing away aboard the *Frostheart*, hidden in the depths of its hull. She had to protect Ferno's son, and she had to protect the frost-heart, at all costs. She stood before the heart, its blue-white glow drawing riverlike lines in the wood of the mast in which it was set. She was determined to keep it safe, a determination she now stressed upon Ash with her Song—and the frost-heart itself chimed with gratitude at his side. Ash sensed the deepness of the despair Rook had felt when it was stolen by Shaard. She had failed. The outcast had won. Shaard's face flashed before Ash, those vivid turquoise eyes, that knowing grin etched onto his face. Rook Sang that he had hunted for Ash, for now that Ferno was gone, Ash was the only one who could guide him to Solstice. But the Fira were remote and forgotten. Ash had remained safe there for many years, just as Ferno had intended. But in his sinister quest to steal the frost-heart, Shaard had happened to climb aboard the one sleigh that still traveled so far north. The one sleigh that would take him unknowingly to Ash's hiding place. The *Frostheart*.

How lucky Shaard must've felt. How very pleased with himself he must've been that he'd foiled Ferno's plan with this single, unknowing act. Rook's anger at herself bubbled up in her Song. She should've hunted him down. She should've gone to Aurora and killed Shaard when she'd had the chance. But she'd made a promise. She had to stay in Skybridge, waiting for Ash. At least that was what she told herself.

But deep down she knew she'd been scared of him. She'd known that Shaard was stronger than she was. Visions of the battle they'd had with Shaard at the Isolai Stronghold flashed in chaotic procession, fury and hatred bubbling within both Ash's and Rook's Songs.

"Who is he?" Ash Sang out. *"Who is Shaard? What does he want?!"*

"Enemy. MURDERER. Wants. Frost-heart. DEATH. VENGEANCE."

Rook's Song was desperate for him to understand what she had to tell him. It was burning through every one of her nerves. She had to warn him, she had to!

"Warn me? Warn me about what?"

Rook tried to answer, but something stopped her. It was like an invisible wall, a shield that would not let her delve any further into her thoughts.

"*Cannot. Hidden. Forgotten . . .*" She'd put the shield up in her own mind, to protect herself from something, and was too frightened to remove it for fear of what lay beyond. Something colossal, something unfathomably malicious and appalling.

"*You have to tell me!*" Ash was getting frustrated. He pushed, his Song pressing for more, despite Rook wavering with fright.

Rook gasped, and the two of them were ripped out of the Song Weave, back to *Frostheart*'s deck. Ash grasped his head as Rook collapsed onto the deck, her breath short and ragged. Crows cried out into the night, flocking to her from around the sleigh, trying to comfort their friend. Ash stumbled backward and was caught by Tobu.

"What happened?" Tobu asked.

"I–it's okay," Ash managed. But he knew that it wasn't. He felt chilled and hollow, a freezing grip scratching at his heart and mind. It felt disturbingly familiar, though why he couldn't recall. And as he watched Rook's terrible trembling, not even Aurora's humid warmth could make Ash's world feel any less cold.

8

Hearth Home

Ash awoke to the shifting of Tobu's muscles after a very uneasy night. He discovered he'd scooted as close to Tobu as possible, curling up against his warm, cozy fur. He rolled away hastily and acted as though he'd been nowhere near the yeti as Tobu rose. "Up. It is time for training."

Half an hour later Tobu shook his head in disbelief, casting his critical eye over the numerous pebbles scattered about the jetty.

"Surely, even by simple luck, you should've at least *nicked* the target by now . . ."

They'd been training with the sling for most of the early morning, and Ash had not managed to hit the bottle target once.

"You're still too tense, your movements too strained.

You're trying to impress me, instead of bettering your-self. You must breathe. *Concentrate*."

How can I concentrate after what happened last night? Ash thought, but said, "I'm getting better, though, don't you think?"

"No."

The rest of the crew were beginning to stir, bleary-eyed and disheveled from the celebrations the night be-fore. All, that is, except for Captain Nuk, who had been up almost as early as Ash and Tobu. She was rushing about the sleigh preparing for the Council Moot, Master Podd scurrying around in her shadow.

"These Moots are as rare as a laughing Lurker, and I have a reputation to uphold!" Nuk was saying as she rummaged through chests and barrels.

"Indeed, captain," Master Podd said. Ash swore the vulpis might've even brushed his fur for the occasion.

"Which is exactly why I need to find my fancy hat,

Master Podd! I know it's around here somewhere . . ."
Ash looked about the rest of the ragtag crew and spotted
Rook, slumped and disheveled in the far corner of the
jetty, feeding her loyal crows.

Ash still couldn't quite believe what they'd accom-
plished the night before . . . that Song Weaving could
show you a person's *memories*. It was mind-blowing. *The
amount you could learn from others, to see their past as
though you'd been there too* . . . Ash felt dizzy at the possibilities. Occasionally Song Weaving could feel like a real
blessing, and not just a curse. *Very* occasionally.

*I wonder what else it might be able to do. Other things
I don't know about simply because I've never been taught.*
Ash found the scope of it all almost scary. *I can't do this on
my own . . . I need lessons from someone who knows this kind
of stuff. Tobu teaches me all he can . . . and he'd teach me
even more if he could. But the simple fact is he's not a Song
Weaver. No. I need another teacher . . . someone like Rook.*

But the memory of the cold aftershock still haunted
Ash. It had felt as though there'd been a . . . a *presence*
there, something behind Rook's mental shield, watching
them. Trying to break through. What had happened to
Rook to make her this way?

"Tobu? Can I ask you a question?" Ash said as Tobu gathered the pebbles together again.

"I believe you just did," Tobu replied.

Ash prepared himself. "I know I asked you over and over to let me learn about Song Weaving from . . . from Shaard. And I know I should've listened to you when you said he was dangerous. You were right." Tobu said nothing as he turned to Ash. "So, this time, I'm only gonna ask you once. I would like to use some of my downtime to Song Weave with Rook, instead of having survival lessons." Tobu's brow lifted. "I—I think I could learn so much from her, if I just had the time to try to understand her."

Tobu was quiet, gazing in the direction of Rook. "It is something I too have been considering."

"I-it is?" Ash had been expecting him to fly off the handle at the mere suggestion.

"Apparently you have made a greater connection to the World Weave than I first realized. Perhaps you don't hear it as we yeti do, but there is no doubt in my mind that you hear it in the stars. In the Leviathans. In your father's lullaby. I agree that you could learn much from her." Ash waited for the criticism that was inevitably going to follow. But the criticism never came. Ash wasn't sure whether it would be in bad taste to leap for joy.

"Well, that's—that's *great*! Thank you, Tobu! I'll work so hard to learn from her, just as hard as in our lessons!" Tobu snorted, but seemed unable to hold Ash's gaze.

"We shall ask Rook if she'll teach you. You have shown potential in your Song Weaving. The way you connected with the Lurkers back at the Isolai and gained their allegiance against Shaard . . . it was . . ."

Impressive? Amazing? Stupendous?

"Adequate," Tobu finished. "Clearly your Song Weaving will be of better use to your survival than conventional weapons." Tobu gazed at the sling in Ash's hand, and his eye gave an involuntary twitch. "You must promise to work hard, that you will listen well to Rook's expertise and wisdom."

Rook chose this moment to scratch behind her hood with her foot, resembling some kind of dog, before she ruffled the feathers of her cloak and cawed in chorus with her crows.

"*Expertise* and *wisdom*," Tobu repeated, as much to convince himself as Ash, who nodded eagerly.

"I won't let you down, Tobu." At this Tobu did hold Ash's gaze. He stared long and hard, thoughts flashing by unseen, but certainly there. At last he turned away.

"I know."

Captain Nuk began to address the crew who had

gathered on the jetty. She was wearing a very fetching, very fancy feathered hat.

"Right, you lot! It's time I was heading off to the Moot! I'll report back when it's done. There's a change on the wind, and I can't say I like the way it smells."

"Aye aye, captain," the crew murmured as one.

"You mean . . . we don't get to go to the Moot too?" Ash asked, disappointed.

"Moots are just for Pathfinder captains and their right hands, I'm afraid, lad," Nuk confirmed. "But where Stormbreaker's concerned, I can already tell you what we'll be talking about—she'll be listing all the Leviathan necks and the best ways we can wring them."

"Good, I say," Kailen said. "I think she has the right idea about those things."

"You only say that because you model yourself on her," Yallah teased, which got a laugh from the crew. "Missing eye, unshakable scowl. Yup, it's all there . . ."

"Laugh all you want—she's a person of action, an' I respect that."

Nuk looked dubious at where Kailen was placing her respect, but continued regardless. "I'll meet you all back here once the Moot's over." And with that Nuk headed off to the Hearth Home, the Council's seat at the highest level of Aurora, her right-hand vulpis in tow. "You don't think I should've tied ribbons round this old thing, do you, Master Podd?" Ash heard her say anxiously as she walked off, gesturing at her peg leg. "Too much? I think it would be too much. Well spotted, Master Podd, well spotted. Whatever would I do without you?"

"Has Tobu got you trainin' for the rest of the day?" Lunah asked Ash as they watched their captain leave. The rest of the crew were creeping back to their tents for a much-needed lie-in, while Tobu had disappeared from sight.

"No, actually!" Ash said brightly. "In fact, he's being really . . . *nice* to me all of a sudden . . ."

"Tobu? *Nice*?" She raised an eyebrow.

"I know—it's pretty weird to say the least."

"Maybe the wolversbane poison did somethin' to his brain?" Lunah said, pulling a face and making claw motions with her hands.

"It can do that?"

Lunah shrugged. "Dunno, to be honest. Never been poisoned; still on my to-do list. So, you got the day free? S'a real shame we can't go to the Moot, eh?"

"Yeah, I was really excited to see it," Ash admitted.

"Yup. You could count on one hand the amount of times a Moot has happened in the last hundred winters. Almost every Pathfinder captain will be rockin' up. The very fate of the Snow Sea'll be decided, an' we're stuck out here."

"It's rubbish," Ash agreed.

"Shame we're too well behaved to sneak in or anythin', otherwise we might get in on some of that action . . ." Lunah gave Ash *a look*.

Ash returned it. "Yes. We wouldn't even dream of it."

"Good to hear you're so willin' to follow orders, Pathfinder. Cause there's no way you could persuade *me* to sneak in an' see that once-in-a-lifetime spectacle, absolutely no way at all."

Hearth Home turned out to be a massive complex of spires and domed halls, and it sat at the highest point of Aurora, so high its towers peeked out of the volcano's crater and gazed upon the sprawling frozen landscape that stretched beyond it. Thankfully, its massive size and twisting corridors provided many hiding places, especially for two children who didn't want to be found.

"I can't believe that worked!" Ash whispered, his nerves at being caught topped only by the rushing excitement at what they were doing. Lunah had ingeniously incited a snowball fight outside that grew so large and chaotic they'd been able to slip past the guards unnoticed.

"The ol' snowball trick? Works every time." Lunah grinned, peeking round a corner to make sure the coast was clear. Together they rushed up the levels of the tower, having no time to admire the beautiful carvings that adorned the walls.

"Through here!" Lunah gestured at a grated panel in the wall. Ash lifted the grate and got on his hands and knees to climb through. It was a very narrow shaft that led off into pitch darkness.

"Is it . . . safe?"

"How innocent you are, Ash, thinkin' this is the first

time I've done this. It's a ventilation shaft, leads right into the Moot Hall." Together they crawled through the tight, dark space. It was slow work, and Ash didn't even want to *think* what the creepy, crawly things he could feel skittering over his hands and face were. Not soon enough, he saw light ahead. With a gasp of relief Ash stopped at the end of the shaft, Lunah climbing unceremoniously onto his back so that she too could get a view of what lay beyond.

They were above a cavernous amphitheater, a ginormous domed roof covering the space above, which was held aloft by large stone pillars. The spaces in between the pillars were open to the outside world, the chill air barely warmed by the huge raging braziers that had been placed round the hall's circumference. Large circular steps led up from the main stage, with hundreds of banners placed round them, each displaying an icon from a Pathfinder sleigh. Each captain and right hand stood proudly beside their respective banners, as varied as the icons themselves.

The place was *heaving*.

You could almost taste the tension and excitement as the Pathfinder captains talked among themselves, filling the hall with a cacophony that sounded

almost like the volcano was awakening once more. After some searching, Ash spotted Captain Nuk and Master Podd, standing by the *Frostheart*'s banner. Ash's heart swelled with pride at the sight of it, and the frost-heart gave a little trill too. He still found it hard to believe he was a part of all of this, that he'd been lucky enough to join what he was sure was the best crew in the entire fleet.

"This. Is. So. Cool. See that?" Lunah whispered, pointing at a large sleigh enjin that sat in the middle of the main stage. "Said to be the *actual* enjin from the Wayfinder's *actual* sleigh. The first Pathfinder sleigh ever made!" As Ash looked at it in awe a large gong was struck, filling the hall with its booming call and quieting the voices of the captains into an expectant silence.

"*Shh!*" Lunah whispered to Ash, her eyes as wide as his with the thrill of it all. "The Moot's about to begin!"

The Council Moot

Hefty wooden doors boomed open at the base of the Moot Hall. Ash shifted his weight so he could get a better view, enthralled. Three elegant robed figures strode in: an elderly man with dark skin and a stark white beard, a pale middle-aged woman with hair so long it trailed behind her like a tail, and a prim-looking vulpis, archeomek trinkets dangling from the elaborate headwear she wore. "The Council," Lunah whispered into Ash's ear; he had already assumed as much. The Council stood proudly upon the Wayfinder's enjin in the center of the hall.

"We declare this Moot in session!" the man announced.

"Aye!" the gathered captains resounded.

The councilman's serious face slipped into an easy

smile, his eyes disappearing behind well-worn wrinkles, suggesting it was something he did often.

"My comrades. Fellow Pathfinders. *Friends*. It warms this old man's heart to see so many courageous heroes of the Snow Sea gathered in one place."

"We realize the inconvenience caused by grounding the fleet and halting your valiant missions to help the Strongholds of the world, and for that we apologize," the councilwoman said, "but the Moot is only called in desperate times, and, make no mistake, these *are* desperate times. We need only look at the frightening number of empty spaces where our companions once stood to understand the true scale of the situation."

The crowd murmured in sullen agreement, looking about at the many empty spaces among them, banners with no captains to represent them.

Sleighs lost to the wilds . . . to the Leviathans, Ash thought, his mouth going dry. *There's so many . . .*

"We are losing Pathfinders faster than we can replace them and sleighs faster than we can build them. The whole Pathfinder mission is at risk of collapsing."

The crowd rumbled with uneasy agreement.

"This has been a long time coming, and still we do nothing!" a captain shouted.

"The Leviathan attacks get worse each day!" yelled

another. "Not to mention the dark spirits that haunt us! The Wraiths are becoming as hostile as the Leviathans they're in league with! There's even been word that the Great Horned One has been spotted at our borders!"

The crowd shifted and murmured in horror at such a suggestion.

"Truly dark omens. Signs of the End Times," an elderly captain said, shaking his head.

To see the Pathfinders this frightened, adventurers whom the tales painted as utterly fearless, was enough to send a chill down Ash's spine. *I had no idea things were this bad*, he thought.

"Captain Stormbreaker of the *Kinspear* has proposed a possible solution," the vulpis councilwoman said, raising her small arms to try to calm the crowd. "It is a drastic plan, but perhaps drastic is what's needed. It is this we shall discuss today, yes yes. Captain Stormbreaker, the floor is yours."

The captains fell silent as a woman stepped down from a banner displaying a Leviathan with an arrow piercing its heart. She made her way to the center of the hall, steady and determined. Ash held his breath, and Lunah gripped his arm with increasing tightness. It was as though the captain had stepped right out of a legend. She was dressed in scarred leather armor and walked with total confidence, shoulders back and head held high, a large fur cloak flowing behind her. Her expression was stern and humorless, one eye hidden by an eyepatch, her long black hair pulled back into a ponytail. She looked more like a warrior than a Pathfinder, and there was something about her that made Ash's head tingle and his hair stand on end. The way she looked, her face, the way she moved . . . it was . . . it was . . . well, he wasn't *sure* what it was. But it was mesmerizing.

Stormbreaker stood before her fellow captains, the entire hall silent as if under a spell.

"You all look like me"—she spoke in a husky voice—"*tired.*" She received a rumble of laughter from the audience. "So, I'll cut to the chase. Who here has lost a crew member?"

A captain quickly broke the silence and said, "I have."

The captain beside him nodded. "Aye, me too."

"I've lost five," said the Tekko captain Ash had seen at the market.

"I've lost seven!" shouted another.

Voices rose with the numbers of those they'd lost.

"And who here has left a Stronghold behind, knowing deep down in their heart that it was likely the last time they would see it before it fell to starvation or attack?" Stormbreaker asked.

Voices grew louder and angrier as the captains agreed.

"Who here has gone out into the wilds and struggled to survive, convinced that they would never make it back to see Aurora's light?"

The hall burst into agreement, captains shouting out their terrible stories.

"Aye," Stormbreaker said, looking at the crowd with a burning eye. "You *are* tired like me. Tired of hiding. Tired of being scared. Tired of living just to survive. But our enemy does not tire. The Leviathans grow more aggressive with each passing moon. They adapt to suit whatever environment they are in, and, mark my words, they will not stop until we are all *dead*." She paced the center stage, gazing intently at all those around her. "The question I ask is: Why should it only be the Leviathans who adapt? We have done the same old thing for countless centuries. We have risked the lives of the few to try to keep the Strongholds connected. The Strongholds . . . or should I call them what they really are: our *prisons*?"

The hall resounded with shock.

"And while the Pathfinder quest is undoubtedly valiant, it is *not working*. We wouldn't be having this Moot if it were. Well, I say *enough*! Enough hiding! It is time we adapt, take up arms and fight back!"

A few captains cheered at this, but most remained still. Someone in the back coughed.

"What are we supposed to do, poke them with our spears and arrows?" a captain asked. "You know more than most that our weapons are almost useless against the Leviathans' thick hides and thrashing claws."

Stormbreaker nodded solemnly. "You are right to question me, my friend. I have dedicated my life to fighting the Leviathans and would be the first to admit that, as things stand, it is a fight we cannot win. But, as I said, we must adapt. BRING IN THE WEAPON!" Large doors burst open at the top level of the amphitheater, and a group of chittering vulpis wheeled in a large contraption.

"What is *that*?" Lunah said. The crowd appeared to share her wonder as they whispered to each other.

The device was shaped like a curved spear point and seemed to be made of some kind of ceramic. The whorled patterns and runes carved into it were unmistakably from the World Before. Sunstones lined its top, glowing brilliant and bright.

"My desperate search for a way to fight the Leviathans led me into the very depths of the earth. Literally," Stormbreaker explained as the vulpis pushed the device to a space in between two pillars, facing it out toward the gray distance. "With the aid of my crew and our vulpis accomplices, we discovered something in a ruined settlement of the World Before, far to the south. Something that will change *everything*." Pathfinders that Ash guessed were Stormbreaker's crew rushed into the Moot Hall and lined its top edges. One held up a tall red flag and waved it high, as others took hold of handles that steered the machine. It was then that Ash noticed another red flag waving back, way out amid the haze of the snow plain that stretched from Aurora to the inner wall. The distant flag waver stood next to some large wooden structures that Ash could just about make out had been shaped to look like Leviathans.

"Fire when ready," Stormbreaker said, giving her vicious-looking crewman a nod. The sunstones on the

device began to hum, growing brighter as energy crackled around them. With a sudden, deafening CRACK, a ball of brilliant light burst from the archeomek's point, making the crowd cry out in fear and alarm. CRACK CRACK CRACK, the device went, firing with such rapidity it was hard to keep track. The balls of energy tore through the air at incredible speeds, the air rippling in their wake, before ripping through the distant wooden structures as if they weren't even there.

CRACKCRACKCRACKCRACKCRACK.

The weapon increased its rate of fire as it warmed up, the blasts now just a blur of pulsating light, and the terrible cracking sound becoming a high-pitched whine. Stormbreaker raised a fist, and her crewman abruptly

stopped firing. The sunstones dimmed, the air around the weapon shimmering with heat.

All that remained of the wooden Leviathan targets were smoldering craters, the scattered debris that lay strewn about the blackened, pulverized ground alight with flame.

The silence in the hall was deafening, or was that just thanks to the ringing in their ears? The Pathfinders stood, mouths agape in stunned and horrified awe. It was a devastating weapon. Ash took a breath, Lunah gripping his arm so tight it hurt. Captain Stormbreaker allowed herself a smile, clearly satisfied at their reaction.

"It takes monstrous weapons to fight monsters. This is but one. The vulpis have managed to construct many from the knowledge we have gained, and they are ready for our use."

The quiet carried on for a few more beats . . . and then the audience erupted into rapturous applause. "Incredible!" they cheered. "Amazing!"

But a voice cut through the noise. "The World Before had these weapons in greater numbers, and still they fell."

The cheering stalled, all eyes trying to find who had dared doubt such an awesome display of power. Ash's eyes widened when he saw that the voice belonged to Captain Nuk. "I daresay their weapons were of better quality . . . ?

But we would all do well to remember that the World Before are a *lost* civilization. What makes you think we won't follow them into oblivion? Pathfinders are agents of peace, not warriors."

"Ah, Captain Nuk." Stormbreaker smiled. "Ever the thorn in the side of reason. What would you have us do? Hide behind our walls until we fade into the blizzard of history?"

"Not that it's in your nature, *Wurmslayer*, but the path to peace does not always involve war and bloodshed. Your obsession with the Leviathans is personal. You have my greatest sympathies, but I cannot condone you dragging us into war for the sake of revenge."

Some of the captains nodded in agreement at this, but most laughed and jeered. "Nonsense!" "Craven!" "Coward!"

Stormbreaker held up a hand for silence. "You're right. It is personal. I lost my family to the Leviathan scourge. But as we've established, the scourge has hurt us *all*. This is personal to all of us! We are already at war and have been for centuries. But this may just be our chance to *win it*. This weapon is the least of what we've found."

"The *least*?" Captain Nuk gasped in disbelief.

"We have found other weapons that make this one look like child's play. Even one that never had the

chance to be used in the World Before's war against the Leviathans, the war that saw their empire fall." Wide eyes and frightened faces followed this statement.

Ash's stomach turned. The idea that something of even more power could exist was frightening to say the least.

"Unfortunately there is a catch," Stormbreaker continued. "For reasons we cannot fathom, the mightier weapons can only be activated by the Songs of Song Weavers."

It was Ash's turn to grip on to Lunah's arm. The hall exploded in protest.

"That's madness! We can't give the Song Weavers that kind of power—who knows what evil they will use it for!" someone roared.

"The Leviathans will use them to turn the weapons against us! I bet that's how the World Before fell! This is absurd!" The crowd were all in agreement.

Ash's heart sank at the familiar accusations. His hope that Aurora might be more forward-thinking now seemed misplaced. A resentment grew like an icicle in his belly, just as chilling and sharp.

"Which is why I propose that we turn the Pathfinder fleet into an armada," Stormbreaker shouted. "We will gather Song Weavers from across the Snow Sea, and under our strict watch and guidance turn them into a fighting force the world has never seen before."

This was a world-changing suggestion, and nobody seemed to know how to react. Ash breathed hard as he thought what this could mean.

"The Song Weavers need not be our enemy," Stormbreaker went on, and Ash's heart lifted. "They have been outcast and feared, but I believe that if we work together, they can be used as a force for good! Give me command of the Pathfinder fleet, and I will see to it that human-kin will become a force to be reckoned with. I will make the world safe for us all. Never again will we have to raise our children in fear. We have the sleighs. We have the brains. We have the unyielding bravery of the Pathfinders, and now we have the tools we need to fight back. Let's wipe the Leviathans from this land once and for all! Let us set ourselves free!"

The hall rocked with cheers and applause. Pathfinders threw their fists up into the air, and some even drew swords and spears and held them aloft to show their support. It seemed that Captain Stormbreaker, the Wurmslayer, had won the Pathfinders over.

All, that is, except for Captain Nuk, who was looking at her comrades as though they'd all lost their minds.

Gathering Storm Clouds

Aurora changed after that. The Pathfinder captains had overwhelmingly voted for Captain Stormbreaker's plan at the end of the Council Moot. *Commander Stormbreaker now*, Ash corrected himself.

The Pathfinder fleet was being transformed into a battle armada, armed with the terrible weapons of the World Before, the worst of which would be controlled by Song Weavers. The whole world had changed with just one meeting, and Ash was struggling to keep up.

The idea of a war with the Leviathans frightened him. He'd been close enough to Leviathans to make his bones quiver at the mere *thought* of trying to fight them. But even though he was scared of the Leviathans, he couldn't shake the niggling feeling that there was more to them than met the eye—that they were more than mindless monsters. He'd always had a connection with them through Song Weaving. During his loneliest moments back with the Fira, the Leviathan Song had kept him company, much like Rook and her crows.

And back at the Isolai Stronghold . . .

"*PLEASE. HELP,*" sounded the memory of the Lurkers' Song.

Ash had helped to free the Lurkers from Shaard's control, and Ash knew they'd been thankful to him, had even aided him in return. "*ALLIES. FRIENDS,*" they'd Sung.

I know it sounds crazy, Ash thought, *but maybe . . . maybe the Leviathans* don't *have to be the enemies we think they are . . . ?*

He chuckled. No one would ever believe him. Ash wasn't even sure *he* believed it.

Then there was the matter of the archeoweapons and Song Weavers. Ash didn't know how to feel about it all. On the one hand Song Weavers were feared across the Snow Sea, though Ash had found that people mostly just tried to forget about them. But now Song Weavers would be actively searched for and gathered. He'd always wished people would give him a shot to prove that Song Weavers weren't enemies of the Strongholds—and now Stormbreaker was giving them that chance—but Ash had already seen the mistrust in the other Pathfinder captains, and did not want to think what might happen if they suspected any Song Weavers had lost their minds to the Leviathans. If they couldn't *control* that, why should they be punished for it? It was all very worrying. More than ever, Ash wanted to get to Solstice and find his parents.

I'm sure once I tell Mum and Dad and the Song Weavers at Solstice what's going on out here, they'll rush to the Strongholds' aid, Ash thought. *They'd have to—it's the right thing to do! We'll all fight together, Song Weavers, Pathfinders, and Strongholders, side by side, and everyone will see that Song Weavers are just the same as everyone else. That we can be the good guys too.* Ash's heart swelled at the idea.

At any rate, Captain Nuk certainly knew how she felt about Stormbreaker's plan. "Has everyone taken leave of their senses?!" she yelled to the others at a table in the Pathfinder's Rest. "This will only lead to needless death, I tell you! Leading untrained civilians into battle with the Leviathans, what is she *thinking*?!"

"She lost her life-mate and child

to the Leviathans," Kailen said. "She has long sworn to rid the Snow Sea of the wurm scourge."

"Oh, I understand why she's so bloodthirsty—I just didn't expect everyone else to blindly follow her!"

"The world is gripped by fear and mistrust," Tobu said to himself more than the others.

"People are desperate, captain," Teya said, sipping her drink. "They'll cling to anything that gives them hope."

"Not you too, Teya? And what about the poor Song Weavers? Being rounded up like tools to be used." Nuk gave Ash a worried glance. "Don't you worry, Ash, my boy, I will fight this with everything I have. This simply will not stand."

"What . . . what if we're able to help?" Ash replied in a small voice. "I'm sure many Song Weavers would want to help if they could . . ." Nuk gave Ash a sad smile.

"Brave child. I would love nothing more than for everyone to live together in peace, and if I believed that would happen, I'd be first to cheer Stormbreaker on. But I fear there's too much history, too much mistrust between the Song Weavers and Strongholders, for us to suddenly throw them all together in a deadly war. This'll end in trouble, you mark my words. We're losing Aurora to fear."

Splintered

Ash sat on the edge of the *Frostheart*'s main deck, absent-mindedly playing his ocarina, but truly getting lost in his thoughts. Tobu sat cross-legged beside him, his huge bulk hunched over the small chunks of wood he carved in his careful, methodical way. The sculptures had started to look a bit less like blobs, and a bit more like yeti now, which Ash guessed was Tobu's intention. Well, they did if you pretended that yeti looked like egg-shaped lumps with faces. As Ash watched he thought he could make out what appeared to be a female yeti . . . and a child.

With a sudden gasp of recognition Ash realized what he was looking at. *Tobu's family!* It was easy to forget that Tobu had been exiled from his home too, just like Ash. Mostly because Tobu absolutely refused to talk about it. Once, and only once, he had mentioned his son—but

Ash had never felt brave enough to ask Tobu about what had happened, and why he'd had to leave them behind. *He must miss them so much*, Ash thought, watching Tobu handle the carvings with uncharacteristic tenderness, his eyes wistful and distant—as they often were these days. Right then, Ash wanted to give Tobu a big fat hug, but knew there was a good chance he'd end up in the canal for his efforts.

Instead he turned his attention to the rest of the crew, including Lunah, who was hanging upside down from the *Frostheart*'s rigging, her dreadlocks and cloak draping down toward the deck, somehow still managing to concentrate and mark notes on her map. Twinge was rolling heavy barrels along the main deck, chewing Kob's ear off about that other time he'd rolled barrels across the main deck. Kob looked like he was contemplating dropping the crates of rations he was carrying and leaping overboard. Master Podd was scurrying about the sleigh, double-checking that everything was in its place. He licked a paw and touched it to the mast, inspecting it for dust. Apparently satisfied, he gave a nod, his big ears flopping forward as he did so. The *Frostheart* was preparing for its next run. Captain Nuk wanted to leave Aurora as soon as possible.

"It's getting too heated around here for comfort. A breath of fresh air will help clear all our heads and show us the path we need to take," she'd said, and Ash couldn't blame her. But he was worried he wouldn't be able to solve the riddle of the Wayfinder before they left. At the thought of this Ash fluffed the note he was playing on his ocarina, and Lunah grimaced at the sound.

"Mate!"

"Sorry!" Ash said.

So far the statue of the Wayfinder had remained stubbornly silent and appeared quite unconcerned with revealing anyone's fate.

Ash's feelings toward his father were increasingly seesawing between a desperate yearning to be with him and a seething annoyance at the overelaborate trail he'd left for Ash to follow.

How did he ever expect me to solve all these stupid puzzles? Ash thought bitterly. *Every time I get close to solving one, another obstacle gets in the way. Who knows how many other clues I have to solve after this one, if I even manage to solve this one at all!*

Ash lowered his ocarina and let out a long, exhausted breath. Tobu glanced at him. *Don't you start*, Ash thought, not in the mood for criticism.

Ash put a hand to his head, trying to steady himself, but it was no use. He felt like he was being consumed by an overwhelming snowstorm, one he'd never find his way out of again. There were too many things to think about, to worry about . . . Ash wrung his ocarina in his hands.

My parents should've never left me in the first place. This is all their fault.

People often describe anger as something hot, but Ash had found it to be cold and biting—as if it gnawed on your senses like frost. A chill of fury clawed its way into his mind now, and his hands began to shiver. Could he even make the journey to Solstice now that Song Weavers were being collected? *How could my parents do this to me? Was I really that awful, that terrible, that they had to abandon me?* The chill grew colder, rising up and tightening round his throat, draining him of all his hope and replacing it with rage . . .

"Ash, are you okay?" Lunah asked, her voice nearly making him jump off the sleigh in shock as he was wrenched from his dark thoughts. He realized Tobu's hand was on his shoulder, his face creased with concern, and Ash became aware that his breaths were ragged, hard, and fast. His hands were clenched into trembling fists, gripping his ocarina so tight his knuckles hurt.

"I'm *fine!*" Ash said far too defensively.

"Be calm, boy. Deep breaths," Tobu said in a low voice. "You are safe with us."

Ash's heart rate settled as the presence of his friends helped quash the cold that had been rising up inside him. But that wasn't all. Ash sensed a warming aura flowing around him, a comforting, faint voice, a Song. It urged him to not give in to hopelessness in words Ash couldn't understand, but which were no less comforting.

Remember, he felt it say, like the whisper of a ghost, *you are not alone.*

As long as Ash had his friends, he had hope. And as long as he had hope, there was nothing he couldn't overcome. With a jolt of surprise, Ash realized he was hearing the Song of the frost-heart, its now familiar chime radiating from his side. Its cold glow was pulsing brighter than usual. Ash had once found it hard to hear the frost-heart's ethereal Song, as though he were trying to listen to a voice in the past. But Ash now found he was able to sense, to hear, to *feel* it, and it appeared to be reaching out to him more and more.

He wondered if it was thanks to Rook's lessons. Ash had spent every moment he wasn't puzzling over the Wayfinder statue training with Rook, deep within the *Frostheart*'s hold, keeping a low profile. Tobu trained close by, and would take regular breaks from meditating or stabbing the air with his spear to say things like "Chin up, boy" and "Sing from your diaphragm, not from your throat." This was nearly always followed by a cold silence from Rook, and Tobu would catch himself, remembering he was no longer the teacher. "*Ahem*. As you were."

But Ash was glad of Tobu's company. He was still wary of Rook, both curious and cautious of what she was hiding. He knew that valuable answers lay within her hidden memories, but thoughts of the cold fear that had taken hold of him the first time still prickled up the hairs on the back of his neck. But they Sang for practice, for Rook to see what Ash was capable of, and for the simple joy of having another Song Weaver to Weave with. And Ash swore that after every time he could understand Rook just a little bit better.

"*Song is essence. My soul. Your soul. World's soul,*" Rook answered when Ash questioned her about it. "*My soul splintered. But Weaving mends. Weaving heals.*" Ash could still not see her face, but he had suspected, right at that moment, he had heard a smile in her voice.

Back in the present Ash reached his own Song out to the frost-heart, thankful it was there. Thankful that he sat by his friends. And *of course* he hadn't simply been abandoned—his parents had good reason for fleeing, he was sure of it. He took a deep breath and let it out slowly. It helped. The chill within him receded.

"I'm okay . . ." Ash gasped. "I'm okay." And, taking a deep breath, he knew he was. Tobu and Lunah shared a glance, before Lunah looked out at the other sleighs in the dock.

"Didn't realize you found sleigh watchin' so excitin'." Ash laughed. "But, Ash," Lunah continued, more serious, "if it's that riddle that's worryin' ya, don't let it. We'll figure it out, together. Cap' wants to leave, but she'll wait a few days for you if she has to. Course she will—we're all in this together!"

Ash nodded, but couldn't help noticing the frown on Tobu's face, the worry that was barely concealed behind his eyes as he watched him. Unable to hold his gaze, Ash looked away, and it was then that he saw it.

Another cloaked figure, hidden in the shadows between two dock buildings close by. They had removed a loose stone in a wall and were placing something in its space. An object Ash was sure they'd just been Singing to.

Ash knew this not because of the volume of the Song, which was far too faint to be heard at this distance, but because of the ghostly, unmistakable shimmer of a Song-aura that flickered and bent the air round the stranger, before fading like mist once the Song was finished. It was an aura that only other Song Weavers could see. The stranger put the stone back in place, and after a quick glance to check the coast was clear, disappeared into the crowds upon the dock.

"Did—did you guys see that?" Ash pointed.

"What?" Lunah asked, looking in the direction Ash was pointing. "That guy with the massive nose? It's *huge*, isn't it?"

"No! The—the person in the alley!"

"What did you see, boy?" Tobu asked, raising an eyebrow.

"I don't know," Ash admitted. "But I'm going to find out."

12

Night Watch

The stone came away from the wall easily. Ash tentatively reached into the gap it left behind, Lunah watching so closely her chin was practically on his shoulder. Standing guard behind them at the mouth of the alley was Tobu, his huge bulk blocking out the light from the main street.

Ash pulled out the object that had been hidden in the hole in the wall. Ash and Lunah gasped together, and even Tobu's eyes widened ever so slightly as he peeked over their shoulders with curiosity.

"It's the same as the Wayfinder's thingamajig!" Ash said, holding the cylindrical object aloft.

"Her *water bottle*," Lunah corrected.

Ash turned the object round in his hands. It had some weight to it and was made of the same ceramic-like

material as many archeomek relics. He clicked all the
rune-etched buttons along its length, he tapped it and he
prodded it, he even Sang to it under his breath. But nothing had an effect. The object remained still and mysterious.

"Those shadowy figures are clearly usin' these things
to hold secret messages," Lunah deduced.

"I thought you said it was a water bottle?" Ash teased.

"A thing can be two things, Ash the Unflatteringly Smug. Why else would they hide 'em around Aurora? They must be hidden in special places only they know where to look. *Man*, there could be hundreds of these things right under our noses! A whole network of shady communications. Maybe—maybe they're some kinda dark-spirit-worshipping cult? Or a revolutionary group plotting to take down the Council! Why else would they have to hide in the shadows?" Lunah's face looked far too excited at her sinister ideas. "This is sooooo cool!"

"I suspect a code is required to open the device," Tobu said, not taking his sharp eyes away from the throng of the busy docks, just in case they were being watched.

"Maybe . . . maybe my dad hid a message in the one on the Wayfinder's belt?" Ash thought aloud. "And if I figure out how to open these things, I can finally solve the riddle?"

"But that could take forever!" Lunah pointed out.

Ash looked at the device's runes, which meant absolutely nothing to him. "And we're leaving Aurora in a few days . . ."

"Well then, it's time to take matters into our own hands!" Lunah said, punching a fist into an open palm, a mischievous grin stretching across her face. "Can I interest any o' you boys in a *stakeout*?"

Night had drawn in, the curtains of sunlight that beamed through the apertures in the mountainside replaced by the cold glow of the moon outside. Aurora had grown quieter, but voices, laughter, and the sounds of Stronghold life were never far here, even in the dead of night.

Ash, Tobu, and Lunah watched the alley from some distance away, hiding on a jetty behind a cluster of crates and barrels that were destined for the *Frostheart*'s hold.

"What are you lot up to?" Yallah asked, spotting the suspicious trio as she and Kailen were making their way back from the Pathfinder's Rest. They had a little wobble in their steps, and Kailen's cheeks looked strangely flushed.

"Shhh! You'll blow our cover!" Lunah replied. "We're spyin' on a clan of creepers. We need to be super secret!"

Kailen pulled a face. "Creepers?"

"Creepers," said Lunah.

Yallah had looked surprised at the answer, but shook her head, chuckling.

"Of course you are. I don't know why I felt the need to ask."

Time passed uninterrupted after that, by friend or stranger alike.

Most of the crew had gone to bed. Ash had been excited at the idea of a stakeout, but as the evening wore on he found himself getting a bit bored, truth be told. He dared to take his eye off the alley for a moment to gaze up at the giant tiered Stronghold that dominated his view. He still couldn't get his head round the fact that such a thing had been built by the hands of human-kin. It was weird to see the place so peaceful. It almost sounded to him like the Stronghold itself was Singing, as though the steady, calming rumble of the distant sounds were drums, and the twinkling lights of windows and torches were the melody, the voice of Aurora.

"Slow night for shady sneakin', I guess," Lunah said, resting her chin on a crate.

Hours passed.

Hours and hours.

Nothing stirred in the alley, not even a squink. Occasionally Pathfinders and Strongholders walked by, going about their business, oblivious to the group keeping a close eye on a certain loose stone in a wall.

"Maybe they won't come back tonight?" Ash whispered, stifling a yawn as a heavily armed patrol of the Guard marched across the dock.

"Patience," Tobu remarked, having not moved a muscle since their watch had begun, despite sitting in what Ash assumed was an uncomfortable, hyperalert position.

"Least we have eyes above . . ." Lunah said, nodding toward the rustling mass of feathers and shadow that was Rook, perched high above them on the *Frostheart*'s crow's nest. She shifted and fussed more than usual, looking out for *something* with some agitation.

"Who do you think *she's* looking for?" Lunah asked.

Ash shrugged. As with everything involving Rook, it was a complete mystery. She hadn't spoken to Ash that evening and knew nothing about their vigil.

"*There*," Tobu said all of a sudden, muscles tensing.

The children's eyes darted back toward the shadowy alley. Sure enough, as their eyes adjusted, they could make out the shape of a person tampering with the stone in the wall.

"*It's them!*" Ash whispered, adrenaline rushing through his veins.

The trio remained as still as statues, watching the shadow-figure tinker with the cylindrical device. They took something out of the relic, but what, Ash couldn't see.

"It's now or never!" Lunah warned.

"Right!" Ash said.

As one the children vaulted over their hiding place and dashed toward the alley. The figure's hood darted up at the sound of their footfalls. Seeing they'd been spotted, the figure leaped to their feet and fled into the shadows.

"WAIT!" Ash cried out. He and Lunah sprinted after the stranger, who led them round a corner into a maze of dark, narrow paths and back streets. The stranger was fast and agile, turning sharply down lanes they clearly knew well, slipping this way and that. Ash stumbled a few times on the smooth cobblestones in his effort to keep up, clipping his shoulder on walls as he rounded tight corners. He was dimly aware that Tobu was no longer behind them, but he didn't have time to worry about where he'd gone. The stranger bolted toward a tall wall that they clambered over with surprising ease. Ash hit it hard, scrabbling to climb it despite having the wind knocked out of him.

"C'mon, Ash, they're getting away!" Lunah cried, making short work of the wall and running ahead. Panting, Ash landed hard on the other side, stumbling after Lunah and the stranger who was pulling farther and farther away.

We're losing them! Ash panicked, knowing that this might well be the only chance he got to solve the lullaby's riddle. The figure sped round another corner, disappearing out of sight. But just as Ash's heart began to sink he heard a cry and a thump.

Turning the corner, they saw that Tobu had leaped down from a roof and blocked the alleyway. The stranger had stumbled straight into him, and drawn a dagger in defense. Tobu growled, unflinching, but kept his distance.

"Please," Ash pleaded, hoping to calm the stranger down, "we just want to talk!"

"Who are you?!" the figure hissed in a male voice, shifting his weight as if to prepare for an attack. His jaw was wrapped behind a long scarf, which covered most of his face. His eyes peeked from under his hood, vivid and wild. Despite the weapon in his hand, he clearly didn't want to fight. The man was terrified. "I won't come with you. I won't be forced into your war!"

"Calm down," Tobu said, taking a step toward the man. His words had the opposite effect. The stranger skittered away from him, brandishing his dagger with trembling hands.

"Relax, man, we're not here to hurt you!" Lunah said, holding her hands up. "We're friends!"

"Friends who set an ambush, who chase me through the streets?"

"Well, if you'd stayed still for one minute, we wouldn't've *had* to chase you, would we?"

Ash could see they were getting nowhere fast, so he did what he did best: He Sang. He Sang the most soothing Song he could muster, a Song of goodwill and alliance, of reassuring peace. His aura of swirling starlight reached out in friendship. The man did not Sing back, but he did lower his weapon ever so slightly.

"*A Song Weaver . . . ?*" the man said, still wary. "And them?" He pointed his dagger toward Lunah, his eyes narrowing further as he indicated the intimidating size of Tobu. "They don't seem like Weavers . . ."

"What you expectin', fangs, claws, an' scary armor?" Lunah said, folding her arms.

"They're friends. They're on our side!" Ash assured him.

"And your spy on the rooftops?"

Ash was baffled, and then realization washed over him. He looked up to a nearby roof and, lo and behold, saw Rook crouching there in the shadows, watching the scene play out from the darkness of her hood.

"I heard some Song Weavers have readily joined Stormbreaker's cause and are more'n happy to sell the rest of us out! How do I know you're not with *them*?"

"We're not from Aurora!" Ash assured him. "We're just passing through."

"Then might I suggest you keep on passing." The man went to dash past Ash, when Rook swooped down in a flurry of feathers, hissing at the man and causing him to back off, yelping in fear.

"Stop it, Rook!" Ash insisted. "You're not helping!"

Rook backed away.

"Safe. For now. Careful. Trust no one. Enemies everywhere!"

Ash nodded and looked back to the frightened man. "Please, I need your help."

"What makes you think I can help you? Seems to me

you have all the help you need!" The man had backed against a wall, his eyes darting for potential escape routes.

"I'm looking for my father. He was a Song Weaver too, like us! He went missing when I was a baby, but—but I know he used to visit Aurora a lot. His name was Ferno?"

"Never heard of him."

Ash's heart briefly sank, but really what were the chances that this man would just happen to know his father? "He left me a message to—to help me find him. I think it's in one of those archeomek cylinders you hide in the walls . . ."

"A cylindra? Then open it and stop bothering me!" The man pushed past Ash, but Ash grabbed hold of his sleeve.

"I don't know how!" There was a moment of silence, as the man stopped in his tracks. "*Please*," Ash begged. "All I want is to find my dad. This—this may be my only chance . . ."

The man was still for a while, his back to the others. He sighed, before turning round.

"You've come to Aurora at a bad time. Song Weavers have sensed a storm on the horizon for a while now. We've been forced into the shadows of Aurora, and every day we live in fear of when people might turn against us. Known Weavers have been given a curfew, and are forbidden from meeting in groups larger than two for fear that we'll plot against the Stronghold."

"That's why you leave the secret messages?" Lunah asked.

The man nodded. "Yes."

"And *are* you plotting against the Stronghold?" Tobu asked.

"Of course not! We just want to be free to live our lives! We leave the secret messages to keep our community alive, to help each other, 'cause spirits know no one else will! We're looking to getting people out of here, to—" He stopped midsentence, fearing he might've already said too much.

"To search for somewhere safe for Song Weavers?" Tobu asked carefully.

"Be sure to tell me if you ever find it," the stranger answered. "Look, I'll help you, Song Weaver to Song Weaver. But spirits curse you if you betray my trust, boy."

Ash raised a hand to his heart. "I'll keep your secret, I swear it. You're my people too." The man looked deep into Ash's eyes, hunting for any sign of a lie. Ash did his best to stare confidently back, despite how uncomfortable he felt.

Eventually the man took a deep breath, and relented. "Each cylindra has a Song that is 'imprinted' on it. They're ancient Song Weaver machines from the World Before," he said, before pointing to the rune-etched depressions. "Each of these runes corresponds to a note on a scale. Once you know the Song that matches the cylindra, you tap in the first notes of the Song by pressing down these buttons. If you enter them correctly, the cylindra will open."

Ash nodded as though he understood, but unfortunately he didn't know what half of those words meant. What was a "scale"? Music had been banned at the Fira, and any Song that Ash Sang came from his heart, not from runes and symbols.

"How about the cylindra on the Wayfinder statue? Do you know what runes I have to press for that?"

The man laughed. "No one's known how to get into that one since someone changed its Song, what, ten years ago now? That cylindra will likely keep its secrets till the end of time. Unless, of course, it was your father . . . ?" He gave Ash a look, suddenly understanding.

"Can you tell me what notes match the runes? Please—I have no idea what buttons to press!"

A noise startled all those standing in the alley, the sound of marching footsteps close by.

"I don't have time to sit around writing codes for you, kid . . ." the man said, eager to be on his way.

Tobu stepped forward, a deep rumble in his throat, convincing the man to reconsider.

"Okay, okay . . . I could Memory Weave with you. But quickly. And *quietly*! I'll show you my memories of the code. Remember them well, 'cause you won't find me again."

"I will!" Ash nodded in excitement.

He assumed Memory Weaving was the same technique Rook had shared with him on the *Frostheart*'s deck, though he was a little perturbed by the man's confidence in suggesting it. Did all Song Weavers know how to do it except for him?

"Thank you," Ash said earnestly. "I can't thank you enough!"

"Yeah, well, can't say it's been a pleasure." The man looked from Rook to Tobu, still nervous. "But promise me one thing."

"Yes?"

"Promise me the moment you get your father's message, you'll leave this place far, far behind before you're discovered. Song Weavers aren't free in Aurora. Not anymore."

13

The Greater Good

Lunah led Ash, Tobu, and Rook up through the hustle and bustle of Aurora's early-morning streets. The watery yellow light that washed down upon the Stronghold echoed the brightness in Ash's soul and the reignited hope he felt.

This is it! I have the answer to the riddle! Weaving a Song of memories, the exact same technique Rook had used, the Song Weaver had shown Ash which runes corresponded to which musical notes. Ash had concentrated as hard as he could, particularly memorizing the runes he suspected would unlock the Wayfinder's cylindra.

"Hope you 'preciate this, fire-boy," Lunah said. "I'm missin' breakfast for you! An' you know that breakfast is, like, a sacred meal to us Drifters! Almost as special as lunch an' dinner . . ."

"I'll make it up to you, I promise," Ash replied, a grin across his face and an extra leap in his step. *I'm so close! Mum, Dad—I'm coming!*

What if this was the last riddle he had to solve? What if, at long last, the statue revealed the way to Solstice? Ash picked up the pace.

Somehow Rook got even more funny looks from passersby than Tobu did. Ash suspected it had something to do with the way she would leap and dash from corner to corner, rushing through the lanes like a wild animal, her crows screeching and crying out in her wake.

"I like her," Lunah said as Rook lurched past an embracing couple, who shrieked in shock.

"*FASTER*," Rook hissed at Ash. "*Aurora not safe. Can't stay.*"

"There's definitely a tension building . . ." Ash admitted. It felt like that heavy, pressing feeling you get before a thunderstorm. Aurora was less busy now that the Pathfinders had begun to leave, but there was still an underlying energy, a buzz among the people. They had a purpose now, after all—a plan to reclaim the world.

"*Not Guard. Not Aurora worry about. They come. Come for you*," Rook Sang.

Ash swallowed. "Who're *they*?" Was this who Rook had been looking out for the night before?

"Hear them. Fearful World Weave Sings. MUST. HURRY."

"What—what do you mean?" Ash's nerves tingled.

"Riddle. Must solve. Fast escape. HEART TO SOL-STICE. To safety."

"Everything okay?" Lunah asked, an eyebrow raised. "She seems more . . . fidgety than normal . . ."

"She's . . . she's just keen to solve the riddle, I think . . ." Ash said, watching Rook rush ahead, past a flustered street performer who'd been surrounded by two stern-looking guards. The performer had been singing to passersby, but was now quivering with fright, his eyes wide and brow beading with sweat. The guards loomed over him in their heavy armor, the man looking small and frail in comparison.

"I-I'm not a Song Weaver, I swear to you!" Ash heard the performer say as they passed. "I just sing folk songs! Y'know, toe-tappers, singalongs! Name a tune, I'll—I'll sing it to you right now!"

"Witnesses claim they've seen you in the dark of night, Singing the Leviathan Song in secret . . ."

"*Lies!* I've never—"

"All Song Weavers need to come with us."

"Please, no—I'm not—" the performer pleaded, looking like he might burst into tears.

"If you don't like it, that's *fine*," the guard said. "If you won't help, you can leave Aurora, though you won't be welcome here, or in any other Stronghold in the Embrace."

Ash's heart tied into a knot as Lunah gasped and shouted, "Says who?!"

The guards turned, anger flashing across their faces.

"*Lunah, leave it!*" Ash mumbled under his breath, not wanting to attract attention.

"Says Commander Stormbreaker, under the authority of the Council themselves," one guard replied, stepping toward Lunah menacingly. "You'd do well to watch your tongue, girl."

Lunah stared back defiantly, not giving up any ground. Tobu stepped behind her, a deep growl emerging from his preposterous beard. The guard hesitated, decided that anyone with a beard like that was probably someone you didn't want to cross, and took a step back.

"It's for the greater good of all the Snow Sea, and I'm sure any honorable Weaver would see that," the other guard said, shoving the performer to make his point. "There's been a call to arms, and you're honor bound to answer it." The guards grabbed the man despite his protests.

Ash, Tobu, and Lunah watched in shock as he was carried away, Lunah cursing while Ash kept his head down, trying to look as invisible as possible.

"Hysteria rules here, and we are in danger of being drowned under its depths," Tobu said. "We must take refuge in a place outside Stormbreaker's reach."

"We'll make our way to Solstice!" Ash said. "No one here knows where it is. We can hide there until things calm down, and we can figure out what to do . . ."

Tobu bared his fangs with distaste. "Our situation requires substance over rumor and legend."

Ash furrowed his brow and scrunched up his face. Why was Tobu showing such resistance to the idea of traveling to Solstice, even doubting its existence? He'd always been the one telling Ash how important it was to listen to the World Weave, and now that he was actually doing it, and was apparently being led to Solstice, Tobu seemed to have lost his faith in his own beliefs. Surely he, of all people, should be eager to follow the signs? Ash pushed on, more determined than ever. "I'll get us there. The statue will show us the way."

The Wayfinder stood noble and silent, gazing proudly over the square she called home.

"Be glad yer made of stone," Lunah said to the statue as they approached. "Whole Stronghold's gone flippin' mad! You'd lose yer mind if you could see it!"

Ash wasted no time. He checked to make sure no one was watching too closely. He could hear a gentle rumble

of loud voices, but for now it sounded far off. The cylindra was firmly attached to the statue, so Ash stepped up onto the plinth so that he could reach it, with Lunah joining him.

"You need someone to cheer you on!" she said when Ash gave her a look. The plinth was barely large enough for them both, so Tobu and Rook kept watch from below. Ash concentrated, thinking on everything the Song Weaver had told him.

Surely there's only one Song my dad would've used to lock the cylindra . . .

He focused on the memories the Song Weaver had shown him, of what runes corresponded to what notes. Rook had helped him understand what he'd seen and heard, and Ash had done his very best to commit it all to memory. So, taking a deep breath, Ash whispered the notes of the lullaby, matching each note to a rune engraved on the cylindra. He pressed the buttons one after the other and then waited, his heart thumping fast.

Nothing happened.

Had he done it wrong? Had he not keyed in enough notes? Was it the wrong Song entirely? *I have no idea what other Song it could be!*

The distant rumble of raised voices was drawing closer, becoming almost distracting.

"You remember the code, right?" Lunah asked.

Sweat trickled down Ash's neck, and his breathing grew faster as he tried to push down the rising panic tightening round his throat. "*Please . . .*" Ash pleaded, "*please don't do this . . .*"

He keyed in the runes again with trembling fingers, slowly, carefully, paying extra attention to make sure he wasn't entering the code wrong. He jerked his hands away once he was done, not wanting to mess anything up.

There was a pause . . .

And then . . .

Click.

To almost overwhelming relief Ash saw the top of the cylindra shift, and heard Lunah gasp. He carefully lifted it with one finger, opening the device. Reaching inside, he fished out a folded scrap of paper and a small, perfectly spherical stone. He held the sphere up and examined the patterns and whorls that had been etched into it. "Archeomek . . ." Ash whispered. He shook it and he poked it, but nothing happened. Tucking it into his furs for safety,

Ash ducked away with the others to a more inconspicuous spot to investigate the parchment. Fira symbols had been scrawled onto it using red ochre. Ash's heart skipped a beat to see them—and then again when he thought who'd written it. To think he was actually holding something his father had once held! He read the note.

> Through forest unbroken and shimmering sky,
> Follow the gaze of the giant's eye.
> The sleeping warrior watches the door,
> Where we shall meet, and you'll search no more.

"Is it what you came for?" Tobu asked.

Ash squeezed the parchment tight between his fingers, trying to absorb all he could of his missing father.

This was it. It sounded like the end of the lullaby—the last riddle he had to solve! He rolled the words around his head, not yet knowing their meaning, but overjoyed to have them.

"I think so . . ." Ash said with a smile, which Tobu didn't return, nodding grimly instead. Ash would've puzzled over this strange reaction, were it not for the angry bellow that echoed through the square.

14

Call to Arms

A crowd flooded the square, a commotion in their midst. Ash and Lunah peeped out from behind Tobu, watching the throng approach as Rook hissed ominously behind them, keeping her distance. Ash had a sinking feeling.

A line of about fifteen people were being marched within the center of the crowd, men, women and children of all ages, urged forward by the spear points of ten guards. The rest of the crowd were onlookers, spectating as the prisoners were marched through the Stronghold. Ash went cold, the sinking in his belly dragging at him like a great weight.

"They're . . . they're Song Weavers, aren't they?" he asked his friends, afraid he already knew the answer.

"What is *happening* to this place?" Lunah said in disbelief.

Tobu watched on, his expression unreadable.

"You can't do this to us!" a prisoner shouted.

"We're people too!" shouted another.

"We've lived here as long as any of you; we have every right to be here!"

"You'll receive new homes!" announced the captain of the Guard. "All Song Weavers are to be moved to the training ground outside the Stronghold where you shall learn discipline and be trained for battle! Rest assured you'll all be taken care of!"

"You're stealing us from our homes!" a young girl squeaked, clasping her mother's robes.

"You're being given the chance to fight for all of human-kin," growled the captain. "You should be thankful!"

"We've been given no choice!" a woman shouted to the captain. "There are children and elders here. We're not warriors!"

The small group of Song Weavers roared in agreement. Ash gritted his teeth at the injustice.

"LET US GO! LET US GO!" the prisoners chanted, pushing toward the guards, who were fast to level their spears and stop the rush before it started.

"You're lucky we let your kind live in our great Stronghold at all!" the captain spat. "Monster-lovers, the lot of you. I'd have had you out long ago if it were up to me! Now back in line, before we use force!"

The onlookers cheered at the guard's show of strength, but Ash's cheeks grew hot as he balled his trembling fists. He'd imagined finding other Song Weavers countless times, and in each daydream it had been a moment overflowing with joy.

Not *this*.

This was a nightmare.

Cold anger gnawed at his nerves, flowing through his blood like ice.

Imagine if Song Weavers did actually use Leviathans for evil, if we did use them as weapons! Then the Strongholds would actually have something to be scared of . . . Maybe Shaard was right. If they're gonna treat us like this, maybe we should make them fear us!

Ash felt himself pulled into a sudden embrace. It felt like he'd been drawn into a protective, loving hug, as real as the shouting surrounding him. It came as a shock to discover that it wasn't a person at all, but the gentle Song of the frost-heart pushing back at the hatred building up in Ash, easing his building fury.

"Fight the anger." It didn't Sing with words but with

sensation and emotions that were nowhere yet every-where. *"Step away from that path. It wants you to hate. You must resist."*

"Be calm." Ash startled as Rook's whisper joined in harmony with the frost-heart. *"Listen, Heart. Hate makes monsters. I know."*

Their Songs pulled Ash from the biting mist of fury that still clawed at him and he breathed deeply, a little shaken at how horrifyingly vengeful he'd just felt. He'd been someone he was not. The cold, hollow feeling released its grip on his heart. He caught Tobu's eye; the yeti was watching him with a deep concern. Ash nodded that he was okay, though Tobu didn't look convinced.

"Wait till Cap' hears 'bout this!" Lunah said, raising a fist. "She'll knock 'em flat! Or maybe we should save her the trouble an' do it ourselves!"

"How—how can they treat us like this . . . ?" Ash asked in a small voice.

Tobu placed a massive hand on Ash's shoulder and gave it a reassuring squeeze. "I believe most people just want to live their lives in peace but wear fear like a shield against a frightening world. They lose sight of what they truly believe in."

Ash hoped he was right. He simply didn't want to believe that all these people were bad. He watched as

the crowd allowed the imprisoned Song Weavers to be marched by, their faces disturbingly indifferent to the injustice of the situation.

"*Get to Solstice. Not our concern,*" Rook rasped over Ash's shoulder.

But Ash didn't want to just hide in Solstice. He wanted the people of the Snow Sea to like Song Weavers, to be on their side.

Is this why Dad left everything behind, Ash wondered, *to get away from being treated this way?* If so, Ash couldn't blame him, not really. *But why didn't he take me with him? Why would he leave me behind?*

And where did his mother fit into all of this? Was she even with Ferno? All Ash knew about her was that she wasn't a Song Weaver. He didn't even know her name! The Fira were a superstitious people and refused to utter the names of those who left the Stronghold for fear that their names would bring misfortune down on them all.

Me and Tobu will never be named there again, Ash realized with a surprisingly painful pang. *They will do their best to forget us, just like they did my parents . . .*

But Ash was doing all he could to remember them. And one thing he *did* know about his mum was that she hadn't trusted Shaard, so at least they had that in common. The thought warmed his heart.

His thoughts were broken by a scream. At first Ash assumed it was one of the prisoners, but then he realized it had come from farther away.

Suddenly the air was split by an even worse sound— an ear-piercing inhuman shriek.

A sound so jarring, it rattled bones and thrummed against eardrums. Everyone in the square ducked instinctively, looking about wildly for the source.

"*What—*" Ash began.

"THERE!" a guard called out, pointing up into the air. Three dark shapes tore past overhead, high above the streets. Ash squinted to try to make sense of what he was seeing. The shapes had leaped off the top of a tall spire and were gliding upon wings that were attached to their four limbs like fabric pulled over the frame of a kite. They circled above Aurora, deftly guiding themselves with tails that ended in sail-like fans. Were they gliders of some kind? No, Ash could see now that they were long and serpentine, round, feathered heads craning in search of an unknown target. A sound worried the back of Ash's head, an annoying buzz that felt like the beginning of a headache.

"What—what's happening?" a guard asked.

No one seemed willing to believe their eyes. Two of the creatures tore away and out of sight, but the last one dived straight down toward the square.

"SHRIEKERS!" the captain bellowed. "BOWS AT THE READY!"

Terrified screams erupted from the crowd in the square as people tore off in all directions, pushing and stumbling over each other in their desperation to get away. The Song Weavers tried to run too, but were hemmed in by the guards, who were grasping for the bows slung over their shoulders.

"Let us go!" the Weavers cried out helplessly.

"How on earth did they get in?" the captain cried, ignoring them. "Leviathans have never breached Aurora's walls!"

Leviathans?!

"I didn't know Leviathans could *fly*!" Ash gasped.

Lunah watched the air with wide eyes. "Technically they don't," Lunah said. "These ones glide. But they need a high perch to leap off to ride the wind. They're mountain 'viathans. They don't come from these areas—they shouldn't be here!"

"Behind me," Tobu said, stepping in front of Ash and Lunah.

Our weapons, Ash thought, seeing that Tobu carried none. *We left them on the* Frostheart!

"*If Sing, be arrested. If not Sing, be eaten*," Rook whispered. "*No good choice . . .*"

"We need to get to cover—those things'll pluck us up like berries from a bush!" Lunah cried.

A Shrieker hurtled toward the crowd at tremendous speed, letting out a shrill scream.

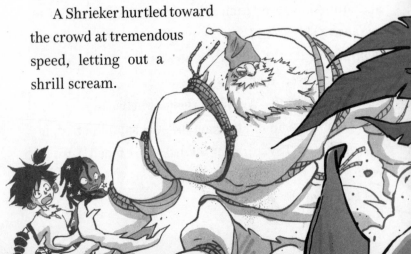

"Spirits help us . . ." the captain whispered, before yelling, "OPEN FIRE! Bring it down!"

With a thrum the guards let loose their arrows. The Shrieker was swift, twirling and weaving its way through the volley, but it couldn't dodge them all. Arrows caught it in the wing, and with another screech, it plummeted to the ground. It crashed into the Wayfinder statue in a cloud of dust and broken stone, right before Ash and the others. A writhing shape whipped around frantically in the dust.

"READY!" the captain behind Ash and the others

cried, holding up a fist. The guards nocked more arrows.

A tail coiled out of the haze, then claws, which dragged the beast to its feet. It emerged from the dust, snarling deep within its throat, its six milk-white eyes focused on its attackers.

Ash thought it looked a bit like a small Gargant, which is to say horrifying, but it was more streamlined, its movements on the ground clumsy compared to the grace it had displayed in the air. Ash's muscles tensed and his throat went dry. He felt so exposed.

No walls.

No sleigh.

Just an unarmed yeti between him and this incredibly disgruntled predator. The monster bared its daggerlike fangs. A deep thrumming sound came from its throat as it tensed its muscles. Then, with a terrible scream, it charged right for them.

15
Control

The Shrieker's awkward gait allowed Tobu time to dive out of its path, pushing the children back with him.

"*No choice . . .*" Rook rasped, and as soon as they were out of the way her broken voice filled the air and her damaged Song-aura darted toward the Leviathan in the hope of calming its rage.

"STOP HER!" the captain yelled. "Do not let them Sing! They'll use the beast as a weapon!"

Rook was tackled to the ground by two guards before her Song could properly get under way. She kicked and screamed, and the guards struggled to keep her pinned down.

"FIRE!" the captain ordered.

Arrows rained down on the Leviathan, blue blood leaking out of the wounds that pierced its tough hide.

The Shrieker gave a scream, and leaned heavily to one side. But it scrambled toward the guards nonetheless, who thrust their spears as one. The Shrieker caught one in its jaws, thrashing its head so violently that the guard was thrown to the ground, his spear snapping. The beast whipped round and caught another with its tail, and the guard hit a wall hard and collapsed in a limp pile. But the others managed to strike true. The Shrieker screeched and wailed, its legs buckling under the strain of its injuries.

A voice suddenly filled Ash's head. *"HELP."*

Ash recoiled as he realized who—or rather what—it was. It was the Shrieker's Song. It didn't sound aggressive or furious. It sounded desperate, small and scared.

"HURT. DYING. ESCAPE. FLEE."

When Leviathans attacked, their Song-auras lashed out as blood-red tendrils of fury. But this one's aura was glowing a pale blue, weak and fading. Ash sensed that it was confused, and hurt, and caught in the wrong place. It was desperate to escape, to get away from Aurora. He looked harder, and saw a tendril of darkness coiled round its aura, strangling the life from it. A buzzing sound pressed down on Ash's head, forcing him to narrow his eyes. With terrible realization Ash recognized it as the same droning buzz that had tormented him back at Shade's Chasm.

Is that . . . the Wraiths?

Ash spun round, fear tickling the back of his neck, but he saw no sign of them.

"Wait!" he shouted. "It doesn't want to be here!"

The guards stabbed at it with their spears, more arrows *thunking* deep into its flesh. The Shrieker let out a piteous whine, its limbs trembling.

"STOP IT!" Ash yelled. "IT'S BEING CONTROLLED! IT DOESN'T WANT TO BE HERE!"

Tobu and Lunah gave Ash an astonished look.

The guards prepared their weapons, ready to put the beast down.

Time seemed to slow.

And it was then that Ash decided to act.

He knew it was reckless.

But deep down he also knew was that it was the right thing to do.

It felt like he was wading through water, his mind sluggish and struggling to keep up, not quite able to comprehend what he was doing. He was surprised to discover that he'd run toward the Leviathan, standing between the guards and the monster, arms outstretched.

"ASH?!" Tobu and Lunah cried out as one, having reached out to stop him but missing his furs by a hairs-breadth.

"GET OUT OF THE WAY!" the captain bellowed in disbelief.

"Something is forcing it to do these things! It doesn't want to be here!" Ash cried.

The guards looked at Ash like he'd completely lost his mind. Maybe he had. But he began to Song Weave regardless. His Song-aura swirled around him, the frost-heart filling him with confidence, a Song of strength and defiance rising out of him.

His aura shot toward the writhing darkness, his voice tearing at it, trying to help the Shrieker escape its grip. The Shrieker lent its weak strength to Ash, fighting back against the controlling tendrils of shadow.

The buzzing drone was not as powerful here as it was in Shade's Chasm, and it vanished like smoke with the combined strength of both Songs weaving together.

The Shrieker shuddered, its white eyes flicking toward Ash. He flinched as the creature moved, but instead of attacking, it began clambering up onto the roof of a building, slow and pained. Blue splats of blood marked its trail. The guards prepared to open fire once more.

"DON'T!" Ash shouted. "You'll just anger it! It wants to leave!"

With one last glance back at Ash, the Shrieker leaped from the building, wobbling here and there in the air until it disappeared from sight.

Ash breathed out in relief, before being spun round by a furious Tobu. "What was going through your head, boy?! You could have gotten yourself *killed.*"

"N-no! I had to help it—it was being forced to attack us!"

"By *what*?! The only things here that could do that are you Song Weavers!" the captain shouted, striding toward them, angry flecks of spit spattering from his mouth with every word.

All the guards were looking at Ash with horrified expressions. "Song Weavers get mind-controlled by Leviathans, it's well-known!" one said.

"The boy's mind has been taken over by the Shrieker, and it used him to escape!" the captain agreed, Ash shrinking away with every word. "Now it's free to wreak havoc elsewhere in the Stronghold! The boy cannot be allowed to leave, he's a menace to us all! Who knows what else the beast will make him do!"

"No, I—it *wasn't*—" Ash began, but the guards were already pacing toward him.

"Ash!" Lunah cried out, Tobu beside her, looking as if he were debating whether to attack the guards.

"ENOUGH!" shouted a Weaver.

"The boy's one of us! We need to help him!" yelled another.

"Don't you *dare!*" the captain roared. "We are the law!"

The Song Weavers began to protest, pushing toward the guards, who brandished their spears threateningly.

"We need to stand and fight! We need to stand together!" The Song Weavers let out a defiant roar and fell upon the guards in a wave, pushing, punching, and kicking their way through their line, the guards having no room to maneuver their spears.

The square broke out into an absolute riot.

16

Undercover

Ash ducked out of the guard's grasp and grazed past the hands of another, slipping and dodging his way through the chaos. He saw Rook kick her way free of her captors, but she was instantly lost in the tumult. Ash could hear Tobu's roaring voice calling out for him, but couldn't see his friends anywhere. He spotted a gap in the heaving, violent mass. Desperate for an escape, he took the chance, guards close behind.

"GET HIM! DON'T LET HIM ESCAPE!"

Ash ran from the square as fast as he could, twisting through crooked streets, leaping over pots and walls, trying his hardest to lose his pursuers.

He could hear the heavy footsteps of the guards behind him, but he dared not look behind to see how close they were. Though he was being chased by angry guards, they were not what had sent Ash's mind into a spin. Was the captain right? *Had* he just been tricked? *Controlled* by the Leviathan? He'd felt no different from any other time he'd Song Weaved. But then he'd never actually *seen* a Song Weaver have their mind taken over by a Leviathan; he'd only heard the stories. Perhaps this was exactly how it felt. Perhaps they'd been controlling him since the very first time he'd Song Weaved, and Ash just didn't know it.

Bile rose up into his throat, the idea of Leviathans controlling his mind somehow worse than simply being eaten. It was true he hadn't been feeling himself recently . . . the cold anger that would gnaw at his insides . . . was that *them*? Panic threatened to flood him when a shadow passed overhead, making Ash instinctively duck.

The other two Shriekers! He could still hear the terrible drone of the Wraiths too, somewhere close.

He ran in and out of the crowded streets, ignoring the protests of people as he pushed past, the angry shouts of the guards never far behind.

Where shall I go? Ash fretted. *Can I make it to the docks?*

He skidded to a halt, the guards lost in the maze of streets for now, though their cries could be heard close by. Ash stumbled back in fear—and was suddenly grabbed from behind. He shrieked, then realized it was Rook, rushing him round the corner as fast as she could.

"They're here. We must flee!"

"Wh-who are here?!" Ash stuttered, running alongside Rook. "The guards?"

"The enemy."

They dashed into another lane—and saw two figures.

"Tobu! Lunah!" Ash cried out in joyful relief.

"Here! *Quickly!*" Tobu said, tearing his disguise off, ripping at the wrappings and ropes that were tangled about him until they dangled from his middle like a shredded kilt. "Underneath!" he said, pointing at it.

"Errrr . . ." Ash said, unsure why he'd want to voluntarily get quite so close to Tobu's behind, but rapidly changed his mind as he saw two guards round the far corner, heading toward them. He dived under Tobu's makeshift kilt and pressed tightly against the fur of his leg, hoping the guards hadn't seen him.

"He went that way!" Ash heard Lunah tell the approaching guards.

"He . . . er . . ." the guard replied, trying to comprehend the sight of a young girl keeping company with a bizarre kilt-wearing yeti and a scary crow-woman.

"Quick, else you'll lose him!" Lunah urged.

"I—er . . . R-right, thank you, girl!" the guard man-

aged, before, to Ash's huge relief, the guard's footsteps
thumped away down the lane. When the coast was definitely clear Lunah spoke.

"I gotta hand it to you, Ash. You make an *excellent*
rear end."

Kinspear

They met the rest of the crew halfway back to the docks.

"Goodness, Tobu, what's happened to you?" Nuk exclaimed, seeing the state of the yeti's clothing. "It looks like you've been wrestling with a sleigh propeller!"

"I had to sacrifice my disguise to remedy the boy's brash, ill-judged actions." He gave Ash an angry look, one Ash couldn't face returning.

"Indeed, you're the talk of the town, lad."

"As is so often the case . . ." Kailen grumbled.

"We must leave, right away. The Guard will not rest until they find Ash," Nuk insisted.

Ash's belly twisted. This was the second time the crew had been forced out of a Stronghold, all because of *him*.

"I-I'm sorry—I—" he stammered. "I'll turn myself in. You can't be exiled from Aurora. You'll all be done for if—"

"Don't worry, lad. They don't know you're with us," Kob said with a kind smile. "We just need to make sure we get you out safely."

Ash let out a long breath, relieved.

"Come. Back to the sleigh. It's high time we set off on another run, wouldn't you say?" Nuk said, guiding the crew down a steep lane that led to the dock.

The Stronghold was trembling in chaos. There was no sign of the Shriekers; they'd either escaped or been killed by the Guard, but people were still rushing about with terror in their eyes. It seemed Aurora had never been attacked like this before, and it showed on the face of every single person they passed. Their fear only heightened when they saw a yeti in their midst.

"Why are the yeti here?" Ash heard passersby saying. "Has the Mountain's Ward finally gone on the attack?"

Who's the Mountain's Ward? Ash wondered, looking toward Tobu, who strode forward without so much as a glance at his accusers.

"*Enemy close,*" Rook hissed at Ash. "*Good we leave.*"

"Did they do this? Who—who were they? What do they want?"

But no answer came from Rook; her hood just twisted this way and that, betraying her skittish nerves.

They made it to the lowest level of the Stronghold,

the huge docks coming into view, but before they even set foot on the jetties a large group of Pathfinders marched up from the docks straight toward the *Frostheart* crew. Ash's heart leaped into his throat as he saw Commander Stormbreaker leading them.

"Spirits above, of all people to bump into!" Teya whispered.

"Quick, Ash, behind us!" Nuk hissed, and the crew stopped to form a line for Ash to duck behind. The crew stood awkwardly, forcing smiles on their faces as Storm-breaker's crew approached them.

"Hail, crew of the *Frostheart!*" Stormbreaker greeted

them, her eyes lingering on Tobu. "Thank the spirits you're all safe."

"Aye, you too, crew of the *Kinspear*. A terrible business, all of this," Nuk said. "Any news on the Shriekers?"

Ash clung close behind Tobu, his knees trembling. *Please don't see me, please don't see me . . .*

"They've been dealt with," Stormbreaker said. "But this shows the seriousness of our situation. This was a blatant attack. Shriekers do not come from these lands. The only ones who could bring them here are Song Weavers."

Ash held his breath.

"What about Wraiths?" Lunah suggested. "Leviathans follow them round like pets; we've seen it with our own eyes."

"The thought crossed my mind, but no black sleighs have been spotted in the area, let alone through the checkpoints on the walls. We'd know if those *fiends* had made it inside."

"So you think the Song Weavers are turning against us?" Kailen said.

"No, I think the *Leviathans* are turning them against us. Leviathans rule the wilds, but they can't penetrate our Strongholds. I believe their new strategy is to make Song Weavers do that for them. We're heading toward Wayfinder Square right now, in fact. Word is a child Weaver up there was turned, and he *must* be found. The Leviathan influence spreads like rot once it gets into their minds. I've seen it happen before. If the boy is not found fast, we could have an uprising on our hands." Ash went cold. The *Frostheart* crew drew tighter together, doing their best to hide him. Stormbreaker took a step closer. "You haven't seen him, have you? A small boy, black hair?"

Ash clung to Tobu's back, trying to stop trembling.

"I've seen many boys with black hair, commander," Nuk replied. Stormbreaker remained silent, eyeing the crew suspiciously. "But I'll be sure to pay more attention, going forward. We wish you the best of luck in finding him." As one, the *Frostheart* crew saluted, and then rotated in a line round Stormbreaker's Pathfinders, turning as though they had been stuck together. Ash wheeled round with them, his heart thumping.

"Aye, thank you, captain," Stormbreaker said, pulling a face at their strange behavior as they backed away while facing her.

We've done it! We've got past her! Ash's racing heart thrummed with hope.

"Hold on!" Stormbreaker called.

The crew stopped, Ash stumbling to a halt.

"Where are you going? We could use your help in the hunt."

"We're heading out on a run, of course, doing our bit for the cause," Nuk replied.

Stormbreaker's eyes narrowed. "I'm surprised at your sudden change of heart, captain. You were my biggest critic back at the Moot."

"Well, if you can't beat them, join them, as my dear mother used to say."

"Mm. I'm glad to hear it," Stormbreaker said, looking anything but convinced. "Will you be heading back north?" Her voice was almost wishful, probably hoping Nuk would journey far off and out of her way.

"Wherever we're needed, as always," Nuk said. Stormbreaker nodded, but didn't dismiss the *Frostheart* crew, who stood there, looking ever more awkward. She took a step closer, eyeballing each one of them.

She knows, Ash fretted. *She knows I'm here!*

Suddenly Kailen stepped from the line. "While I have you here, commander, can I just say that I really am happy to have you as the leader of the fleet." She placed her arm round Stormbreaker's shoulder and tried to turn her from the others, but Stormbreaker resisted. "It's about time someone with guts took charge. I for one can't wait to hit back at the wurms, show 'em what we're made of!" Stormbreaker finally relented, allowing Kailen to turn her round, flustered with the outburst of compliments.

"Th-thank you," she said.

The rest of the *Frostheart* crew then swarmed round the Commander, all smiles and laughs, except Tobu, Rook, and Ash, who slowly backed toward the sleigh.

"It's true—she doesn't stop goin' on about you!" Yallah laughed.

"Story after story, Stormbreaker this, Stormbreaker that . . ." Twinge added.

"I try to tell her, but does she listen?" Nuk added. As they crowded Stormbreaker, keeping her occupied, Kailen waved her hand behind her back, signaling for Tobu and Rook to make a break for it. They wasted no time, spinning round and herding Ash, still somehow unseen, toward their sleigh.

18

Out of Sight

The large gates rumbled open and the *Frostheart* passed through the outer wall, away from Aurora and back into the wilds. Ash sat alone at the sleigh's stern, watching the mountain Stronghold grow smaller and smaller. A Stronghold he had dreamed of seeing, and a Stronghold that had been more wondrous and spectacular than he'd ever imagined. But a Stronghold he wasn't welcome in, just like every other one in the Snow Sea. His throat felt scratchy, and tears streaked down his cheeks. Whether they were tears of sadness or anger, he couldn't say. He wanted the Strongholds to accept him so badly, and yet he *hated* the Strongholders for rejecting him, for treating the Song Weavers like that. Why would he want to be accepted by people he hated? He didn't know what he felt anymore. Memories of the Shrieker attack darkened

Ash's thoughts, and he tried to quash them, finding them scarier than the idea of being an outcast. Had Wraiths really attacked Aurora with the Shriekers, even though there'd been no sign of them, or had the Song Weavers done it as Captain Stormbreaker believed they had? Had they had any choice, or had they had their senses stolen from them by the Shriekers, as Ash feared had happened to him? The more he considered it, the more likely it seemed. Why else would Ash have helped the Shrieker; why else would he feel a connection with the Leviathans? They weren't allies; they were bloodthirsty monsters! Even the crew, his only friends, seemed to be eyeing him worriedly. *Probably worried I'm not myself after hearing I saved that Shrieker . . .*

Ash pretended he didn't care, but his stinging eyes told a different story. It had been particularly hurtful to see that Tobu was among those watching him from a distance.

Ash wished the *Frostheart* would go faster. *So I can get to Solstice quicker, the one place where I belong*, he told himself—but he also knew it was because he hoped he could outrun the awful things he'd just experienced.

At least it wasn't a complete disaster, he thought as he rolled the archeosphere his father had left for him, still puzzled about its purpose. The main thing was he had the next verse in the lullaby, and that was really what he'd come here for.

"I checked the Council records as you requested, captain," Ash overheard Master Podd say to Nuk up on the bridge directly above. Normally Ash would've gone on minding his own business, but a word caught his attention. "Indeed, I found the records for the sleigh known as *Trailblazer*."

Trailblazer. Ash's heart skipped a beat. *My mum's sleigh!*

"And?" Nuk asked.

There was a pause. "A fire. Burned it to ashes."

Ash's world came to a sudden, stomach-lurching stop.

No, he thought. *No. It can't be. Not after . . . everything. . . It's not true!*

His body felt utterly numb. His aching heart, and the news he'd just heard, thundered around his head.

"I see," Nuk said. "And the crew?"

"Unaccounted for, captain."

"Well, thank the Valkyries for small mercies. So they could still be alive . . . ?"

"Indeed, captain. Quite possible. The *Trailblazer*'s records ended after that. The rest remains quite the mystery." With these words, these simple, hopeful words, sound and life and movement rushed back toward Ash like a gale.

*They got out safely, I know it! Just because the sleigh
burned doesn't mean that—that—* Ash took a long, shuddering breath. *I know Dad made it to Solstice, even
Shaard thought so. And hopefully my mum went with him.
Maybe . . . maybe they even burned the* Trailblazer *on purpose to throw Shaard off their trail? Yeah—that's gotta be it!*

"And what was the name of the captain?" Nuk asked.

Ash went dead still.

"Captain Ember."

Ash's breath caught in his throat. But this time it was
with excitement instead of dread.

Ember . . . My mum's name is Ember!

"Let's not tell the lad just yet," Nuk said. "Not until we have the whole story straightened out. He's been
through enough, the poor tyke. The last thing he requires is a needless scare."

"I agree, captain."

"Excellent work, Master Podd. I do appreciate it."

"Indeed, captain."

Ember. Ash rolled the name around his head and was
surprised to discover he had a smile on his face. He knew
his mother's name! It was comforting—it brought him
closer to his mother, like she was standing close by, just
out of sight.

I have to find her. She'll make this right, I know it. As soon as I find my parents, everything will be better.

Ash watched as Aurora, the sacred harbor of safety, the cradle of civilization and center of it all, drifted farther and farther away from his view. It looked beautiful. He was glad he had gotten to see it. For he knew, deep down, he would never see it again.

THE WILDS

19

On the Run

The sleigh had been following them closely all day.

The *Frostheart* was heading south from Aurora—though toward what, no one was sure. The peak of Aurora's majestic mountain had disappeared from view. Ash looked to the southeast, where an enormous forest sprawled out toward the horizon before fading into a dark blue smudge in the dim twilight dusk. But in every other direction there was plenty of space upon the vast snow plains that lay between the trees and mountains.

"So why on earth are they tailing us so closely?" Nuk asked.

The crew had gathered on the starboard side to watch the peculiar sight, with Master Podd steering the *Frostheart* at the bridge. Kailen had raised the signal flags, asking if the sleigh needed help, but there had been no response.

"Perhaps they've been sent to keep an eye on us," Arla suggested.

"Aye, perhaps. Stormbreaker clearly trusts us as far as she can throw our sleigh. But if that's the case, they're not being discreet about it, are they?"

As the sleigh drew up even closer to the *Frostheart*'s stern, the emblem emblazoned upon its sails became visible.

"It's the *Ice Runner*!" Teya called down from the crow's nest.

"Captain Norrow's lot?" Kob said. "Not really the types to spy, even for someone like Stormbreaker . . ."

"No, indeed," Nuk agreed, her voice low with suspicion.

Rook was fidgeting at Ash's side, Singing to herself in her harsh whispers. This wasn't exactly unusual, but she did seem particularly agitated. Tobu was on his other side, and Ash couldn't help but notice he had his bow in his hands.

Always ready for anything . . . Ash thought. He strained his eyes toward the *Ice Runner* and could see people moving about on deck, but they were still too far to make out properly. Then something shifted. It was the cargo hatch being raised.

To everyone's surprise, something crawled out of it. Something *large*.

"Um . . . that's . . . not *normal* . . ." Lunah said, watching the thing slither across the deck and claw its way up the mainmast. The entire *Frostheart* crew strained their eyes, trying to make sense of what they were seeing.

Rook suddenly reeled back in alarm. "*They've followed!*" she rasped.

"What the—" Kailen began.

As the thing leaped from the mainmast and unfurled its leathery wings, understanding crashed over Ash like a rockfall. *A Shrieker.*

"LEVIATHAN!" Kailen roared, and the rest of the

crew began swiftly arming themselves as Tobu had.

The crew opened fire, but they were too late. The beast let out an earsplitting cry as it dived into an attack. Its hind claws splayed wide, like the talons on a bird of prey, and it headed straight toward Ash.

"MOVE!" Tobu roared, pushing a stunned Ash out of its path. In an explosion of timber, the monster tore through the side of the *Frostheart*. The tremendous force of it threw Ash high in the air. Everything moved in slow motion. The world spun as he rose up amid a cloud of splinters and the helpless bodies of his friends.

Lunah, Master Podd, and Rook were below him, plunging toward the rushing snow. Kailen was barely clinging to the side of the deck, her hold slipping. Tobu was above Ash, and somehow managed to scoop him into a protective huddle as they fell. And in a snap, time sped up. They crashed into the ground, Tobu breaking Ash's fall, the entire world shuddering with terrible force. They flipped and tumbled and crashed through the stinging snow. Ash's head screamed, his neck cracked, his legs bent in ways they weren't meant to. The world spun in chaos, until finally they came to a stop.

With a groan Tobu released his hold on Ash. Ash sputtered and coughed, rolling over onto his back. Every single part of him hurt—even parts of him he didn't

know he had. His head throbbed. He touched it with his hand and saw it stained red when he pulled it away.

"T-Tobu?" he managed to croak.

"Up!" came Tobu's voice, urgent.

We're overboard! Spirits, we're out in the open! Ash realized with alarm, staring in horror at the sleigh that raced toward them. It was the *Ice Runner*. It looked incredibly large, its timbers creaking, its enjins roaring.

"UP!" Tobu shouted, wrenching Ash to his feet. But Ash's heart had gone cold. He could finally make out the *Ice Runner*'s crew, and couldn't believe what he was seeing. The ragged black cloaks writhing in the wind like smoke. The deathly pale faces, the gnarled horns. It was unmistakable.

Wraiths.

Ash and Tobu began to run, for all the good it would do them.

Ash spotted Lunah and Rook, who had landed nearby. They were picking themselves up, the dire situation dawning on them too. Kailen was already sprinting ahead, Master Podd on her shoulders.

The *Frostheart* was wheeling back round for them, but so too was the Shrieker, streaking across the sky. Ash could now hear the terrible chant of the Wraiths, which seemed to have a hold over the creature, seemed to be *guiding* it. As if things couldn't get any worse, Ash spotted three more sleighs appearing from the nearby foothills. Black rotting timbers and tattered sails, sleighs dragged from a nightmare.

"They've set up an ambush!" he cried as Tobu led them toward the forest, the only cover for leagues around. It was only a few hundred steps away, but it looked like a million miles.

The *Ice Runner* was close now, and getting closer.

"Quick!" Tobu shouted. Ash could feel the tremors upon the snow as it surged toward them.

"We can't outrun a sleigh!" Lunah gasped, and she was right.

"Get to the forest!" Tobu ordered, planting his feet in the snow and aiming his bow at the encroaching vessel. "I'll deal with this."

"Tobu, *no!*" Ash cried out, sliding to a stop beside him. What was the use in running anyway? They'd never make it. The group huddled together defiantly against the overwhelming odds. To Ash's surprise Rook crouched low and touched the snow, murmuring under her breath as strands of her broken Song-aura twisted out of her. He wondered what on earth she was doing—but there was no time to think. The Shrieker was tearing down toward them, the *Ice Runner*'s shadow washing them in a veil of darkness. The *Frostheart* was still too far away, and under attack from the Wraith sleighs. Tobu fired arrow after arrow at the *Ice Runner*'s propellers.

Tink.

Tink. Tink.

Of course, they did nothing to slow it down. The sleigh was upon them, its roaring enjins churning up snow like a cyclone, the ground shifting and heaving about their boots as the sleigh's runners drew near. Lunah was screaming, Tobu was firing, Rook was whispering. There was no way out.

And what's more, Ash could sense the voracious Song of another Leviathan below the snows, racing toward them to finish off anything the Wraiths left behind.

When suddenly—

FWOOM!

With a mind-shredding, earth-shattering *CRUNCH* the *Ice Runner*'s center erupted into the sky. What looked like a gigantic spearhead had torn right through it, as fragments of the sleigh rained down from above, the sleigh's sunstone enjin soaring through the air like a comet. The spearhead was some kind of Leviathan, one Ash had never seen before. Long and insectoid—its head formed a hard, ax-like crest of bone that had cut through the sleigh like a hatchet would a branch.

At the very same moment, the Shrieker dropped out of the sky, seemingly released from the Wraiths' spell.

With a scream of twisted metal, the *Ice Runner* spun out of control, round and round, before skidding to a halt, dead on the snow.

20

Bad Company

The view before them was one of utter devastation. The *Ice Runner* had practically been torn in two, its broken timbers scattered about the snow. The enjin lay open close by, the sunstone that had powered it still glowing, melting its way through the ice. Ash swallowed hard as he saw Wraith bodies among the wreckage. Some stirred, many did not. The giant Leviathan, whatever it was, was nowhere to be seen.

Under the snows again, Ash assumed with a shiver.

Ash was pulled up by rough hands and found himself face-to-face with Rook's black hood. "*MOVE*," she hissed.

"Did—did you call that . . . *thing* with your Song?" Ash asked, unable to tear his eyes from the carnage the beast had wrought, trying to get his head round the

power a Song Weaver could wield. Rook nodded, force-fully turning Ash away from the destruction.

"No person should have that much power . . ." said a wide-eyed Kailen, overhearing Ash's words as she approached, Master Podd still on her shoulders, ears twitching as he gawked at the wreckage. "Not so sure we should be travelin' round with someone capable of that much carnage . . ." Lunah and Tobu also looked to Rook with troubled expressions. Rook recoiled in reply, hissing. It might have seemed threatening, but Ash could sense she'd been hurt by Kailen's words.

"She just saved our lives!" Ash said, staring Kailen right in the eyes. "*Please*, Kailen. We're not all like Shaard."

Kailen stared back, face hard and doubtful, but even-tually she nodded all the same.

"Enough bickering. We must go. NOW," Tobu said.

The largest Wraith sleigh had ceased its attack on the *Frostheart* and pulled away, heading straight toward the wreckage, where Wraiths were stirring like ghosts, ready to search for the prey that had managed to escape them.

"To the forest, now!"

Branches clawed at the group as they rushed through the tree cover, pine needles and coarse bushes scratching and tearing at Ash's cloak, trying to steal it away. When he dared glance behind, he could see the large Wraith sleigh skirting the borders of the forest, the dead faces of its crew staring out among the pines, searching. The group fled deeper into the forest, hoping they hadn't been spotted.

It was then that something large, *very large*, leaped out from the deep shadows. It was the Shrieker that had dropped from the sky. Ash stumbled and backed up against a tree, heart racing as it sounded a threatening *thrum*.

"Ash!" Lunah cried. The Leviathan stood between him and his friends, who began circling it cautiously.

The Shrieker's eyes followed Ash's every movement, its tail whipping about, ready to attack. Tobu and Kailen snarled, spears in hand. Ash shifted along the large tree trunk, desperately feeling for some hole to hide in, some escape.

There was none.

It's too close—what am I gonna do?! he thought, panic rising.

But the Shrieker did not pounce, nor did it roar or try to take a bite out of Ash. It just watched him, almost curiously. For the first time, in a flash of sickening fear, Ash realized he recognized the creature. It was hurt; fresh arrow and spear wounds darkened its tough

hide as it leaned heavily to one side. It was the Leviathan he'd helped back at Aurora. The one he feared might have controlled his mind. Was it planning to control him again, to make him hurt his friends?

I can't let it in. I can't let it win!

Ash scrunched his eyes shut and ground his teeth, concentrating so hard on blocking out any Song the creature might Sing that his head hurt. But how do you defend against something you don't understand? There was a rustle some distance behind Ash. The Wraiths must be getting close. The Shrieker made a guttural sound and just like that it slithered away, off into the darkness.

"What was *that* all about?!" Kailen asked.

Ash shook his head, half deliberately, half from trembling.

"How . . . *rare*," Master Podd pondered.

"Onward. Quickly," Tobu insisted. Close, *too close*, they could see the ghoulish shapes of the Wraiths creeping their way into the forest, silhouetted against the moonlight, bows drawn as they scoured the trees.

The group ran and they ran. Ash's ankle nearly twisted on snow-hidden tree roots, but he managed to right himself and keep going. Everywhere stood mighty trees, some as wide as a house, almost indistinguishable from the deep shadows they cast in the lifeless moonlight. Ash could still hear the roar of the Wraith sleigh in the distance. Harsh voices called out amid the trees. The Songs of Leviathans rattled Ash's ears. Danger was everywhere.

As the group scrambled farther into the depths of the dark forest, they spotted old frozen rope bridges hanging broken from the treetops, crisscrossing high above the forest floor, leading off in every direction.

"The Pinehaven Roads . . ." Kailen whispered, a small smile pulling at her lips. "The pathways of my Stronghold. We stand a better chance up there, above the snows!" They all rushed to climb the nearest tree. Its trunk was as wide as three yetis lying down head to toe, and so sheer there were no obvious footholds or branches to hold on to. Ash couldn't understand how Tobu, Kailen, and Lunah were managing to so nimbly climb it. He sprang up, hugging the trunk's thick circumference, only to slowly slide back down onto his bottom. He looked across at Master Podd, the only one keeping him company on the forest floor. "Want to ride on my shoulders?" Ash offered. Master Podd raised an eyebrow before he pulled out an archeomek device. Vulpis were famously scavengers of archeomek, but Master Podd had never shown much interest himself. "A vulpis of more refined tastes!" Nuk used to say. With a bang the device fired a grappling hook into the treetops, with a rope trailing from the contraption in the vulpis's paws.

"Just a little toy," Master Podd said, and then with a nod he shot up into the canopy at great speed, pulled up by the rope. Ash blinked a few times as Master Podd reached the top before anyone else. Tobu came back down for Ash in the end, who clung on to his shoulders as the yeti climbed high above. They took a moment to rest on a creaking snow-covered walkway. Ash was so glad to be off the forest floor, away from the Wraiths and Leviathans, that the dizzying height almost had no effect on him. *Almost.*

Rook looked like a large crow more than ever, perched as she was on a branch, her ragged feathered cloak hanging off her like wings, surrounded by her loyal smaller crows. Lunah stood on tiptoes, squinting out of the tree cover to the landscape they'd just escaped from, the lantern-lights of the *Frostheart* and its pursuers just about visible in the far distance.

"There's no way the *Frostheart* can come back for us with those sleighs houndin' 'em," she said as she watched the sleigh drift ever farther away, relentlessly pursued by the black sleighs. "We'll . . . we'll just have to join up with them later . . ." Her voice wobbled with doubt.

"Wraith scum, that's the second time in as many weeks they've pulled a fast one on us!" Kailen growled, punching a fist into an open palm. "Next time we meet, they won't be so lucky."

"Difficult to hit ghosts," Master Podd said.

"This was a carefully planned attack," Tobu said. "They targeted us specifically with a stolen Pathfinder sleigh. No doubt they brought the Shriekers into Aurora. But the question is: Why?"

"Might as well try to get the captain to give up the *Frostheart*, for all the good it'll do you tryin' to understand the Wraiths," Kailen said. But Ash wasn't so sure.

"You seemed to know they were coming, Rook. You

warned me they were in Aurora." All eyes fell on Rook. She remained silent. "What do they want?" Ash tried again. They already had Shaard hunting for them; the *last* thing they needed were supernatural ghoul pirates too!

"*Wraiths bound to the Devourer. Will do all to serve it. To stop you hiding frost-heart.*" The frost-heart at Ash's side whispered a lament at Rook's answer, its brightness dimming.

"You knew they would come for us?!" Kailen said. "*How?*"

"*World Weave. Listen. Know things.*"

Kailen shared a glance with Tobu once Ash had translated, both of their eyes narrowing.

"So how do we get away from them?" Ash asked, frightened.

"*Solstice. Only hope.*" Ash told the others what she'd said.

Tobu gazed intently at Ash, his mind seeming to weigh up all the options and possibilities.

Tobu's usually so sure of his decisions, Ash thought. *Why's this one causing him so much worry?*

"Yeah, I don't think we're gonna just stroll over to Solstice, do you?" Kailen scoffed, nodding toward the forest floor below. "There's a coupla obstacles in our way . . ." The gang followed Kailen's gaze. Threading its way between the trees was a large shape, which unraveled its way through the forest like some terrible centipede, its many, many legs moving, reaching, and grasping at the trees as it pulled itself through the foliage. It made Ash's skin crawl.

It's the same type of Leviathan that Rook called to destroy the Ice Runner, Ash remembered with horror. The monster turned its head this way and that, tasting the air with a long tongue that flickered in and out of its ax-shaped snout. And it wasn't alone. Several of the eel-like Leviathans coiled their way through the trees, silent except for the soft purring Song they Sang.

"*Spearwurms*," Rook whispered.

They looked as though they were heading toward the harsh distant sounds of the Wraiths, curious and territorial.

Ash and the others hugged the platform as close as they could, still as statues as the Spearwurms passed them by. It was then that it hit Ash. He looked out at the dense canopy surrounding them, so deep and dark it could well have stretched on forever, his heart sinking with hopelessness.

They were stranded in the wilds.

With only the Wraiths and Leviathans for company.

21

Bearings

Ash awoke with a start. He was surprised to discover that instead of his cozy tent aboard the *Frostheart*, he was now sheltered by the dark branches of a fir tree they had hidden beneath the night before. And rather than the comforting heat of the *Frostheart*'s sunstone enjin to keep him warm, there was only the dwindling fire that Tobu had made, red embers cooling amid the charred firewood. The comforting rumble of the sleigh's movements were gone, as were his soft bedding furs. Everything was still, quiet, and very, *very* cold.

At least the fire didn't attract unwanted attention, Ash thought in relief. To make the fire they'd had to climb down from the relative safety of the walkways for fear of burning the whole thing down. But it was a risk they'd needed to take. "The cold out here will kill you faster than any Wraiths," Tobu had warned the others.

Lunah lay fast asleep under her cloak, a thin line of drool hanging from her open mouth. The others were gone. *I already miss the* Frostheart *so much*, Ash thought. After what had happened in Aurora, it had felt so good being back aboard. He knew that no matter how the world saw him, he was welcome on that sleigh. Anger that he'd been quite literally torn from it gnawed at his insides, giving him a headache.

He poked his head out through the pine needles into the dim early-morning darkness. He spotted Rook perched in the tree high above, keeping watch. She was Singing quietly with her crows, who rested on the branches around her. He guessed Tobu and the others were out scavenging for food.

Even though he wasn't the best with heights, a lifetime of fearing what lay beneath the snow made Ash very uncomfortable standing on the forest floor indeed, despite Tobu having picked a tree that sat upon a massive rock as a precaution. Ash (rather awkwardly) clambered back up to the rope bridges above and surveyed his surroundings. The forest was dark and dense. Amid the gigantic pines squatted uncountable smaller fir trees, poking their pointy heads out of a thick blanketing mist. Anything could be hiding in there. Looking up, Ash saw a gap in the canopy wide enough for a view of the last remaining stars in the purple-blue morning sky.

I haven't seen the stars in ages, he realized. Quietly, so as not to break the forest's almost sacred-feeling silence, Ash began to Sing his lullaby. The forest around him faded, but his other senses heightened. High above, the stars that were guiding his way to Solstice blazed with brilliance, and Ash's shivering body warmed with comfort at the sight of them, especially after the horror of the night before. And yes, a new one had joined the others, thanks to the fact that he'd solved the Wayfinder riddle in Aurora. Were these stars forming a constellation that would allow him to find Solstice? Were they pointing him somewhere, trying to tell him something? All he knew for certain was that he had the next verse in the lullaby.

Through forest unbroken and shimmering sky,
Follow the gaze of the giant's eye.
The sleeping warrior watches the door,
Where we shall meet, and you'll search no more.

They were certainly in a big ol' forest, which he supposed was a good start. But *shimmering sky*? Did that mean the kind of sky where the spirits danced bright and green above the sleeping world? Ash certainly didn't have the first clue about giants and sleeping warriors. He retrieved the archeosphere he'd found in the cylindra out of his pouch. Turning it round in his hands, he ran his fingers over its surprisingly smooth texture, tracing the patterns etched into its surface. He knew next to nothing about archeomek. What was he supposed to do with this? Was it part of a device he was yet to find? Did it need a power source? Was it broken? Ash sighed. *More mysteries, but mysteries I have to solve, if I ever want to get to Solstice. To safety, away from Wraiths, Stormbreaker, and angry Strongholders.*

As he Sang, more for comfort than anything, Ash felt something tug at his Song-aura. He'd almost grown used to hearing the frost-heart's Song, as warm as the voice of a friend. But this time its Song felt different— like a guiding hand, trying to direct his attention—and it seemed to be pointing him southeast. Ash looked, but all he saw was unending forest.

"*You . . . you want me to go that way?*" Ash Sang with curiosity.

The frost-heart sounded pleased, making a twinkling sound Ash imagined stars would make. It had turned into a right old chatterbox. *And now it's helping me with the riddles?* Ash touched the archeomek it was encased in, braving its chill. He increasingly suspected the stories were true, that the stone was indeed the heart of some ancient, powerful creature. *But what? Surely a Leviathan would never be so helpful and kind?* All the same, Ash felt he could trust the frost-heart. Perhaps that was a mistake, perhaps he was being tricked again, but deep down, it felt right.

Ash took a long breath.

"Southeast it is then."

22

Rising Anger

Ash, Lunah, and Rook ate the breakfast of berries that Rook had gathered during her night watch, and sipped a surprisingly nice pine-needle tea. It wasn't much, but it was warm and incredibly welcome.

Tobu and Kailen returned as they ate, dropping two snow hares before them. "We need a *proper* breakfast. Got a long way ahead of us, an' we need all the energy we can get," Kailen said, looking sidelong at Rook and the simple berries she'd supplied, a hint of triumph in her eyes. At that moment Master Podd erupted out of the snow where he'd been burrowing, shaking his fur vigorously and laying out a bountiful haul of edible roots he'd found under the ice. Kailen went a bit red as the roots were piled up, towering above the hares. Rook simply nodded and shared the rations out to the others to

prepare over the fire before noisily chomping into her
share raw. There was something quite unnerving (and
definitely a bit gross) about watching the meat disappear
into the darkness of her hood, bits tumbling down into
the feathers of her cloak, her crows fighting each other
for the scraps.

"Do you know where we are?" Ash asked as they ate.

"The Endless Forest," Kailen said proudly. Ash's ears
perked up at the name.

Through forest unbroken . . .

"The Pinehaven Stronghold, my people, watch over
this land."

"Yeah, a forest 'bout as welcomin' as Kailen herself," Lunah teased, chewing on a root as she brought out her map and pointed to a massive forest south of Aurora.

"*Ha ha ha* . . . Very good. So. We're about . . . here." Kailen indicated a spot on the outskirts of the forest. "It's what we Pinehaven call the 'Absolute Middle of Ruddy Nowhere.' The Stronghold itself, right in the center of the forest, is way too far to travel on foot. Our best bet is to head for one of the border outposts linked by the Pinehaven Roads." She pointed at dots that were spaced out round the edges of the forest. "They'll shelter us, an' from there we can try an' meet up with the *Frostheart*."

"Do you know what paths we should take?" Tobu asked.

"I, er . . . no," Kailen admitted, flushing red again. "I became a Pathfinder, not a hunter, so I was never stationed at the outposts."

"I think there's a border outpost northeast of here, an' one bout the same distance southeast," Lunah chipped in.

"Let's head southeast," Ash suggested quickly.

"Why?" Tobu asked suspiciously.

"Well . . ." Ash took a breath. "The frost-heart wants me to go that way." The heart trilled its approval. Tobu straightened. The others exchanged a *look* before Lunah shrugged.

"S'all the same to me, fire-boy. Nothin' seems weird with you anymore. We just need proper shelter, an' fast."

Tobu nodded. "Our situation is grave. Leviathans find it harder to move through trees, but it does not mean the forests are without them. The risk of starvation or freezing would be challenging enough to contend with, without an army of Wraiths hunting us down too. We must keep moving and cover as much ground before nightfall as we can. Our lives depend on it."

Nausea worried Ash's belly; his meager breakfast was not sitting well. So this was it, then. All Tobu's dire warnings and training to survive the wilds were about to be put to the test. Ash was less than sure he was up to the task.

After hiding their campfire under piles of snow, they prepared to leave. "Which way is southeast?" Ash asked, snatching back the archeosphere he had lent to Lunah to "investigate," which apparently meant banging it repeatedly with a stone.

Lunah shrugged, then got up and shielded her eyes as she gazed off in all directions. She popped a finger into her mouth, then held it up to the wind before kneeling down and tasting the snow on the ground. She looked back with a smile.

"I'm just kiddin', it's this way." She pointed before drawing a small knife from her belt. "Gotta leave a trail for the rest of the crew, so's they know how to find us." She was about to start carving into a tree trunk when Tobu caught her wrist.

Lunah wiggled the blade about in his grip, still trying to reach the tree. "Not sure what yer up to here, big guy, but you ent makin' this any easier . . ."

"Markings will not lead just the *Frostheart* crew to our whereabouts." Lunah lowered her blade in understanding. "Besides, no Pathfinder sleigh can pass through these trees."

"Then they'll walk. They'll come for us."

"Indeed," Master Podd said as Kailen nodded. "The captain will not abandon us."

"Then we'll need to disguise the trail we leave, something that only the *Frostheart* will recognize." Tobu thought for a moment. "Mursu are said to have an incredible nose for scents. Tying morsels of hare high up in the trees should keep most predators from reaching them, but leave enough of a trail for Captain Nuk to follow, with the Wraiths none the wiser."

Rook Sang something in response.

"What did she say?" Tobu asked.

"Rook said that your plan is good, but she *could* just send her crows to lead the others to us," Ash translated. Tobu's fur bristled, his mouth moving, lost for words.

"Well—well, yes. That . . . could work too." He cleared his throat. "A less time-consuming solution."

Rook immediately whispered a Song to the crow on her shoulder, who cawed in response before taking flight into the early-morning sky, leading a flock of its brethren in search of the *Frostheart*.

"We're far from any outpost," Kailen said, looking out at the icicle-adorned rope bridges of the Pinehaven Roads. "So I doubt these paths've been maintained all that well. Be careful."

Master Podd trotted along one without any problems, his little legs carving a trail through the snow that sat atop the wooden planks.

"Seems fine to me!" Lunah said, following in Master Podd's footsteps. Her foot fell through a rotten plank in almost the same instant, but luckily she was alert and pulled herself up.

"To be honest, it's not that different from the *Frostheart*'s deck, is it?" she said as Ash rushed to see if she was okay.

Carefully the group ventured deeper into the Endless Forest. "Boy, a word," Tobu said as they settled into their stride. Ash warily stepped behind the yeti at the back of the party, out of earshot. Was he going to talk about what the Shrieker might've done to him? How Ash's mind had appeared so easy to take over? Or was it just another standard telling-off?

"Do you consider yourself to be a hateful person?"

The question took Ash by surprise. "N-no! At least . . . I don't think so?"

"I do not think you are either," Tobu agreed. "So, I am forced to wonder why your temper has been so short of late. Why your anger has been so quick to rise. It seems . . . at *odds* with who I know you to be."

Ash was shocked. Was this why Tobu had been watching him so closely?

"I've not been any angrier! I don't know what you're talking about!"

Tobu came to an abrupt stop, and Ash walked straight into his back.

"OW! What'd you do that for?" Ash said, annoyance flaring in his veins. More annoyance than he should've felt, in truth. A little anger even.

Tobu gave him a knowing look.

"Well, a lot's happened lately. Bad stuff. Storm-breaker's army, the Wraiths . . . what Shaard did to us all . . . You'd be angry, too!" Ash explained, Tobu nodding as he spoke.

"So you do not suspect that the

Song Shaard taught you has anything to do with it? A lingering effect of that sinister, hateful Song that forced others to do your bidding?"

Ash looked at his feet, aghast at what Tobu was saying. "*No!* I mean, I don't—I don't really know . . ." But deep down, Ash did know. It made perfect sense. He *had* been feeling out of character recently. The cold that had been gnawing at his insides, the bitter thoughts that always followed; they were the same cold, spiteful sensations as when he'd Sung *that* Song in Shade's Chasm, and, rage-fueled, forced a Leviathan to act against its will. He'd felt the corruption sink its claws into him then, but the thought that it hadn't let him go had never occurred to him. The realization horrified Ash. Was that Song turning him into someone he wasn't? Someone like *Shaard?*

"You are a fast learner, boy, in spite of what I might sometimes say. I am proud of what we've achieved in the small time I've had to teach you. But if you learn one thing from me, let it be this: Leave that Song well alone, for the good of us all. I know what it is like to lose oneself to anger and resentment." Ash dared to look at Tobu, and saw his face strained with painful memories. "It narrows your mind. Closes your heart. It is a destructive path that has only one end."

Ash went quiet, terrified that Tobu might be right, while feeling wholly embarrassed that he might be being influenced by a Song as well as a Leviathan. Was he really so easy to manipulate? He'd only Sung Shaard's Song a few times, yet it already appeared to have had a great effect on him. Ash promised himself he would never Sing it again—no matter what.

"Do not follow in my footsteps," Tobu finished, almost too quiet to hear.

This was a rare mention of Tobu's past, and Ash decided to seize it.

"Tobu—who is the Mountain's Ward?"

Tobu's eyes widened. "Where did you hear that name?"

"I—I heard people at Aurora say it. They saw you, a yeti, and said that the Mountain's Ward might've gone on the attack . . ."

Tobu's face was dark. When he answered, his voice was quiet and dangerous. "The Ward is of no consequence to you, or our journey." And with that, they walked on in silence. Ash knew Tobu well enough to know that was the end of the discussion.

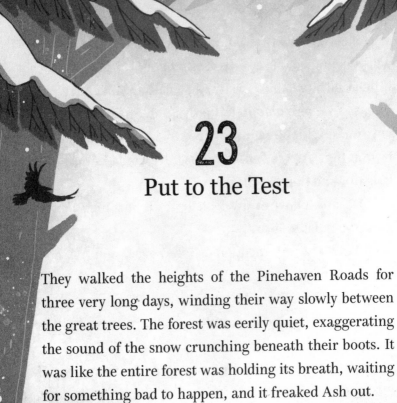

23
Put to the Test

They walked the heights of the Pinehaven Roads for three very long days, winding their way slowly between the great trees. The forest was eerily quiet, exaggerating the sound of the snow crunching beneath their boots. It was like the entire forest was holding its breath, waiting for something bad to happen, and it freaked Ash out.

They kept as quiet as possible, constantly on alert for signs of danger. When they had to communicate, they resorted to the sign language that hunters across the Snow Sea used when out in the wilds. The only hint of their passing was the odd dusting of snow their boots would send slipping between the wooden planks of the walkways.

Rook's crows confirmed to her that they'd found Captain Nuk and the *Frostheart*, and were leading the sleigh toward the group, hoping to meet up at the southeastern border outpost. Kailen listened to Ash's translation with a raised eyebrow. "She got all that . . . from her *crows*?" Ash nodded sincerely. Kailen held his gaze, her eyebrow rising so high Ash was worried it might leave her forehead altogether. "We're never getting out of this forest alive, are we?" she said with a sigh.

In spite of all the hardship, Ash was pleased to discover that the six of them made a good team. Lunah led the party, using Mother Sun's position in the sky and her wrist-mounted compass to navigate their way. Ash and Rook both listened carefully for any signs of Leviathan Song. Master Podd used his remarkable scavenging skills to supply the party with much-needed food, as his footsteps were light enough to allow him to walk across the forest floor unnoticed. And Tobu and Kailen brought up the rear, bows in hand and arrows nocked, keen eyes and senses watching for anything the Song Weavers might've missed, and hunting down the bigger game Master Podd could not.

Rook moved like some kind of animal, sometimes literally on all fours, skittish and jumping at the slightest sound. She would occasionally whisper to herself or to her crows, and the crows Sang back reports of what they saw up ahead, or at least that was what seemed to be happening to Ash.

He noticed that the others kept their distance from her, especially Kailen, who shot Rook the same suspicious looks as she had when Ash first came aboard the *Frostheart*, before she'd learned to trust him. It made Ash's heart ache. He knew how lonely Rook had been, and he hated the thought of her having finally found some companions, only to find she was still isolated from them because she was . . . *different*. It felt all too familiar.

So he stuck close to Rook, and tried to learn as much as possible from her. Rook was much better at hearing the Leviathans than Ash, but he'd gotten used to the rhythmic thrumming sound of a Leviathan on the hunt, the way they would silence their Song as the group drew near. He started to get a better sense as to what direction the Songs were coming from too, though the dense forest did not make it easy. The deep ferns and pine needles were ever shifting and rustling, though whether it was from a wild animal or something worse was always hard to tell.

Sometimes the walkways would be broken or too weak to cross, and they'd have to risk traveling across the forest floor. It was tough going, and dangerous. The snowdrifts were deep and hard to navigate, and the extra effort could make them careless about how much noise they were making, how keenly they were keeping watch and listening for danger.

While struggling uphill one dark afternoon, they passed a small herd of ulk. Rook Sang to them in a gentle, quiet voice, surprising the rest of the silent group. Despite its rough edges, Rook's Song was tender. The ulk raised their heads and twitched their ears but did not run. To Ash's amazement he could've sworn he heard the ulk Singing back, just quiet and subtle enough to convince him he was imagining it.

"Are those ulk Singing? I thought it was only us and the Leviathans!" Ash whispered to Rook, who nodded.

"Everything has Song, some clearer than others."

"We could lure them over, make them easier to hunt!" Ash suggested.

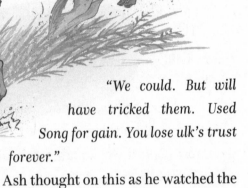

"We could. But will
have tricked them. Used
Song for gain. You lose ulk's trust
forever."

Ash thought on this as he watched the
ulk leap gracefully over ferns and out of sight.

As they trekked on, Ash began to notice the
treetops occasionally shifting as though something large
had bounded off them. He got an increasingly creeping
sensation that they were being watched. At other times a
large shadow would cast over them, only to disappear as
fast as it arrived. Whenever Ash looked up at these moments he could see nothing but looming trees and gray
skies. He asked Rook if she'd noticed it too.

"Curious. Inquisitive. But not sure if it trusts . . . yet."
Ash craned his neck but could still see nothing but forest
and cloud. "Seems you've made friend." Ash wasn't sure
what he found more unsettling—the mysterious stalker
or Rook's apparent rediscovery of humor . . .

As the days passed, Ash couldn't stop his teeth from
chattering. A vicious chill had pierced through his thick

cloak and furs, and he found himself stumbling over his feet ever more frequently, his body feeling heavier by the hour. The stories of old never mentioned the cold of the wilds. Sure, they talked about the ice and snow, but always as sweeping, dramatic landscapes for the hero to journey across. But they never spoke about how the cold makes your nose run *all the time*. Or how your fingers go so numb you can't even use them to wipe a runny nose. They never mentioned how soaking wet the snow makes you, or how hard it is to dry your clothes. They never told how you shiver so hard you begin to fear you may never know what it's like to be still again. Ash remembered the times he had sat by the warmth of a cozy campfire back with the Fira, wishing he could have an adventure outside the Stronghold walls. *What an idiot.*

Sometimes Ash would feel the cold annoyance rising in his stomach, but he would remember Tobu's words and do his best to push it back down. It was at times like these the frost-heart would pipe up, its voice heard only by Ash's despairing mind.

"Onward," it said. *"One foot in front of the other. Don't give up!"* Its Song would give Ash the strength he needed to push forward when he was sure he could go no farther. But it was right. No one else was giving in, and Ash would be a bovore's bottom if he was the first who did.

24

Hunted

Something was wrong with Lunah.

As they set off on the fourth day, her usual perkiness and optimism were nowhere to be seen. She looked from her map to her compass and the position of the sun almost obsessively, gazing about the thick forest with unmistakable concern etched on her face.

"Everything okay?" Ash signed at her.

"Yes, why wouldn't it be?" she signed back, scowling.

Ash put it down to how exhausted they all were, and how bleak the situation felt. This forest seemed unending. How had his father navigated this ceaseless sprawl of trees? Had he left some kind of marker for where Ash could find the next clue? Ash hoped so. The thought of trying to find something hidden in this forest felt the same as trying to find a particular snowflake in the entirety of the Snow Sea.

They arrived at a river that cut through the forest, with thin, broken ice bordering its edges. After following it for some time, Lunah stopped them at a ford made up of smooth stepping-stones. "This way," Lunah signed, but Tobu stopped her.

"Southeast is *that* way." He pointed farther down the river.

"This is Sky Shimmer River," Kailen signed. "Leads to Pinehaven, a hundred leagues south."

Ash's arm hairs stood on end.

Through forest unbroken and shimmering sky . . .

"Tobu's way feels right," Ash confirmed. He was rewarded with a sharp, wounded glance from Lunah. She consulted her map and squinted up at Mother Sun, who barely pierced the gray clouds.

"Yes. That's the way I meant."

"Never a doubt in my mind," Master Podd assured Lunah, but Tobu watched her lead the way with a troubled expression.

They continued on for some time, Lunah's steps becoming ever faster and more determined. Ash grimaced as her boot snapped a twig and the sound thundered through the otherwise silent forest.

"*She's getting careless . . .*" Tobu said under his breath.

At that exact moment, Ash's ears itched, as though

someone had whispered into them from behind. The hairs on his neck stood on end. Before Lunah took another step, Tobu dived into her, tackling her into the snow under a boulder.

"Tobu! What are you doing?!" Lunah said aloud, angry.

He clasped his hands over her mouth, and urgently signaled to the others. "GET DOWN."

They did so behind the trunk of a fallen tree. They waited, belly-down in the snow.

Everything was still.

Quiet. Too quiet . . .

Ash noticed that the forest birds had gone silent. Rook's crows had taken wing and were perched in the branches above, rustling their feathers with agitation.

And then Ash heard it.

The chanting.

That malicious, *hateful* drone. This close it sounded

like a rhythmic, spiteful shout. Ash gritted his teeth as the sound battered his head. He peeked out from beneath the log, and saw long dark shapes racing toward them. Sleighs, five of them, but small two-man vessels, able to weave in and out of the trees. The dark ghostly figures of Wraiths rode in them, their pitch-black eyes searching the forest for any sign of movement. But it was what was pulling the sleighs that made Ash's heart beat so fast he thought he was going to be sick.

Lurkers.

The scrambling monsters hissed and roared as they pulled the sleighs at surprising speed. Tendrils of smoky shadow twisted from each Wraith driver and wrapped round the necks of the Lurkers like reins. A sleigh drew dangerously close to their hiding place, and Ash darted back from the gap he'd been spying through. The driver raised a fist, and the sleighs came to a stop. The Wraith that rode this sleigh was tall, its horns particularly large and twisted. All Wraiths were threatening, but there was something about this one. A sense of malicious power oozed out of it like a scent. Could it be their leader? It turned its head from side to side as the others continued their chant.

It was listening.

Listening for *them*.

Had it heard Lunah? Did it know they were there?

A Lurker groaned, right on the other side of their log. It was *so close*. Ash held his breath. He felt Rook tense, saw Tobu and Lunah trying to shrink themselves to the smallest shapes possible behind their boulder. Master Podd had buried himself under a snowdrift, only the tips of his ears visible as they poked out of the snow. Ash had to suppress the overwhelming urge to jump up and run as far away from these monsters as he could get.

Moments felt like hours. The chant barked on and on, shredding Ash's nerves.

Go away, go away, please go away, Ash prayed, clenching his eyes shut, sweat dripping down his forehead despite the cold. He clutched the archeosphere his dad had left for him, as if that would somehow keep him safe. Opening an eye, he saw Tobu giving him a stern yet supportive look. Kailen had a dagger in her hand, ready to fight. Rook squatted stone-still with her back against the log, fingers curled like a beast's claws.

Suddenly the Great Horned One gestured to the hunting party, and they tore off into the forest depths, as fast as they had come, their terrible chant fading with them. Tobu poked his head above the rock to check that the coast was clear. "They now have the advantage of speed," Tobu said, before looking back at Lunah. "It is essential we get behind the safety of walls. *Fast.*"

Lunah swallowed hard and nodded.

Ash had never seen his friend look so terrified.

He knew just how she felt.

25
Freedom

The forest was changing. The atmosphere felt . . .
different. The cold air almost sparked with tension, and
strange shapes began jutting from the snow like large
stones, plants and tree roots creeping over their rough
surfaces as the forest attempted to reclaim them. As
the group pressed on, cautiously keeping their distance
from these strange objects, Ash saw that they were, in
fact, not boulders, but archeomek machines. Huge ancient relics that had lain frozen since the countless eons
of the World Before. Each looked distinct and dangerous,
and Ash could only guess at their purpose. They were in-

credibly intimidating, and Ash couldn't shake the feeling the relics were watching the group pass with harmful intent.

"War machines . . ." Tobu signed. "This is an ancient battlefield."

Ash gulped, remembering the power of the weapon Stormbreaker had displayed. He felt like they'd somehow walked back in time, to a place where they were unwelcome and most certainly did not belong.

They trudged through the battlefield all afternoon, the war machines watching their trail like silent guards. As evening drew in, the group made camp in a long-abandoned Pinehaven watchtower. It reminded Ash of a large seed-pod hanging from tree branches on lines of fraying, frozen rope, which appeared to still hold it safely above the unsettling archeomek below. Ash was afraid that old-world magic might jolt these unknowable things back to life at any second. The watchtower was ramshackle, but it had a roof, or at least *most* of a roof, and at that moment it felt like the homeliest place in the world.

Ash helped Master Podd collect firewood while Lunah furiously studied her map and the others set out to hunt for food. "This," Master Podd said, holding up a branch, "is a good stick." He handed it to Ash, who held a pile of similar sticks they'd collected in his arms. "This one," Master Podd said, raising another, considering it carefully, "this too, is a good stick."

"How about this one?" Ash asked, showing the specimen he'd found.

"No, Ash. That is not a good stick." Master Podd shook his head, disappointed at Ash's obviously poor choice. After collecting enough firewood and kindling, they got a toasty fire going back in the watchtower's hearth. Ash absentmindedly fiddled with the archeosphere as he warmed his frozen bones. He'd wanted to talk to Lunah, but she was currently tucked away in the corner with a clear come-near-me-and-I'll-bite-your-head-off vibe, so Ash thought better of it. That left Master Podd, who was staring into the flames intently, sitting straight-backed and cross-legged.

"Master Podd? Do you . . . do you think Tobu's happy that I'm trying to find Solstice?" Master Podd seemed surprised that Ash would choose to confide in him. He shifted a little, his tail swishing back and forth. "I'm starting to think that he's not, or that he maybe doesn't even . . . *believe* in it. I dunno. Whatever it is, he's acting weird."

Master Podd nodded. "Indeed."

"Indeed?"

"Indeed—my suspicions were correct. The captain is much better at these kinds of talks than I am."

"S-sorry, I didn't mean to disturb you . . ." It had been worth a try, but Ash knew full well that Master Podd wasn't the most talkative of types.

"Not to worry, young Ash. As second-in-command, keeping the crew's spirits high falls to me in the captain's absence." He took a deep breath, as though preparing for a daunting task. "Perhaps Tobu is acting strangely because he'd rather you didn't *go* to Solstice," Master Podd suggested, firelight reflecting off his white fur.

"Why . . . why wouldn't he want me to go to Solstice?"

"You often speak of finding a place where you'll be safe, where you belong. Of finding your parents. Up until now, Tobu has been tasked with providing these things. Perhaps he is not yet ready to hand over that job."

Ash had never thought about it that way. But the idea just seemed too far-fetched.

"*Tobu?* Being upset at not having to look after me? Are . . . are we talking about the same Tobu?" The more Ash considered it, the more preposterous it seemed.

Master Podd looked as serious as ever. "No matter how hard he may seem on the outside, I suspect underneath all that rippling muscle you'd find Tobu about as soft as the rest of us." Ash raised an eyebrow, a powerful technique he'd learned from Kailen. Master Podd blinked. "I *did* say the captain was better at these talks than I. But trust me when I say I know soft when I see it." With that, he gave his fur a squish to prove the point. Ash rolled the archeosphere from hand to hand as he stared into the dancing flames, lost in the theory Master Podd had left for him to think on.

Later that night, Ash jolted awake. The sorrowful Song of the Leviathans echoed throughout the forest—the same Song that had kept him company so many times at the Fira Stronghold, and which stirred something deep within him. *Probably trying to sneak into my mind*, Ash thought, though he had to admit the Song didn't sound aggressive.

It sounded as though it mourned the loss of something.

Longed for something taken.

Ash rubbed his face, relieved they weren't in danger, but annoyed he'd been awoken. The others were asleep, huddled together on the wooden floor, but to Ash's surprise, he saw that Lunah was awake, away in the corner of the watchtower with her nose still buried in her map.

Something's definitely bothering her. She's obsessed with that thing!

Rook was on night watch, sitting broodingly at the window, muttering to her crows as she gazed outside. Ash went to keep her company, giving Lunah a wave as he passed. Lunah didn't even look up.

"Hi," Ash whispered when he arrived at Rook's side, his breath misting before him.

The crow on her shoulder cawed in response.

He gazed out into the endless expanse of shadow that was the forest. Spirits danced vibrant and green in the cold night sky.

Suddenly powdery snow crashed down from a nearby pine as something large landed on it. Ash gasped as he made out the shape of a Shrieker in the darkness, silhouetted against the deep blue sky. The tree bent under its weight as its six eyes stared unblinking at Ash, glowing like small moons. He made as if to wake the others, but Rook stopped him.

"*Been following us,*" Rook Sang, calm as if she were talking about a puppy. "*Same one from Aurora.*"

"Really?" Had the Wraiths sent it after him? Or did it have its own sinister plans for Ash now that it seemed

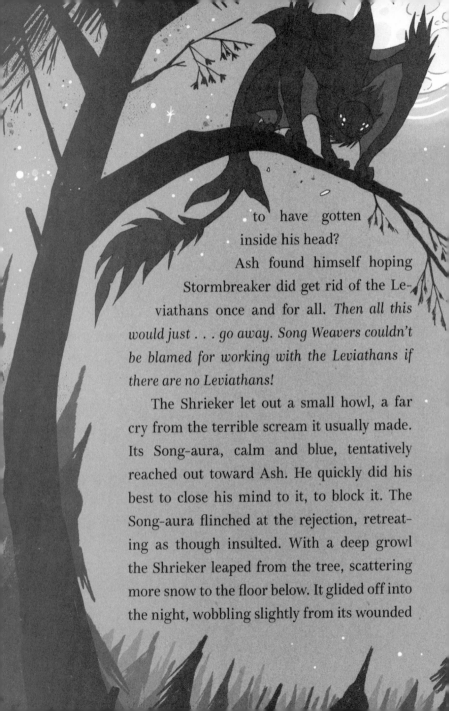

to have gotten inside his head?

Ash found himself hoping Stormbreaker did get rid of the Leviathans once and for all. *Then all this would just . . . go away. Song Weavers couldn't be blamed for working with the Leviathans if there are no Leviathans!*

The Shrieker let out a small howl, a far cry from the terrible scream it usually made. Its Song-aura, calm and blue, tentatively reached out toward Ash. He quickly did his best to close his mind to it, to block it. The Song-aura flinched at the rejection, retreating as though insulted. With a deep growl the Shrieker leaped from the tree, scattering more snow to the floor below. It glided off into the night, wobbling slightly from its wounded wing. Ash breathed out. Master Podd barked in his sleep, his legs moving as though he were running, his tail and ears twitching.

"*Why refuse it?*" Rook asked, surprised.

"Why?!" Ash was shocked she even had to ask. "Because it's a Leviathan! Because it hates us! And this one . . . I think . . . I think . . ." Ash had been keeping this bottled in for so long. His heart beat fast. He hadn't realized how heavily the thought had been weighing down upon him. "It tricked me, back at Aurora. I think it might have controlled my mind with its Song." Ash thought Rook of all people could understand the threat Leviathans posed to Song Weavers. "What does it mean? Will I be okay? Or . . . or is it like a *poison* in the mind . . . ?"

Rook made a sound like a chuckle. "*Only one controls us. Not that one.*"

"S-sorry?"

"*Only one can control us.*"

"Only . . . one?"

"*The Devourer.*"

Ash's mind slurred at her words, his thoughts as slow as if they'd been dipped in tar. *That can't be true*, he thought. *Everyone in the world knows that Leviathans can control Song Weavers' minds. It's why everyone's so scared of us!* He had to be misunderstanding her. "You mean the Shrieker didn't . . . it *didn't* control my mind?"

Rook shook her head from side to side.

"How—how can you know?"

"Know Song Weavers. Know World Weave. I know. We control Leviathans. Not other way round."

"But that's . . . that's . . ."

Ash went white. *That's awful.*

Song Weaving to control the Leviathans had always felt *wrong* to Ash, but he had justified it by telling himself he was only doing what the Leviathans would do to him. But if Rook was right, then Ash had forced a creature to do his bidding, and the creature couldn't fight back. *Spirits,* Ash thought, guilt dragging at his heart as he paced backward and forward. "The way I controlled them . . . I—I . . ." A thought came to Ash. "If you knew all this, why did you order the Spearwurm to attack the *Ice Runner?*"

"I didn't," Rook replied.

"But . . . you did! We all saw you!"

"Didn't control. I asked."

"Asked?"

"See them as others, not monsters."

"But . . . but . . ." Ash was desperately trying to make sense of this. His world felt like it had been turned upside down. Did this mean that Leviathans weren't . . . bad?

No! They still hunted human-kin mercilessly, even if they couldn't control minds! "Leviathans help the Wraiths!" Ash said. "They *must* be bad to help evil things like them!"

Rook made a hacking sound, which Ash realized was a laugh.

"Help? *No choice! Controlled. Forced. Leviathans evil as storm. As raging river. As avalanche. Nature, not evil.*"

"They're vicious—they hate us!"

"*When thought controlled, you felt weak? Defenseless? Angry?*" Ash went quiet. "*Leviathans the same. Isolai free of Leviathan attack—they respected Leviathans. Strong-holders, Pathfinders—make you angry? Because do not understand us. But you're no different. Do not understand Leviathans.*"

"What about this Devourer, then?" Ash asked.

"*Very different.*"

Ash held on to the window frame as if for his life, speechless. His guilt turned to horror at what he'd done . . . what Shaard was still doing! The somber Song of the Leviathans washed over him from outside. They mourned the loss of something, and Ash started to suspect he knew what it was.

Their freedom.

Had the Shrieker truly been trying to reach out to

him? To try to connect? Ash found himself wishing it would come back, so he could say he was sorry.

As if that would make up for any of this . . .

"We . . . we have to tell people!" Ash's spit was thick and sour. "Why haven't you said anything before? This is *massive*, Rook! We have to tell everyone they have nothing to fear from us! The way Song Weavers and Leviathans are treated . . . it's not right. We could stop it from happening!"

"*Sing with me*," Rook whispered, sensing his inner turmoil. It took a few moments before Ash understood she meant to Memory Weave.

He froze with unease. "But . . . the shield in your mind . . ." Rook was frightened of something in her memories and had done her best to hide it, and after last time Ash wasn't sure he wanted to know what it was either. "Won't . . . won't it hurt you?"

Rook thought on this. "*Price I should pay. Sacrifice needed for truth. Sing with me.*"

Ash hesitated. "Rook . . ."

"*Please.*" Her Song sounded pleading. "*I want. I deserve.*"

Ash gulped but steeled his nerves. He began Singing, and as their auras interweaved once again Ash's senses were taken away to a far-off place inside Rook's memories.

26
Trust

Rook's Song-aura swirled like a river, and Ash's consciousness was pulled along as though he'd been caught in the current. He could sense the shield that Rook had raised in her mind—a latticework of her broken Song-aura blocked their path. Her Song was hesitant and full of uncertainty.

She's frightened, Ash thought. Rook was unable to hide her true emotions this deep within her Song. Whatever it was that lay beyond was enough to scare Rook into hiding her own memories from herself. Her fear was everywhere, suffocating and constricting, and Ash felt like he was drowning in it. It took a lot of his willpower not to pull himself out of the Song Weave back to the safety of the watchtower. But whatever was through this wall was important. Answers that Rook felt Ash needed to know. Finding his courage, Ash surged his own aura round Rook's, lending it strength.

"Don't worry," he Sang as confidently as he could. *"We can do this. Together."*

Rook braced herself as their auras entwined. *"Together."*

As one Ash and Rook pierced the shield, and fell deep into memories. Terror threatened to overwhelm Rook, but she also shuddered with relief, as though a great weight had been lifted. The deeper they went, the colder it got. And although Ash lent Rook as much of his support as he was able to muster, he couldn't shake his own feelings of dread at what they were about to uncover.

Horror. Desperation. A weak, fading hope, so close to being snuffed out by a creeping despair. All these feelings crashed into Ash like a frightful wave. All things Rook had felt at this moment, whenever *this* was. Ash trembled and choked. He saw shapes, small details, two figures meeting at a dock. The figures felt safer in each other's company, but that didn't stop them from looking over their shoulders to see if they'd been followed. Their forms were blurred, but Ash could sense that one was Rook.

"Who is the other one?" Ash asked.

Rook's Song grew in warmth and hope for a brief relieving moment.

"The other one?" Rook Sang. *"The only one."* The only one who had ever trusted her, the only one who had ever been a friend. A blurred image flashed in Ash's mind, a face, too hazy to make out. *"Ferno."*

Ash's heart fluttered. *"My . . . my dad . . . ?"*

Ash clung to Rook's memories of his father as though they were a life raft. But no matter how much Ash focused, his father remained a vague shape. *"How do you know each other?"*

Ash was almost afraid of the answer. Shaard had said that his father had once been an ally, and Shaard clearly had a history with Rook too. But Ash was still desperately clinging to the hope that it was another of Shaard's lies—he couldn't bear the thought of his father as Shaard's companion. Visions flashed in Ash's mind, of Rook and Ferno side by side. Together in Aurora. Often on the docks, or aboard sleighs, sometimes even in the wilds. They were in this mess together, and would not let the other down.

"Both cursed. Both lost," Rook Sang, her voice cracking. *"Both there for the other."*

Rook's voice broke away, overwhelmed at rediscovering the only happy memories she'd ever had, lost to her for so long. She held on to them like they were delicate, and precious, for they surely were. Ash knew she would have tears in her eyes back in the watchtower and felt like an intruder in such personal memories.

In the next vision, Ferno and Rook were perched precariously upon a cliff face, Leviathans scrambling to reach them from the snows below, jaws snapping and claws scratching. Ash was stung by the fierce frustration Rook had felt at the time. She was so close to achieving something, only for it to slip away from her at the last second. If they were ever to heal the poison in their souls, they had to learn how to properly Song Weave, how to connect with Leviathans without using force. But the Leviathans had rejected them despite their pleas for peace.

"*Leviathans sensed corruption in us,*" Rook now explained to Ash. "*Did not trust.*"

"*What do you mean?*" Sang Ash.

"*Trees have souls,*" Rook Sang back. "*Mountains have souls. People, wolvers, ulks, insects, all have souls. Song is souls talking, reaching, connecting. Cannot lie in a Song. It is truth. It bares open soul.*"

"*Somehow I think I . . . I always knew that,*" Ash Sang in wonder. Song Weaving came without thought or words.

It just *was*.

It was a part of him.

It expressed his innermost feelings and desires—his joy, his pain. *And that means that . . . that the Leviathans can't lie either. They can't trick us, their Songs can't deceive.* Guilt crept through Ash again. *No wonder the Leviathans hate the ones who use them . . . ones like Shaard . . . like . . . like . . .* Ash's belly twisted. *Like me.*

"*So . . . so if you were cruel, or selfish . . . the Leviathans would know . . . ?*" Ash Sang.

"*Yes. Would know. Would not trust. Leviathans here long before us. Closest to world's soul, to World Weave. Will do all to protect it.*"

Rook had once wanted to give up. It was too late for Ferno and her. They were broken, and there was no forgiving what they had done. But Ferno would not allow it. He Sang with the Leviathans, day and night, trying to convince them he was on their side. One day they would wake from their nightmare; they would break free from the darkness.

Rook's Song bloomed with warmth, then a deep thanks that felt to Ash like the laughter shared between friends, like a warm fire after a cold day. Ferno's soul had been as wounded as Rook's, but he believed that she of all people deserved a second chance. He insisted there was good in Rook, more good than bad. No one had ever thought that way about her, no one had ever cared enough in the first place.

She'd always been the weirdo.

The odd one out.

The outcast.

Rook knew she owed Ferno a great debt for not allowing her to give up, one she would do everything to repay.

"*What happened to you both? What hurt your souls like this?*" Ash asked with an ever-increasing dread. "*What could you possibly need forgiveness for?*" He had to ask the question, even though every instinct in his body screamed at him that ignorance was bliss.

Rook's Song twisted and contorted. She strained and she struggled and cried out in despair.

"*I—I can't!*" she managed. "*Hidden . . . Forgotten . . . But . . .*" She paused, sifting through her thoughts. "*Ferno saved me, though . . . though I could not save him . . .*"

"Dad . . ." Ash whispered . . . before feeling the sting of a severe chill. Was it back at the watchtower? No . . . it was within the Memory Weave, within Rook's mind. A biting tempest wind froze the vision still, so frigid it hurt all of Ash's senses.

Something was here.

Something had been searching the whole time they'd been in the Memory Weave, and whatever it was, it had found them.

Ash could sense Rook fighting against it, trying to tear herself out of its grasp. It wanted her. And now that Ash was here it would take him too. Whatever Rook was hiding from, it was here, and its grip was tightening round them.

Ash joined her in the fight, trying to break free of its clutches. He'd never felt something so merciless and unforgiving. He pulled and he squirmed, but with every struggle, the thing seemed to drag them closer. Then, just as he was losing hope—

"*Fight it,*" Ash heard the frost-heart Sing, its voice a world away, and yet Ash could've cried at how welcome it was. It reached out its Song like a rope, and Ash clung on to it like he would've his parents' hands, like he would've the *Frostheart* crew; he clung on to it for dear life and refused to let go.

"*Do not let it win!*" the frost-heart Sang. "*Do not let it take you!*"

"*Rook!*" Ash screamed out into the swirling, freezing darkness, unable to find her in that chilling hate, desperate to escape with her.

"*I'm here!*" Her aura tethered to

Ash's, and as one, the frost-heart pulled them from the Memory Weave back to the watchtower, deep in the Endless Forest.

Both Ash and Rook were back in the watchtower, shivering, huffing mist with every heaving breath, in spite of the

warmth of the fire. Their companions watched them with wide eyes, having been woken by the commotion.

"I mean, yeah, sure, go for it. None of us wanted to sleep or anythin' anyway . . ." Kailen said, though when she saw Ash's tears she went quiet.

Ash cuffed his hand at his cheeks, sniffing. "What—what *was* that thing?" Rook only shook her head. "What happened to him? To my dad?"

Had the dark presence that had so nearly dragged them into oblivion been what had cursed his father's soul too? Rook was trembling, her crows gently nipping at her in comfort. She looked up at Ash, her face hidden within the shadow of her hood.

"*I . . . I do not know. I miss him. He . . . he was only friend I ever had.*" A crow cawed with indignation. "*Yes, yes. Apart from crows.*"

Ash managed a laugh. "Well, I'm your friend now too."

"*Spirits help you.*"

Rook had taught him so much, which was impressive, considering she couldn't talk. But Ash still had so many questions. And the closer he got to the answers, the more frightened he became.

27
Intruders

The ancient remains of the battlefield became ever more abundant as their journey continued to the southeast.

Frost-coated vehicles, snow-buried weapons, machines that Ash couldn't even comprehend. "Pinehaven whispered of this place," Kailen signed, eyes narrowed and bow fingers twitchy. "A place haunted by ghosts of the past, a place many wouldn't dare tread . . ."

The group walked in fearful silence, as though the slightest sound might stir these timeworn titans. They seemed so dead and unnatural among the trees and plants of the forest, yet the idea that they had once moved and fought was somehow even more disturbing.

All of a sudden the frost-heart began to Sing at Ash's side.

He clasped its casing, worried it was making too

much noise, its chime cutting through the ominous air like a blade.

"*There!*" it was Singing. "*There!*"

Confused, Ash looked up, and thought he could see something beyond a steep ridge to his left. The others were giving him strange looks.

"Wait . . ." Ash signed to them, before clambering up the slope, slipping a few times in the snow. He reached the top and, lying belly-down so he wouldn't be seen, peeked over the ridge. There, squatting within the entrance of an icicle-adorned cave, was a ruin from the World Before. And even more impressive, half buried in snow and ice, an enormous figure sat to the cave's side. Even seated as it was, it still towered higher than many of the buildings in Aurora. It looked to be made of stone,

its lifeless eyes gazing at the doorway to the ruins. The others arrived, lying down at Ash's side.

"Do not run off like that!" Tobu whispered angrily, before his mouth fell open as he saw what Ash had been looking at.

It must be impressive, if even Tobu's jaw dropped, Ash thought, unable to take his eyes from the spectacular sight.

"*Here,*" the frost-heart chimed. "*Here.*"

"The heart's reacting to this place . . ." Ash signed. "But why . . . ?"

"*The heart . . . ?*" Rook Sang, curious.

"There must be something in there . . . underneath that statue . . ."

"Not a statue," Lunah signaled. "Drifter legend says they used to move. Stone warriors that stomped about, shooting fire and crushing anything that stood in their way . . ."

"Warriors . . . ?" Ash gasped.

Through forest unbroken and shimmering sky,
Follow the gaze of the giant's eye.
The sleeping warrior watches the door,
Where we shall meet, and you'll search no more.

Could it be? Ash took the fact that the frost-heart was incessantly chiming its encouragement as a big, fat yes.

"I need to get in there," Ash whispered. "The final answer to my riddle is in there, I know it! Maybe even Solstice itself!"

Rook straightened at this, almost as excited as Ash. Kailen and Master Podd shot him a questioning look, while Lunah's eyes widened. Tobu shifted his weight, but kept his eyes focused on the ruins.

"The answers you seek may be inside the ruins, though they may not be what you expect, or even want to hear. Whatever you discover, you will never be able to turn back from this moment. Are you sure this is what you want?"

Ash couldn't believe Tobu even had to ask. Why was he always so weird? Ash's parents could be in there *right now*, Ferno had said so in the lullaby! *Where we shall meet, and you'll search no more . . .*

Ash nodded, so eager he nearly leaped over the ridge and sprinted to the ruins there and then. "Yes, I'm sure."

Tobu took a deep, tired breath. "So be it."

He was acting *really* strange now. It troubled Ash, but he still got up. Checking that the coast was clear, Ash crept down the ridge, his friends following behind.

He reached the middle of the clearing, his heart thrumming, his smile widening.

At last—we've done it! We've made—

His thoughts were blasted from his head as he was knocked off his feet, snow exploding before him. He lay on his back, and was dimly aware of shouts and screams, of frantic movement all around. Something wet landed on his shoulder. He touched it, mind thick as sludge.

Drool.

Drool dripping from the massive, snarling head of

the Spearwurm that rose above him, gazing down with hungry eyes. A Spearwurm at the head of a pack of at least fifteen that were circling the clearing, coiling round the trees. They slithered down the cave's mouth and over the stone warrior, blocking the entrance to the ruins, blocking any means of escape.

Kailen stood behind Ash, aiming her bow. Lunah had a dagger in her hands, while Master Podd raised his little fists. The closest Spearwurm reared back its head, preparing to attack Ash, when Tobu leaped between them, his spear clasped in his hands. The Spearwurm let out an earth-shaking roar, its jaws so close to Tobu that he was showered in spit, and so large it could've bitten him in half. Unfazed, Tobu returned the roar, unleashing a bellow so mighty and defiant that even the Leviathan pulled back in surprise. Rook was the only one not in a defensive position.

"NO!" she screamed, pulling hard at Tobu's shoulder. "Don't attack!"

Rook began to Sing, pushing Tobu out of the way. She weaved a Song of peace and patience. It stalled the Spearwurms, her Song-aura keeping them at bay, but they were straining against her, fighting her message of calm.

"Help me!" she urged Ash. "Connect. Weave with them!"

"I—I *can't!* There's too many, and I—they'll—"

"You can. Song Weaver. You must show trust. Show you're not enemy. Show you're on their side! Be clear. Be true."

Rising to his knees and furrowing his brow, Ash joined his Song with Rook's. He Sang the most soothing Song he could, his star-light aura reaching out in friendship, trying to send out calming emotions toward the growling Spearwurms.

"Peace. We mean no harm. Please let us pass!" The Spearwurms hissed threateningly. Ash held out his hand, palm open in what he hoped was an unaggressive gesture, but it only revealed how much he was trembling.

"Peace. Friends."

The Spearwurms drew closer, their jagged teeth bared.

"HUMAN. ENEMY. TRESPASS?" they Sang as one, their twitching purple auras flailing about, turning a vicious red. The Spearwurms' hatred for human-kin sizzled through Ash's blood, giving him pins and needles.

"I'm not your enemy!" Ash insisted, although he wasn't sure he believed his Song. *"I'm on your side!"*

Sides.

What side am I on? Ash fretted. *I thought I was a Pathfinder . . . just like my parents . . . I . . . I wanted to help the Strongholds. But they don't want to help me. They hate me. They want to use me, like Shaard uses the Leviathans!*

The Leviathans' Song delved deep into his, searching out who he was, who he *really* was. They heard the Song of his confusion, all his sorrow, his desperate need to find where he belonged.

I'm a Song Weaver. And Leviathans hate Song Weavers, I can feel it! They are our enemies, of course they are! They hunt us! They kill us!

He looked from the Spearwurm to the ruins, which stood so, so close, and reeled at how cruel fate could be. His parents might've been waiting for him right there, just beyond those doors. He'd traveled halfway across the world to be here. The moment he'd been waiting for his entire life was almost within his grasp, and yet was about to be stolen from him by these hateful monsters. Fury stung Ash's insides, frustration burning his senses. At that moment he would've done anything to get rid of the Leviathans. To force them out of his way, to erase them from the world. But there was no escape from this, not now. Unless . . . ?

The familiar chill had risen up inside him, and now begged him to use its power. Ash *did* have an option, a way out of this terrible situation. A Song—so powerful it could bend the will of Leviathans. But Ash had made a promise to Tobu, to himself, that he would never use that Song again. Rook had only just spoken of its corrupt nature. *But . . . but I only have to use it this once*, he assured himself, *and then it'll all be over*. One Song, and these Spearwurms would be his to control.

He was aware of the frost-heart chiming wildly. *"Don't give in to hatred!"*

Ash clenched his fists and gritted his teeth, trembling with fear, or was it with anticipation?

You could make them do anything you wish, the coldness within him seemed to whisper. *Anything at all.*

"Don't listen to it!"

"I NEED TO!" Ash barked back with anger. *"Just this once!"*

With the oath made, Ash cried out Shaard's Song. His Song-aura began to bleed from star-white to inky-black, the star-light blizzard warping into thrashing serpentine tendrils. The Spearwurms reared back and let out a terrible bellow.

"NO!" A voice tore through Ash's mind, louder even than a Shrieker's scream or a Gargant's roar. *"Never Sing that Song. Do you hear me? NEVER!"*

It was Rook. She pulled Ash back, throwing him to the snow, her Song so intense it was enough to shock Ash out of his Song-trance, his aura dissipating. He gasped

and trembled. The Spearwurms
slithered toward him, their thrumming vibrating through his ribs. *Rook's
mad. You can't reason with monsters like these!*
They were going to kill him. Overwhelmed, he yelped
out loud, ducking away, arms over his head, preparing
for the worst.

But the Spearwurms did not strike.

Peeking through his hands, Ash saw Rook walking calmly toward them, Singing her broken Song, her
hands held out, steady as stone. Her Song-aura weaved
round theirs. Ash could feel the emotion in her Song, the
feelings she was revealing.

"*Sorry to intrude. We ask to pass, and with permission
we shall be gone. We're not your enemies.*" That was what
Ash could make out, but there was also a depth to her
Song that Ash could not delve to; things were being said

that he could not understand. The melody was unthreatening and entirely entrancing, as warming as being held by a loved one you hadn't seen for years. Her Song was earnest, and she meant everything she Sang. Finally, the Spearwurms seemed convinced, their Song-auras turning from red to a tranquil blue as they danced round Rook's.

Ash's jaw dropped as the Spearwurms slowly withdrew to the edges of the clearing, uncoiled from the ruin's entrance, allowing them passage.

"*Thank you,*" Rook finished, before striding across the clearing toward the ruins.

Tentatively, the others followed. They couldn't believe their eyes. Lunah was staring in openmouthed bewilderment.

Ash's nerves were on edge as he followed in Rook's footsteps, the retreating Spearwurms following his every move with suspicion.

"Okay, maybe she *is* useful to have around," Kailen dared to say, shaking her head in disbelief, Master Podd at her side, stroking his chin with interest.

"Indeed, the captain will be most impressed when I tell her."

Tobu was the last to follow, his muscles tense and ready for the slightest show of attack, fangs bared.

This—this is mind-blowing, Ash thought in awe, his limbs trembling. In all his years alive, Ash would never have dreamed such a scene possible, and yet here they were.

They passed under the looming archeogiant, Ash hoping beyond hope that it didn't choose this moment to wake up. When they arrived at the heavy stone door to the ruin they all pushed against it, but it didn't budge.

"Do we need a key?" Ash panicked, all too aware that the swarm of Spearwurms were still watching them, eyes glaring and Songs thrumming. "Or some hidden, advanced ancient archeomek device to open it or—" The rest began crawling through a large crack in the door. "Or we could go through that big hole, yes." Ash followed them through as fast as he could, not wanting to push his luck and risk the Spearwurms changing their minds.

28

Past Glimpses

It was dark inside the ruins. *Very dark*. But not so dark that Ash couldn't hear Rook telling him off. *"Never Sing that Song. NEVER!"*

"I-I'm sorry, but what else could I do?"

"NEVER. Song hateful. WARPING. Destructive!"

"I—I only tried to help!"

Ash flushed with shame. He found himself glad that the others couldn't understand what Rook was saying to him, that they wouldn't have been able to see his Song-aura and know what he'd been about to do. He swore he could feel Tobu's judgmental eyes boring into him regardless, his powerful yeti senses sussing out what was going on. Ash backed away from Rook, straining his eyes and feeling his way around, the only light coming from the crack in the door. The smell of damp and undisturbed air filled his nostrils, his heart still beating wildly.

"Watch out, there's stairs here," Lunah warned, her voice somewhere ahead.

Following Master Podd, whose eyes allowed him to see in the dark, they all climbed down the stairwell, farther and farther under the cave, pushing their way through another heavy stone door at the bottom. Fear tingled at the back of Ash's neck. What if the place was cursed? What if ghosts, or even worse, *Wraiths* came from the depths of these old ruins that may have gone as far down as the underworld itself? The air was close, suggesting this new chamber wasn't very big. Ash bumped into something hard as if to prove the point.

"Ow!" Then his hand clipped something else. "Ow!" He then stubbed his toe. "Ow!"

"Ash!" Lunah chided.

"Sorry!" he whispered, before hitting his head on something that hung from the ceiling. Whatever it was, it began to click and whir. The air shifted as the sounds of machinery buzzed to life. Lines of blue-white light flared into existence, blinding at first. They danced across the walls and ceiling, whorls and patterns glowing as though they'd had luminous water poured into them. The room the group found themselves in was indeed quite small, and chockful of aged archeomek.

"Nice work!" Lunah said.

Ash rubbed his head. "Th-thanks . . ."

He stumbled back as his boot stepped on something crunchy. He yelped when he saw that it was a skeleton, its armor rock-hard with ice. "*Gah!* There's a dead person!"

"Four of them," Tobu murmured, indicating another three scattered about the glowing room. The others wore helmets and held strange weapons in their death grip, skulls grinning at the new visitors. "Warriors . . . *once.*"

"What is this place?" Ash whispered, wondering why his dad had led him here. What kind of gateway to Solstice was *this*?

"Looks like some kind of ancient shelter," Kailen surmised.

"Look at all the archeomek . . ." Ash said.

Most of it was dark and dead, but some blinked with light or had parts that clicked and moved. *Shaard would've loved this*, Ash found himself thinking. Master Podd's nose wiggled and ears twitched at the sight of so many relics. His natural-born scavenger ways were threatening to break through his indifferent exterior.

"*Is Heart Singing? Know what to do?*" Rook Sang, dragging a pale finger through the thick frost that coated a dashboard.

"No . . ." Ash admitted. It had gone silent, though Ash could sense it vibrating with what felt like anticipation.

They looked around, trying to make sense of the place. Rook sniffed about in nooks and crannies while Master Podd pocketed a few choice archeomek devices.

"You never know when one might come in useful," he said in answer to Lunah's raised eyebrow.

Ash found himself drawn to a control panel which had a small stone sphere set in a cavity at its center. Patterns of light glowed round the sphere's shape and radiated out from it across the panel's flat surface. Slowly, Ash reached for it . . .

And a Song burst from the sphere the moment he touched it, his mind erupting with visions.

Explosions flashed red and orange against a smoke-choked sky. Archeoweapons blasted crackling balls of lightning across a ravaged land, toward a swarming mass of Leviathans. A mountain rose dark and grim in the distance. Gigantic machines and stone giants, things that had no right moving, belched fire at the encroaching tide. A terrified warrior wearing the same helmet as the skeletons in the shelter looked straight at Ash, his face covered in sweat and dirt. Ash recoiled as the man began to shout, unable to understand the words he spoke, but their meaning and emotions were clear enough, translated through the sunstone's Song much like Rook's memories had been. "It's over! We can't hold them! We've fallen!" A Hurtler leaped into a group of warriors behind him, biting down with its powerful jaws. "It's coming! It's coming!" It was then that Ash heard it. The terrible, awful drone, the same one chanted by the Wraiths, but so thundering that it sounded like a ferocious scream, a world-shaking roar. To Ash's amazement, human-kin ran among the Leviathan tide, charging the armored warriors and attacking them in a wild frenzy of weapons, fists, and teeth. Suddenly the mountain, or what had appeared to be a mountain, *moved*. It shifted its weight, heading straight for the panicked warrior. "We can't stop it! It's coming! *It's—*"

The vision came to a sudden end. It had all happened so fast.

"Are you okay?" Lunah squeaked; the others looked just as worried.

"Y-yeah . . ." Ash muttered, clutching his head. "The machine, it . . . I heard a Song . . . I saw through some- one else's eyes . . . It was a . . . battle? People from the World Before fighting Leviathans, people dying . . . It was *horrible* . . ."

Lunah put a hand on Ash's shoulder as he shivered.

"*Heard of such things. Songs burned into stones. Fro- zen in time,*" Rook explained, closing in on the device, running her hands along it, sniffing at it.

"There was something else . . ." Ash said. "It was . . . I think it was a Leviathan. As big as a mountain . . . They were throwing everything they had at it, but they . . . they couldn't stop it . . ."

"*Impossible,*" Kailen scoffed.

Rook remained quiet as Tobu's eyes narrowed. Lunah appeared almost as scared as Ash felt. Master Podd swiped another relic.

"Ash . . . look," Lunah said, pointing to a rack filled with other archeospheres.

Tentatively, Ash picked another one up, turning it in his hands as Rook removed the previous one from the device. Ash placed the next stone into the device, adrenaline pounding through his veins. Taking a deep breath, he placed his hand on the sphere.

He was prepared for it this time, so the shock was not as great. But the Song was just as terrible.

Another warrior from the World Before sat in front of Ash, this one gaunt and exhausted, deep, dark rings under his eyes. He stood in the room Ash and the others were in, but all the archeomek devices surrounding them were working, buzzing, clicking, and illuminating the space with an eerie blue glow.

"This is General Ario," the man said, "of the Ninth Legion, report- ing from the Pineridge front." His voice sounded as defeated as he looked. "Gods, I don't even know if I'll get this message-sphere out. Why am I even making it? Fear, I guess. Loneliness? The sad ramblings of a man with no hope left." He chuckled joylessly. "We've been ordered to pull back. But what's the point? There's no outrunning this. Our weapons have no effect. They don't even slow the thing down. It destroys anything in its path, consumes anything it touches. Even took out one of those Leviathan Ancients." He paused to rub his eyes. "They say they're workin' on something back at the capital. Something that can imprison it. But you need Leviathans for that, and they hate us as much as they hate it now. No. They won't help us. And even if they could, it's too late. The rumors from the east are true. Its Song claws into your mind. Changes you. Only affects Song Weavers, but that's the whole top brass of the empire. That's *me*." He was quiet for some time, then started grimacing. "I can't escape it. I hear it all the time. That cursed droning! When I'm awake, in my dreams . . . It calls to me. You can't fight it. This God-Leviathan. It's like war taken a form. It's hate personified. How d'you even begin to fight something like that?"

The Song ended. As Ash's eyes readjusted to the darkness, he clasped at his throat, which had gone tight with dread. *What* is *this thing . . . ?*

"Well?" Lunah asked.

With a faltering voice Ash told the others of the frightening, awful message he'd just received.

"It sounds like the fall of the World Before . . ." Lunah said once he had finished. "Say what you want about the World Before, they knew how to have an apocalypse . . ."

Tobu didn't look shocked by the news. "Such a creature is known to the yeti scroll-keepers. It is in our songs and legends, our histories. The World Eater, we call it. But it lives no longer, and has not for millennia . . ."

Ash remembered the mural Shaard had shown him.

The warnings Rook had been desperate for him to understand.

"The Devourer . . ." Ash whispered, as Rook nodded grimly. "Some kind of mega-Leviathan destroyer . . . *thing*."

"Well, that's somethin' I reckon I woulda remembered seein' wanderin' about, so somethin' must've stopped it? Maybe this prison thing they were workin' on succeeded?" Lunah said.

"Maybe . . ."

A line from the lullaby came to Ash's mind, one he had never understood until now.

"Lest shadow break through prison's shell . . ."

The lullaby had instructed Ash to keep the frost-heart safe unless *something* broke from a prison's shell. Had the World Before really managed to imprison the Devourer? Surely it would be dead after all these centuries? Ash reached out to the frost-heart for reassurance, its distant melody a comfort amid all these dark thoughts. His hand brushed the pouch at his belt as he did so.

"Wait! I just remembered!" Ash said aloud, and pulled out the archeosphere his father had hidden in the Wayfinder statue. The sphere was exactly the same size as the others on the rack. With trembling hands, Ash replaced the one in the device. It was a perfect fit.

Could this be it? Was this the end of the lullaby, of all the riddles? Ash imagined a secret door opening, revealing a hidden Stronghold underground, his parents smiling at him, holding him in their arms at long last. But what if it wasn't? What if something had gone wrong? What if Shaard had gotten to them first? He was almost too frightened to find out.

Sensing his worry, Lunah approached his side and took his hand, smiling encouragingly. Ash looked to Rook, who gave him a reassuring nod. Only Tobu wouldn't meet his eye, suddenly very interested in the archeomek relics. "'Bout time we solved this endless riddle, right?" Lunah smiled, before gently guiding Ash's hand to the sphere, stepping back as Ash was once again enveloped by a Song-vision.

29

The Messages

Unlike the other message-spheres, this Song wrapped Ash in warmth. He felt like he sat by a roaring hearth, cozy and safe while a blizzard raged outside. A man came into focus. Even though the man was a stranger, Ash immediately knew him. Black, messy hair sticking up all over the place. A friendly face, quick to smile. Dark brown eyes. The man looked like Ash. Though he was marked with scars and exhaustion, inky lines streaking down from under his eyes like black tears, there was no mistaking it. Ash took a shuddering breath.

It was Ferno.

It was his father.

"My boy," Ferno said, and Ash gasped. His heart ached, a terrible joy swelling inside, a wonderful sadness. "My incredible, brilliant, brave Ash."

"*Dad . . .*" Ash answered with a smile impossible to hold back as tears rolled down his cheeks. "I . . . I did it . . ." Ash began, amazed to be finally standing before this person he'd dreamed of finding all his life. "I did what you asked! I followed the lullaby . . . I solved the riddles, I—"

"I am so proud of you," Ferno said, smiling. Ash laughed, his tears salty on his tongue. "You have come so far, as I never doubted you would. You definitely take after your mother in terms of determination, thank the spirits."

"Like . . . *Mum*? Is she . . . is she here, can I see her, can I—"

"I wish more than anything I could be with you there right now," Ferno interrupted.

"But you are! I'm here, Dad. I'm right here! I—I made it. I—" Ash's breath caught in his throat. He reached out to touch his father, to hold him and hug him and never let go. To show him that they were together at last. But Ash's hand passed through thin air. This was a memory, so, so real . . . and yet. Ash had always known this, but for the most blissful of moments Ash had believed he was about to hold his mum and dad, safe from the world outside. But his parents weren't here. This was just a memory, nothing more.

"I wish I could see the person you've become; I wish

it so much it hurts," Ferno said. "We would often try to guess what you'd be like, your mum and me. Ember, of course, thought you'd be strong, *unstoppable*, even. A capable warrior, a natural leader, just like her. Perhaps you have even grown to become a Pathfinder." Ferno grinned. "She would've loved that. She always wanted to make the world a better place, but she said you'd be the one to do it. I asked her how she knew, and she just gave me that look, the one I couldn't argue with. The look I fell in love with." Ferno laughed sadly. "She *just knew*. As for what I thought you'd be? I tended to think smaller, not that I didn't believe you could do great things if you wanted to. I suppose if you're reading this message, it seems your mother was closer to the mark. She always was. Though you know what?" Ferno paused, thinking, Ash hanging on his every word, desperate to hear more, yet never wanting the message to end.

"Perhaps I did guess some things right about you. I know you're clever, of that I'm sure. Who else could've solved all those riddles? I'm sorry they were such a pain"—Ferno chuckled at this—"but I knew they'd be no match for you. I also know you're as brave as they come. Crossing the Snow Sea, the things you must have had to go through . . ." Ferno's voice broke away at this, and Ash held his breath. "Most of all I know you're compassionate," Ferno continued. "You can't have gotten here alone, which means you must have had the help of friends, friends who I'm positive would do anything for you. Which means you're kind, Ash. You're a good person." A shadow passed over Ferno's face, a shadow that was echoed on Ash's.

Ash swallowed hard, his throat tight.

"I don't have long. I need to tell you what I can. You have the frost-heart? Of course you do." Ash touched the casing at his belt, reassured by the sting of cold, the chime of reassurance. "It is the heart of a Leviathan Ancient, the most powerful Leviathan there ever was. But it's more than that. It is a key. You *must* get it to the safety of Solstice. You *must* keep it away from a terrible, violent man named Shaard. I—I was a fool to trust him. He tore me away from your mother . . . from you. He destroyed the person I was. But I know you will see through his lies, just like Ember did." At this Ferno took a breath, his eyes glistening. "Shaard will be trying to find you. He'll do all he can to get his hands on the frost-heart, but you must not let him. Together we started something that must be stopped at all costs. Shaard intends to use the frost-heart to release a terrible, hate-consumed Leviathan from its prison, but he cannot be allowed to. The entire world depends on it. Get to Solstice, Ash. The Elders there will help you." Ferno took a breath, composing himself. "If anyone can stop this disaster from happening, it's you, my brave, brave boy. You have everything you need to find Solstice. Follow the stars. The North Star marks the start. The others will lead the way from there. Trust in the frost-heart, it won't let you down. But most of all, trust in yourself. Look at everything you've done. A child from the middle of nowhere, as far from anything as you can be. And now here you are at the center of it all. You are nothing like me, and for that I could not be happier. The fire in my heart has been doused with darkness, but know that any good that may still be in me is the love I have for you and your mother. It's what kept me alive. But your heart is strong, I know it, and it still burns bright. Remember that the world is beautiful, and full of good. Never lose that hope, Ash, that belief in others. It is what makes you kind, and generous, and *strong*." Ash trembled at these words. Why did they sound like a goodbye?

"Dad . . ." Ash tried to speak, his vision blurring through stabbing tears. "Dad, where are you?! I want to help you; I want to find you!"

His dad looked at the floor, his messy hair falling over his eyes and hiding his tears. Ash wanted to rush over to him, to pull his chin up and tell him it was okay, that he just wanted to be with him, to help, to do anything—but Ash knew his words were useless.

And at that terrible moment, at the very heights of Ash's despair . . . Ferno began to Sing. He Sang with a hushed, cracked voice, but to Ash it was the most beautiful thing he'd ever heard. Ferno Sang a Song Ash knew better than any other, a Song that was as much a part of Ash as his heart and soul. The Song that had kept him company when he'd grown up alone and unwanted. The Song that had assured him in his darkest moments that somewhere out there he was loved. It was the Song that had taken his hand and led him to his new home, to his new family.

Ash sank to his knees, curling up at the feet of Ferno as he Sang Ash's lullaby. His father, this ghost. Every word, every verse, Ash clung on to them, afraid he might lose them forever.

The message came to an end, the cold, abandoned shelter materializing around Ash once again. His arms were held out, reaching for someone who wasn't there. His cheeks were hot and red with tears.

Ash couldn't face looking at the others, knowing they'd heard his side of the conversation—they would've seen him so vulnerable. He didn't want to be here in this dark, forgotten place. He didn't want to be lost in the freezing, unforgiving wilds. He wanted to be happy, warm and safe with his parents.

Tobu strode toward him. Ash braced himself, expecting a comment about how he needed to pick himself up, that this wasn't journey's end, that he'd wasted their time.

Not now, Tobu, not now . . .

But instead Tobu placed an arm round Ash and picked him up from the floor. Ash gazed up, light flaring through his tears. Tobu looked him in the eye, stern as ever, but there was sorrow there too.

"We will find them," Tobu said.

Ash placed a hand on top of Tobu's before Lunah dived in and gave him a big hug. Her warmth was welcome, and Ash was surprised to discover he was smiling.

"I think . . . I think that was it," Ash managed to say, his throat tight and scratchy. "I think that was the end of the lullaby."

30
Don't Look Down

"So . . . this ent Solstice then?" Lunah asked when, once again, Ash had told the others about the vision he'd had.

"No."

"Well, I gotta say, I'm kinda glad." She looked around at the dim, crumbling room, at the skeletons grinning at them. "Was startin' to feel a bit sorry for you Song Weavers . . ."

"I still have no idea where Solstice is! He said I had all I need to find it . . . it has something to do with the stars, but . . . but . . ." Ash rubbed his face. "Uuuurgh, I need to think about this . . ."

At that moment Tobu's ears flickered. He brought his spear forward, eyes wide with alarm. "We're not alone."

The others froze. Ash listened carefully, and sure

enough, he heard it, his stomach dropping. The chaotic movement of scrabbling claws and lashing tails, scraping through snow and stone. But worst of all, the hateful, vile chanting.

The Wraith Song.

"Just outside the ruins," Tobu whispered. "They've found us. We must move!"

With his heart in his throat, Ash followed the others to the far end of the room, moving as fast as they could without making any noise. They pushed through another doorway just as they heard footsteps coming down the stairs.

Light streamed down into the narrow corridor they found themselves in, a hole in the ceiling created by a rockfall leading to the outside world.

Tobu gave Lunah, Ash, and Master Podd a boost

to climb out, while Rook and Kailen leaped up with incredible agility. Scratches and movement could be heard from the room they'd just left as the Wraiths searched for them. The party scrambled over the large rocks that had collapsed into the ruins, using them to climb out of the cave and back into the forest outside.

Their heads popped up into blinding light high atop a large rocky outcropping. As his eyes adjusted to the light, Ash saw Lurker sleighs darting through the trees, hideous shadows appearing and disappearing within the forest mist.

"Up," Tobu signed, pointing to the Pinehaven walkways that creaked in the canopy above them. They clambered up a ladder as quietly as possible, freezing whenever they thought a sleigh had spotted them. At this height Ash could see that the Wraiths surrounded the front entrance to the ruins,

searching the forest for any sign of their quarry. The Spearwurms were nowhere to be seen.

Perhaps they're hiding from the awful Wraith chant.

"Stay low," Tobu signaled, trying to keep to the center of the wobbly bridge to keep it as still and quiet as possible. They crept along the bridge as fast as they dared, sidling round a wide tree trunk and pressing up against it as Wraiths appeared at the hole they'd just made their escape from. Ash peeked his head out and saw that the Wraiths had also spotted the bridge they'd just crossed and were making gestures toward the ladder. The entire forest seemed to hold its breath. Then, to Ash's horror, the Wraiths began climbing, jagged blades drawn and ready, their companions watching from below, Lurkers snarling at the head of the sleighs.

"Which way?" Tobu signed to Lunah, whose eyes were wide and white. She looked at the network of walkways that sprawled out in almost every direction. She was breathing hard, her brow furrowed.

"This way," she said, pointing, before quickly changing her mind and pointing down another bridge.

"On the count of three, run," Tobu signed. Ash's guts tied into a knot. "One." His legs trembled. "Two." He took a deep breath. "Three." They shot off across the walkway as fast as they could. Without even having to look, Ash could sense the Wraiths springing into action.

The swaying of the walkway made running difficult. Ash misplaced his footing and for a terrible moment thought he was going to fall over the side, but he corrected himself and carried on scrambling after the others. He saw the sleighs below giving chase, the Wraiths training their bows at Tobu and Rook. Arrows thunked into the underside of the walkway, the wooden planks thankfully shielding them. The path forked ahead.

"This way!" Lunah yelled, leading them to the left. The furious chant was growing ever more cutting, forcing Ash to squint and clench his teeth. It clawed at his mind with vicious intent, and filled his vision with vivid red spots. As it reached a crescendo, there was a sudden explosion on the forest floor.

A Spearwurm darted from the snow like an arrow and tore right through the walkway a hairsbreadth behind them, its head crest cutting the wood into splinters, before diving back down into the snow. The bridge had been torn in half. Ash's belly lifted into his throat as the platform dropped. He managed to grab hold of a plank as the walkway swung toward the tall pine it was attached to. It thumped into the tree trunk with tremendous force, Ash just barely keeping his grip.

"UP!" Tobu roared, using his spear to deflect an arrow that had been heading right for him.

The Wraith sleighs gathered below like hungry wolvers, Lurkers scrambling at the tree trunk, snapping and roaring.

Lunah and Rook used the collapsed walkway like a ladder, clambering up as fast as they could while Tobu protected them from flying arrows, hanging off the wooden planks with one hand and foot to allow himself better movement. Ash tried to follow, but seeing how high they were, he went dizzy with a wave of nausea. His sweaty hands began to slip.

"Don't look down!" Tobu roared, clacking another arrow away with a swing of his spear. "Keep your eyes on the walkway. One rung at a time."

Ash steadied his breath. With trembling hands he climbed. He scurried past Tobu, who ducked his head out of the way of another arrow. Tobu pulled himself up, catching Ash by his shoulders and lifting him to the platform where the others waited. "GO!"

They sprinted across another walkway, the Wraiths following closely, their chant unending. The Spearwurm burst from the ground again, ramming one of the trees that held the walkway aloft, its force pulling the tree's roots out of the frozen soil. A second leaped from the snow like some terrifying sea serpent, smashing into the underside of the bridge but not quite managing to cut through it.

"Can't you Sing to them?" Kailen asked Rook as they pushed forward.

"*Wraiths corrupt Leviathan reason. Leviathans won't listen,*" she Sang, but Ash was too busy gasping for breath to translate.

"How far to the outpost?" Tobu demanded of Lunah. Her eyes darted around in open panic. "Lunah, which way? We need shelter *now!*"

"I—I don't *know!*" Her dreadlocks swished from side to side as she assessed the possible options. "*I don't know!*" She began to lead them down one path when the Spearwurms surged up from below, tearing through tree trunks and bridges like they were twigs. She stumbled down another path, fear plain across her face.

"There!" Lunah said, pointing to a large Pinehaven pod that hung from mighty trees some way ahead at the border of the forest, the snow plains stretching out white and endless beyond. Torches could be seen alight within. "*An outpost!*" Lunah was almost laughing in relief. But the relief was short-lived as a Spearwurm ripped through the tree trunk behind them. The walkway shuddered as shards of wood showered the forest floor. Ash yelped as another Spearwurm exploded from its hiding place ahead of them and carved straight through the tree in front. Branches tangled and snapped. Trees began to tumble to the ground, taking the walkway with them. Tobu leaped toward Ash and Lunah, shielding them with his huge bulk as they crashed into the clearing below in a wave of snow.

Rook rolled as she hit the ground beside him. Kailen hit the floor hard, while Master Podd swung down safely with his grappling hook. They scrambled to their feet, covered in snow and pine needles. Backing up into a close circle, they watched in horror as the Spearwurms surrounded them. There were five of them now. No, *six*.

The same ones that let us pass earlier, Ash thought, panicking. He backed as far into Tobu as he could, terror fraying his nerves as the Leviathans bared their fangs and let out low, trembling growls. The Wraith sleighs formed an outer ring, chanting in fury. Ash saw the Great Horned One among them and could sense its grim satisfaction at having finally caught them.

There was nowhere to run.

The Wraiths had them trapped.

Tobu gripped his spear tightly. "First opening you see, *run*. I will fend them off as long as I'm able."

"There's no way you can fight all of them!" Ash cried.

"*You must all run!*" Rook insisted, her Song-aura flowing out of her. "*Do not let them catch you. Protect frost-heart. Get to Solstice. You must!*"

"Wh-what are you going to do?" Ash shouted over the drone, a terrible dread creeping up his back.

"*Leave me here. Do not take me with you. I will become a danger to you all. Promise me.*"

"What're you talking about? I'm not leaving you—no way!"

"*There's no time!*" she screamed, the Wraiths charging forward with their Leviathan slaves. "*Run! Do not come back for me!*" And with that Rook changed her Song. It warped and convulsed, turning as black as the droning mass it fought against. Serpentine tendrils burst from her aura and surged toward the Spearwurms. Ash gasped as he realized it was the same Song he had Sung in Shade's Chasm, the same evil Song that Shaard had taught him.

"Rook!" Ash yelled, frightened that Rook was about to make the same terrible mistake he had, but he could barely hear his own voice over Rook's fury, more scream than Song. Her aura was an unstoppable torrent, tearing through the mass of the Wraiths' shadow-Song like a blade, ripping a Spearwurm from their grasp. The Wraiths reeled back, shocked at her strength.

"*DESTROY THEM,*" Rook commanded the Leviathan.

With a roar the Spearwurm dived for a Wraith sleigh; the two riders only just scrambled out of the way as the beast tore through it, turning it into kindling. The Wraith Song directed the other Spearwurms to attack, but Rook was ready for them. She sent her Leviathan charging to meet them. As the Spearwurms rammed into each other and began thrashing and biting in a madness of limbs and snow, Rook took control of the Lurker that had been freed from the broken sleigh. With a screech it bounded at the other Wraiths, crunching one under its powerful jaws.

Ash and the others watched in disbelief, both amazed and horrified. Then Tobu scooped Ash and Lunah up under his arms. "To the outpost!" he ordered, running after Kailen, who had Master Podd on her shoulders.

"We can't leave Rook here!" Ash cried, looking back at her. She now stood alone against their enemies. The attack had weakened the Wraith Song, its bubbling mass shrinking down as she wrested control of more Spearwurms, turning them against the Wraiths, who scattered back into the depths of the forest.

The Leviathans ripped their sleighs to shreds, clawing and biting at any that passed too close. One was even caught by a Spearwurm's powerful tail swing; the Wraith soared through the air and hit a tree with a horrible *crack*.

"We cannot go back!" Tobu said. "It's too dangerous!"

"We shall not make her sacrifice meaningless."

"No! I won't leave her to die! She's our friend, and after all the help she's given us, she needs us now!" Tobu gritted his teeth, still running. "Tobu, *please*."

Tobu let out a growl of frustration. "Head for the outpost," he said, dropping the children. "Do not stop until you reach it!" And with that he turned on his heel and rushed back to Rook.

Ash saw that the only Wraith that remained in the

clearing was the Great Horned One, who stood defiantly before Rook. It roared and growled its terrible Song back at her, tendrils of shadow choking the life out of her. Terrifyingly, it seemed more than a match for her incredible powers. Rook was on her knees now, at its mercy. It strode toward her as it roared, drawing two blades from its cloak. Ash slowed as he saw the Wraith prepare to strike Rook's helpless body.

"No . . ."

Lunah tugged at his arms. "Ash, we have to move!"

"But . . ."

The Great Horned One raised its blades up high, but something gave it pause before it struck the killing blow. Tobu's spear was heading right for it. It dived out of the way just as the spear landed at its feet. But it couldn't duck the enormous bulk of Tobu, who launched his whole weight into the creature, knocking it to the floor.

Tobu wasted no time scooping Rook into his arms and slinging her over his shoulder before running back toward the children. The Great Horned One roared in fury and struggled to its feet, pulling out the bow it had slung over its shoulders, the Spearwurms having fled.

Ash and Lunah had reached the knotted rope that led up to the outpost and began climbing, Ash arcing his head so he could watch Tobu's escape. The Great Horned

One fired arrow after arrow, but Tobu was quick, sensing their approach and dodging out of their way moments before impact, Rook swaying lifelessly over his shoulder.

"Come on, Tobu, come *on*!"

"He can't dodge 'em all!" Kailen fretted as she climbed the rope, unable to return fire. Just as Tobu dodged another arrow, a mighty call echoed throughout the forest. It sounded like voices bellowing in anger. *Hundreds of them.*

"Warriors!" Lunah cried out.

The sound came from above them, and for the first time Ash saw what looked like an entire warband lining the walkways of the Pinehaven outpost, brandishing their spears and bows, silhouetted against Mother Sun like heroes from legend.

The warriors called out their war cry, preparing for battle.

An arrow struck the snow at the Great Horned One's feet, who recoiled at the challenge. It knew it could not defeat those kinds of numbers, not without the Leviathans it had lost. It could only back away, safely out of bow range, watching its quarry escape. Its shadow crept long and far across the snow, reaching out for Tobu as he grasped the rope and hefted himself up with a grunt. Only at another challenging roar from the outpost's warriors did the Great Horned One shift, raising its head to look straight at Ash. Its eyes were black and pitiless, and made Ash's skin crawl.

With that it turned and faded back into the shadows of the forest.

"Up," Tobu panted from below, Rook's body weighing him down. "Please climb up."

"S-sorry!" Ash said, ascending the rope as best he could. His arms were shaking when he reached the large hatch that led into the outpost, but a hand reached down to help pull him up. He took it gladly and came face-to-face with a smiling Pinehaven hunter.

"Spirits, you do find the strangest things out in the wilds, don't you?"

31
Tea Time

The sky was as white as snow, lighter than the blue-gray ice below it, a thin mist hanging low across the frozen plains. The chill wind filled the *Frostheart*'s red sails, a welcome splash of color in this desolate land, and pushed it happily along the border of the Endless Forest. A flock of crows led the sleigh toward the Pinehaven outpost where Ash and the others stood, watching their friends arrive with wide smiles. Lunah was bouncing up and down, waving vigorously at the sleigh.

Kailen smiled. "Now that's a sight for sore eyes."

Master Podd wiped away a tear.

"Took their ruddy time, didn't they?" Lunah laughed.

Ash couldn't help but laugh with her.

Back to her usual self, he thought with a smile, relieved.

"Would you like some more pine-needle tea?" offered Galon, the Pinehaven hunter who manned this outpost. He approached them on the sheltered outdoor platform where they stood, a large ceramic pot in his hand. He was a tall, thin man and, unlike his fellow Pinehaven native Kailen, he was welcoming and quick to smile. This was the fifth tea he'd offered them that hour. "It's just so exciting to finally have guests! You spend a few moons all on yer lonesome, wonderin' if you'll ever see another friendly face again, and then BOOF, whole crowds of 'em, all appearing at once! I have so much tea to offer. So much."

"Keep it comin', Galon, my man," Lunah said, waving her cup about.

"I'm okay, thank you," Ash said as Tobu shook his head, but Galon poured them another cup anyway.

"Goodness me, but this is exciting, isn't it? Glad I tidied up this week, that's all I'm sayin'!" You could tell Galon had gotten a little lonely manning the outpost all by himself. He followed his new guests around like a joyful pup.

"Just one man to defend an entire outpost?" Kailen had asked in shock when they'd first arrived, three days earlier. "I leave Pinehaven fer a few years and the whole Stronghold goes to shambles!"

"Well, Pinehaven has many outposts circling the forest borders, but not nearly enough people to man them, not these days," Galon explained. "Need our hunters defending the main Stronghold in the forest center, that's what's real important!" Kailen looked guilt-ridden, and Ash wondered how long she'd been away. "I wouldn't say I've been entirely alone, though!" Galon said, dipping his head toward the life-sized warrior figures he'd constructed that lined the walkways, staring vacantly out into the forest as though on watch.

"Got a lot of time on your hands, Galon?" Lunah had asked.

It was easy to tease, as up close they looked a bit strange, silly, even, but from down below they were surprisingly convincing. *Spirits*, it had been enough to scare the Wraiths away. The effect was only slightly lessened by the big smiley faces Galon had painted onto their sackcloth faces. And they'd all been impressed with the strange horn Galon had made. When he blew it, the horn created a hundred angry shouts, making it appear as though the outpost was heavily manned. It might've been a mistake showing Lunah, however, who used it every opportunity she got.

The *Frostheart* had pulled up underneath the hanging sanctuary, cautious of any lingering Wraiths. The crew had climbed the rope one by one, leaving Arla and Kob to look after the sleigh, and each member was greeted with warmth and cheer as they popped through the hatch. And tea. Lots of Galon's tea.

It was a joyous reunion. There was hugging, there was laughter, and even a handshake from Kailen. The *Frostheart* crew were back together again, and Ash's smile couldn't have grown any larger if he'd tried. "Soaring salmon cakes, you went for a bit of a stroll, didn't you?" Captain Nuk laughed. "Wouldn't fancy it myself, a tad too much walking for my tastes."

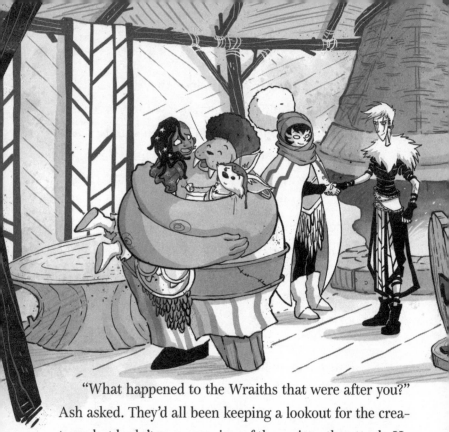

"What happened to the Wraiths that were after you?"
Ash asked. They'd all been keeping a lookout for the creatures but hadn't seen any sign of them since the attack. He
found himself feeling more uneasy than comforted by this.

"They lost interest soon enough, once they were sure
they'd chased us away," Yallah said. "They were clinging
to the forest borders, trying to find you. Still are—we
had to skirt right round 'em to get here."

"Aye, foul creatures," Nuk confirmed. "And Valkyries be thanked we had Rook's crows to follow, else we
would've never found you out here. Seemed rather strange
at first to trust the squawking of crows, but I suspected

anything bizarre and out of the ordinary would probably lead to you lot."

The reassembled crew swapped stories, Twinge making the whole process last three times as long as it should've, but Ash didn't mind one bit, relishing the company and laughter of his friends. The room fell into an astonished silence once Ash had told the others of the ruins they'd found, and the secret messages held within. Even Galon stood transfixed, missing Kailen's cup and pouring tea into her lap. "Watch it!" she cried, pushing him away. Nuk held the frost-heart in her hands, considering it with newfound wonder.

"To think I thought it was a sentimental good-luck charm . . . but it was the key to a Leviathan's prison all along, you say?"

The crew looked at each other with a mixture of fear and skepticism.

"S'all a bit extreme, isn't it?" Teya questioned. "A key to releasing some world-destroying monster? We've seen some crazy things in our time, but *this* . . . ?"

"It's the kind of thing you'd think you'd've heard of before now," Twinge agreed.

"I've heard mention of some King Leviathan in my travels, but I thought it all mere fable and superstition . . ." Nuk said.

"We have just been chased relentlessly by the Wraiths," said Tobu. "If what Rook says about them is true, and they are under the command of the World Eater, then this thing is very much alive, and more powerful than we ever knew. It has reach outside its prison. Its servants will not rest until they find us. Nowhere will be safe. There will be nowhere to run." The group fell silent. Tobu paused, as though gathering strength to say what he needed to. "Finding Solstice is the only way we end this. The only place Ash and the frost-heart will be safe."

Ash shivered. So much so, he could barely react to the amazing fact that Tobu was finally on his side.

"I know it's a lot to take in; I'm . . . I'm still not sure I get it all either. But I know what I saw. My dad was clear about it."

"But . . . why? The Wraiths I can understand—they're evil, heartless ghouls. But why would a human-kin want to unleash something like that upon the world, even someone as awful as Shaard?" Teya asked. "What does he gain from this?"

"I don't know," Ash admitted. "But we all saw the lengths to which Shaard was willing to go to get the frost-heart."

The crew thought on this. "I cannot claim to understand it all, but something caused the fall of the World Before, and it sounds like we might have discovered just what that was," Nuk declared. "It seems the sensible thing to do would be to get the frost-heart to safety, and everything therefore seems to be pointing us toward Solstice."

The tightness in Ash's chest lifted at Nuk's words. *She agrees, we're actually going to do this—we're finally going to set course for Solstice!*

"You really plan to go through with this, captain?" Kailen asked, amazed. "Stormbreaker won't be happy."

"She never is," Nuk said.

"Look, I'll be the first to admit I was wrong about

Ash. His heart's in the right place. But there's a war on, and we have our orders. As Pathfinders we swore an oath."

"Indeed we did!" Nuk answered. "We swore an oath to help the people of the Snow Sea, no matter who they are. We swore an oath to serve those too isolated and helpless to help themselves." Nuk looked at Ash, a fire burning in her eyes. "If we can stop this monstrosity from being unleashed upon the world, well then, I'd consider that a path well run, wouldn't you?"

The room erupted into agreement, all except for Kailen. Even Galon punched his fist into the air, spilling tea as he did so. "I have no idea what you're talkin' about, but I'm so happy for you all!"

"The question, though, is *how*?" Nuk rubbed her chin. "No one has ever found Solstice before. You know the way, my boy?"

"I . . . don't," Ash said, his shoulders slumping. "Well, I . . . kind of . . . It's something to do with the stars in my lullaby. But I'm not sure where to start—yet."

Nuk nodded. "Let us think on it, though we must make haste soon, wherever we go. It is too dangerous to leave the *Frostheart* stationary and unprotected by Stronghold walls."

Yallah smiled. "Well, we're just glad to see you all

alive and well. It is no small feat to cross the wilds like that."

"We were like a crack team of survivalists out there!" Lunah grinned. "Tobu an' Kailen strutted their stuff, Master Podd dug us up some grub, an' Ash used his Weavy-wiles to listen out for the 'viathans . . ."

"And Lunah guided us here! We would've been lost without her," Ash smiled, but for the first time that day Lunah's grin faltered and she looked down at the floor. "R-Rook too, she was incredible. I've never seen anything like it, her Song Weaving, it's . . . it's . . ." Ash trailed off.

"Speakin' of which," Nuk asked, "where *is* our feral friend?"

32
Unveiled

Rook lay unconscious on a bed within the smallest pod in the outpost, her breaths coming fast and ragged. She whispered Songs under her breath, frantic and disturbed. The Songs frightened Ash, and judging by the way the rest of the crew shifted uncomfortably as they looked at her, it scared them too. There was a profound *wrongness* to the sounds. "She's been this way for the last three days . . . since . . . since she saved us," Ash said, his voice shaking with concern.

"What is she saying?" Nuk asked gently.

"Nothing I understand. It's just . . . *gibberish*." He was too afraid to admit that he recognized snatches of it as the same dark, hateful Song she'd Sung before she collapsed.

"I don't know why she won't snap out of it!" said

Arla, the *Frostheart*'s elderly healer, who'd been collected
by Tobu. She approached Rook's bed and laid a crooked
finger on her hands. "She's clammy with sweat, yet she's
deathly cold."

"We should watch her closely. We don't know what
that Song's done to her," Kailen said. Ash shot her a look.
"I ent sayin' she's not our friend, but that Song is *evil*. She
knew it. We know it. And we'd be stupid to ignore that."

Arla reached out to draw back Rook's hood.

"Wait!" Ash protested, stopping Arla with his hand.
Somehow it felt wrong to reveal Rook's face. She'd taken
care to hide it, and it felt like a betrayal to undo that
while she was unconscious, without her consent.

"Ash," Arla said softly, "I need to examine her. It's
the only way I can help."

Ash's lip trembled, but he nodded, taking his hand
away.

Ever so gently Arla pulled back Rook's hood.

Everyone in the room took a sharp intake of breath.

Rook looked as though she had seen about thirty
winters. Her skin was as white as death, her tousled,
spiky hair almost as pale, all matted and sticking to her
sweating, whispering face. What was truly peculiar,
however, was the black and purple darkness that leaked
down from her eyes like dripping paint, spreading out

across her cheeks like spider legs. But it wasn't paint. It was under her skin. Her pale lips did not stop moving, constantly uttering the strange Song, her expression anguished.

"She needs some tea, by the looks of things," Galon said.

Arla put a hand to Rook's head, then pulled back one of her eyelids. Ash's heart skipped a beat as he saw that Rook's eyeballs were not white, but a glossy pitch-

black. Her pupil was as white as snow. *What is she?* Ash thought, his mouth going dry.

"Is this—is this some kind of Song Weaver sickness?" Kailen asked, making a sign to the forest spirits.

"Of course not!" Ash was quick to answer, though truly he didn't know. What if she was right, and Ash could catch it too?

"She has a darkness in her blood," said Tobu. "While I do not sense the same shadow over her as I did Shaard, they are cut from a very similar cloth."

"Reckon she ent safe to have aboard the *Frostheart*, not anymore," Kailen said.

"NO!" Ash shouted.

"You are very trustin', Ash, but her story is clearly more complicated than she lets on. We have to put the safety of the crew first," Kailen insisted.

"I can't believe you'd say that! She *is* part of the crew, and she needs our help! She's saved us more than once; she's on our side, and that's that. We have to make her better." Ash tried to swallow the lump that was growing in his throat. "If she hadn't tried to save us all, she . . ."

"Do not think that way, boy." Tobu raised Ash's chin up. "This was her choice, and she acted bravely." He turned to the others. "While there is certainly something sinister afoot, I do not doubt that Rook cares for the boy and would never want to put him in danger."

Ash looked up at the yeti with gratitude, which Tobu returned with sad, tired eyes.

"Why don't we get her better first, eh?" Nuk suggested, breaking the tension. "Let's see what the lady has to say for herself when she's awake, rather than us flinging hearsay across her sleeping body." Arla had been mixing an herbal concoction, which she put to Rook's babbling lips, helping her to drink it. Rook choked out the mixture, her Singing not allowing her to swallow.

It was only then that Ash noticed Rook's crows were nowhere to be found. He'd never once seen her without them. Looking around and out the door to the small pod, he spotted them. All were perched outside the building. Once inseparable from her, they would now not come any closer to Rook.

And it made Ash's blood run cold.

33

Stars Above

Ash Sang the lullaby for the fiftieth time that night. More than ever, he needed to figure out what the glowing stars meant, and what he was supposed to do with them to find Solstice and get the frost-heart to safety. But more importantly, at least to Ash, he hoped the Song Weavers there might be able to help make Rook better. If anyone could figure out a cure for a Song Weaver sickness, it would be them.

And once we're there, the Frostheart *could use Solstice as a new base,* Ash thought. *A better one than Aurora, one that is welcoming and accepting to all.*

As he'd expected, a new star shone brightly when he Sang the lullaby, gleaming next to the others. The last one. And they still meant nothing to him.

"Trust in the World Weave," Tobu said, trying to help. "You have all you need."

Easy for him to say. Have I missed something? A clue, a missing star that would make up a constellation that could guide us? Ash pointed out the newest star to Lunah to see if she knew what it was.

"It's the North Star," she said, hanging upside down from a roof beam, explaining that it might help to get a new perspective. "S'always in the same place in the sky, and it's the brightest. It always sits between those other two stars, there, the Two Brothers."

"The North Star . . ." Ash repeated. "Dad said it marked the start . . . whatever that means." He looked down at Lunah's star map, where he'd used charcoal to circle the stars that shone when he Sang.

"*Marks the start . . . ?*" Lunah said to herself, before leaping from the roof beam and unfurling her world map, slamming it down on the walkway floor in front of Ash. "Here!" she cried. "The start!" She pointed excitedly at two large mountains, somewhere south of the outpost. "These mountains are also called the Two Brothers, just like the stars. They're named after the same legend! The story tells how two conjurer brothers summoned the great Everstorm in a duel but froze solid in the storm they created. The mountains are said to be their frozen

bodies, cursed to be forever locked in a brotherly battle!"

"Right!" Ash said, as if he had the faintest idea what this had to do with anything.

"Yer dad said the North Star marks the start, right? An' the North Star always sits between the Two Brothers. Well, I reckon that means we start our journey to Solstice right here, between the Two Brothers mountains. The passage between 'em is the gateway to the Everstorm, that ragin' blizzard that's impossible to navigate?"

"Okay . . . ?"

"Well, what better place to hide a Stronghold that don't wanna be found?"

Ash's world froze, then sped forward in its rush to catch up with everyone else. He laughed and clapped Lunah on the back. "You've done it! That—that's gotta be it, right? Lunah, you're a genius!"

"Well, yeah . . . I am."

Ash's mind raced, his belly rolled, and he could barely keep still.

"But how do you navigate the unnavigable?" Tobu asked, ruining the moment. "How do you find the un-findable?"

Ash and Lunah stopped celebrating, going quiet in thought.

"Y'know, furball . . ." Lunah said, "this is why we don't invite you along to our idea sessions."

But nothing could stop Lunah when she was on a roll.

"DING DING DING DING!" she shouted minutes later, running around the outpost like a crazed Hurtler. "CREW MEETING! CREW MEETING! DING DING DING DING!"

The crew gathered in the main pod, confused and curious. Galon served them all tea, having invited himself along.

"Something to share with us, Lunah?" Nuk asked as she arrived, interrupting the story Twinge had been telling the others about potatoes.

"You bet, an' this ent about potatoes or dinner, as important as those are. I have made a great discovery!" Lunah slammed her map on the center table for all to see. "Right, so we're tryin'a find Solstice, yeah? Well, I think I know how to get there." She pointed at the Two Brothers. "The start." She then held up her star map and turned it so that the North Star, sitting in between the Two Brothers, lined up with the mountains. "I bet you anythin' the stars that light up durin' Ash's songie-doo-daa mark the directions we have to follow once we pass through the Two Brothers. They mark a trail to follow, and they'll guide us through the Everstorm!" The crew mumbled, unsure about the idea.

"We still need a north point," Teya said. "Compasses don't work in the storm; they go berserk . . ."

Lunah shot Teya a big grin, in her element now. "That's where our Song Weaver friend comes in." Ash grew nervous as all eyes landed on him.

"Me?"

"When you Sing your lullaby, you can *sense* the stars, as well as see 'em, right?"

"R-right . . ."

"We may not be able to see the sky in that storm, but with you Singin' you'd be able to sense the North Star, as it's one of the stars that lights up for you! You will be our compass, fire-boy. You'll be able to point a navigator north!" She put her hands on her hips, proud of a problem well solved.

"By navigator, you mean you, of course?" Nuk said.

Lunah's smile left her face, her excitement vanishing instantly.

"No . . . no. Not me . . . I . . . You—you need someone more skilled to do this."

"Lunah, you're the best navigator I know," Ash said.

"I'm the *only* navigator you know!"

Ash hated seeing her doubt herself like this. Where was the bold, courageous Lunah he knew?

"Think of your Proving. This could be it; this could be how you chart the uncharted!"

"I *can't!*" She slammed her hands onto the table. "Guys, I can't. I couldn't even find my way through a wood, what chance do I have in the Everstorm?" The entire crew were as shocked as Ash at Lunah's reluctance.

"But, Lunah . . . you did find your way . . ." Ash began.

"No, I didn't. We got here by accident, or because of the frost-heart or whatever. I was tryin' to get us to another outpost, one farther south." She looked miserably at her feet, not willing to meet the concerned gazes of the others. "I shame my ma."

"Lunah, don't you say that," Nuk said softly.

The room fell silent.

"You *do* shame your mother," Tobu said. "You shame all of your people."

"*Tobu!*" Ash cried out as Lunah screwed up her face, looking for the first time ever like she might cry.

"Do not defend her, boy. The Drifters are renowned explorers. They face any challenge that stands in their way, no matter how great, and do not rest until they overcome it. You shame their legacy, girl, by giving up after your first obstacle . . ."

"Tobu, that's quite enough, thank you," Nuk warned.

"I thought the Proving was meant to be just that, a way to prove yourself?" Tobu continued. "Should it be easy? What does that prove?"

Lunah looked up from her boots, annoyance flashing across her face.

"A *true* Drifter would relish the challenge," Tobu said. "Your mother would pick herself up and charge forward, not back down."

Lunah was going red. She looked like she was about to explode, her hands now trembling fists at her side. Then, to everyone's surprise, she smiled.

"Stars above, but you're a bilgeslurper of a motivator." She laughed, wiping a (very tiny) tear from her eye. "I can see why Ash moaned about you so much." Tobu folded his mighty arms and raised an eyebrow. "But . . . *thanks*. I appreciate it, big guy." With that, Lunah slugged him in the arm, but her fist bounced off it as though she'd struck a mountain.

"I'm confused. Is this a . . . *moment* we're witnessing here, or . . . ?" Nuk asked.

Lunah laughed. "Somethin' like that." She rubbed her hand before taking a deep breath. "I think . . . I think I can get us to Solstice . . ."

"We need more than *think*, dear," Nuk said.

Lunah looked from Tobu to Ash for courage, doubt still scratching at her sides. She swallowed, and then a determined grin spread across her face.

"I *know* I can."

34
The Promise

They said their thanks and goodbyes to Galon the next morning before setting off from his lonely outpost. "Come back soon, won't you?" he said as they left. "I'll make sure I put the kettle on!"

The *Frostheart* raced across the snow plains once more, and, *spirits*, did Ash feel glad to be back aboard. He gripped on to the side rails, laughing and crying out with joy as the wind buffeted his hair and cloak. With a smile he remembered feeling just the same when he left the Fira all those moons ago. He was still as excited, but it was different now. It was tinged with satisfaction at the prospect of a journey's end.

Or at least this *journey.*

Ash watched the Hurtlers that pursued the sleigh, too far behind to be a worry. What did trouble Ash, though, was the shape gliding after them in the sky. It was distant, but Ash thought he could make out the silhouette of a Shrieker gliding between the weathered crags that lined the path they were running, a slight wobble in its flight.

It can't be the same one, can it? Ash thought. *Why's it still following me?*

Receiving no answers from the air, Ash decided to visit Arla's healing tent to check on Rook. Her crows perched about the masts and rigging, reluctant to get too close, but unwilling to abandon their friend either.

Ash ducked into the tent and saw that Rook was on her own, unconscious, muttering dark words under her breath.

"Still not with us?" Ash asked.

He sat next to her for some time and took her cold hand in his, hoping that she sensed his company. He felt her weak Song-aura reaching out to him, its dark tendrils writhing and probing.

An idea came to him.

He listened out to hear if anyone was close, but the rest of the crew seemed busy.

He knew it was a bad idea.

He knew it might be dangerous.

But he wanted to help his friend in any way he could. Nerves fraying, Ash began to Sing, and he reached his own aura out to hers. And shadow enveloped his mind.

Ash was suffocated by overwhelming hate and rage in a sea of darkness. It screamed into his ears, it battered his senses, it reached down his throat and clasped its terrible claws round his heart, pressing against his lungs and freezing his blood cold. Ash gasped for air, flailing his Song wildly as he fought to break free of the frightful grip, but the more he struggled, the stronger it closed about his soul. It was never going to let go; he would be dragged into this hate and would be consumed by it. Ash could sense that Rook was fighting against it too. But her Song was faded and distant, lost in the shadow, and Ash couldn't reach her.

Something large, bigger than life, was rising behind him. *She tried to stop me*, the thing said in a voice formed of nightmares, *so I have taken her. I will break her into pieces.* It was a loathsome thing, ice-cold and seething with hostility. *I am glad you have come looking for her*, it said, *for now I can see you. I know who you are. I know what you are.* Ash turned slowly, unable to resist, though he tried his hardest. There loomed a colossal mass of uncontrolled, primal fury. *You too wish to stop me. But I cannot be stopped. I will take you as well, and together you shall be torn to shreds, body and soul.*

It roared at him, reaching out for his very being, bellowing with earth-shattering force, ripping any thoughts Ash had from his mind, any resistance he might've had, leaving only quivering fear.

A glowing thread of light suddenly flared bright, shielding Ash from the onslaught. Tendrils of shadow gushed toward the shield like blood from a wound, but it couldn't reach Ash through the barrier of light.

"*Sleep, Cursed One,*" the frost-heart Sang at the thing as its aura weaved around Ash. "*You no longer belong in this world.*" With these words the frost-heart pulled Ash's aura out of the darkness.

Ash jolted from the vision with a cry. He gasped for air, his chest aching as though he'd been drowning. Sweat shone on his skin. Words echoed in his mind, fading at his return to the real world . . .

"*You cannot keep me here. I have awoken. And I will be free . . .*"

Ash's body was quaking at the horror he'd just witnessed. What *had* he just witnessed? He looked at Rook, still lost to her nightmares, tendrils of her Song grasping out for him.

Ash backed away. *Why—why is that* thing *in her Song? What's happening to her?* Ash screwed his eyes shut, trying to get the visions out of his head.

"*Wounded. Damaged,*" the frost-heart Sang, its own Song-aura trying its best to soothe Ash's frayed nerves. "*Ally resisting, but her strength cracks and weakens. Ally needs aid.*"

Ash stared helplessly at Rook, her eyes flickering frantically beneath her black eyelids. He tore out of the tent, wanting to get as far from her nightmare as he could.

Most frightening of all was how familiar the chill he'd felt had been. It was the very same one that crept into him when he got angry, as when he'd Sung Shaard's Song.

Lost in dark thoughts, Ash headed for the reassuring company of the crew, who were busy taking anything that wasn't nailed down belowdecks in preparation for the Everstorm.

Tobu saw him and waved him over. "It is nearly time," he said as Ash drew close.

"S-sorry?" Ash said, watching Tobu add yet another crate to the already huge pile he was carrying.

"You will soon be back in the care of your parents. Are you ready?"

"Oh! Yes, of course." Ash was still distracted by what he'd just experienced. He dared not tell Tobu for fear that speaking it out loud might somehow make it real. He just wanted to get to Solstice. The sooner they did, the sooner his parents and the Song Weavers could help Rook and get rid of the thing that tormented her. "I'm excited. And a . . . a bit nervous too . . ." Ash admitted. It had been so long; they would barely know each other. Would he live up to what his parents wanted him to be? Would they get along? Would the *Frostheart* even make it through the Everstorm? The swirling in Ash's belly was making him nauseous.

"They will be proud of you," Tobu said, as though he'd read Ash's mind.

Ash smiled. He considered his guardian then, so steadfast and sure. Carrying more crates than any human-kin would find possible. Ash looked at the tiny box he'd just picked up, thinking of what Master Podd had said back in the forest, about Tobu worrying he might lose Ash. He still couldn't believe it. Again, his heart ached that Tobu might ever feel that way. There was no one like Tobu. Ash would never forget what he'd done for him.

"You'll come with me into Solstice, right?" he asked, following Tobu belowdecks. "Even once I've found my parents? I'd love for you to meet them."

To Ash's surprise Tobu chuckled. "I'm not sure that is something you'd want."

"Of course it is! And I'm sure they'd want to meet you! You've done so much for me. You looked after me when no one else would."

Tobu's brow, usually locked in a permanent frown, softened in the gloom of the hold. He let out a breath, a small smile curling at his lips, a look so strange on the yeti, but Ash was troubled to see it tinged with sadness.

"Boy, you now have Rook as a teacher, and you need to learn things I am not able to offer. There are paths you must travel that I may not be able to follow. But whatever happens you must always follow your own path, and find where you belong. We all must." He dropped the heavy load he carried, the timbers of the sleigh trembling as he did so. Ash placed his box carefully on the pile.

He's—he's not planning on leaving me, is he?

Ash honestly didn't know if he could cope without Tobu. Besides, where would Tobu go? No, he must just be trying to prepare Ash for the worst, as he always did. Ash followed Tobu back up to the main deck in uncomfortable silence. The yeti gazed out at Mother Sun as she began to set behind the craggy cliffs that cleaved through the landscape.

"I think the Song Weavers will be different from everyone else," Ash said, not wanting to let the conversation drop. "They know what it's like to be snubbed. I think they'll be welcoming. They'll let you into Solstice, all of you! And then hopefully Captain Nuk will let my parents join the *Frostheart* crew, and we can all run the Snow Sea together."

Tobu continued to squint toward the sunset.

"I am not so sure. The Sacred Yeti Lands live in supposed peace. They have no quarrel with Leviathans, for ours is with the human-kin. It is forbidden for any human-kin to set foot within our borders, on penalty of death. The Mountain's Ward is the leader of the yeti warriors, and they defend the lands with spear and bow."

Ash's ears pricked up at the name he'd overheard in Aurora. "You knew them?" he asked.

Tobu's face darkened. "I did. My point is, the reason for the bad blood between our two peoples is ancient and half remembered, and yet we still find ourselves isolated and in constant conflict. Try to imagine how the Song Weavers will feel about outsiders, when prejudices against them are still very much alive."

Ash didn't like this idea. Not one bit. But he could

see the sense in it. He was angry with the Strongholds for the way he'd been treated. He was even willing to abandon them all, happy to hide away in Solstice. Ash looked over the crew he trusted, the crew who had taken him in and become his friends, and his guts tied into knots at the idea of having to leave them behind. Why did everything have to be like this? *How will anything get better if everyone is always fighting?*

After some time Ash said, "I'm sure whatever path I take, Tobu, I'd want you to be by my side."

The orange sunset glinted off Tobu's shining eyes. "And I have sworn to protect you as long as I am able."

"Hey, guys, grub's up!" Lunah yelled as she bounded toward them, balancing three bowls in her arms. "Look at you two, skulkin' over here all broody an' serious. I've got just the thing to turn them frowns upside down!" She sat, laying the bowls out and patting the deck next to her. Ash and Tobu sat down beside her. "Convinced Twinge to make us somethin' special, seein' as what we're about to do is incredibly dangerous an' all."

Ash took up his bowl and looked inside, his belly rumbling. To his disgust he saw a dirty old redroot inside.

"Redroot?"

"Yeah! A Fira specialty, right? Thought it'd be a nice

treat, an' Twinge seemed more'n happy to get rid of what he had stored." Ash pulled a face as he looked at the tough, leathery excuse for food in his bowl. "Wassup, Ash the Fussy an' Ungrateful?" Lunah asked, seeing Ash's expression and poking his knee. "Has it been cooked wrong? Tobu told me you love the stuff!"

Ash looked at Tobu, whose expression was as unreadable as always. But was it Ash's imagination or did he have a slightly mischievous twinkle in his eye?

Tobu took a root in his hand and looked straight at Ash. "From the beginning of a journey"—he took a bite out of the root. His face began to flush, and water welled up in his eyes at the root's intense spice—"to its end."

Ash and Lunah both took a bite.

"Y'know, this stuff really is terrible," Lunah said with a full mouth. "It tastes like hot mud! Eurgh, how do you love this so much?"

Ash laughed. "Well, I thought it was delicious, but I'm stuffed," he lied, putting his bowl aside, the root barely touched. Lunah followed suit. She must've been nervous to turn down food, even if it was a gross red-root. The idea of navigating the Everstorm was clearly still eating away at her. Ash smiled at her, hoping to ease her nerves. He was just happy to be in the company of his friends, safe and sound, for the time being at least, aboard the sleigh that had become his home.

"So, Solstice, huh?" Lunah said, her voice a bit shaky. "As if finding the long-lost Isolai wasn't enough . . . I'm gonna have so many stories to tell 'em all back on the Convoy!"

"Do you think you'll head back to the Convoy as soon as you finish your Proving?" Ash hoped his voice sounded supportive and didn't betray how much he didn't want Lunah to go. He was already getting worried that Tobu was right, that the Song Weavers might not be as welcoming as he hoped. That to meet his parents, he would have to leave the crew. He couldn't bear the thought of losing Lunah too.

"I've got to do the stupid thing first. Then returnin's the only way I can complete it. I'll be welcomed back, a true Drifter an' everythin'. I'll honor my family. My ma. S'what I've always wanted . . ." She went quiet then, fiddling with her boots. "Just as well Teya's pretty good at navigatin'. I'm worried the *Frostheart*'ll jus' go round in circles without me guidin' 'em." She laughed, but it seemed forced.

Ash swallowed. "Can we make a promise?" he said after a while. "That whatever happens, wherever we end up, we'll make sure we find each other again." He looked Lunah and Tobu dead in the eyes.

Lunah stared back, then offered her hand. She pulled it back as Ash went to take it.

"Only shake if you mean it."

Ash grinned, and took her hand, shaking it firmly. "I promise."

"Me too."

Tobu's face was impassive. He looked as though he was about to tell them how unrealistic that was. That it was a child's dream, and foolish to promise such things. But instead he placed a hand on top of theirs, engulfing them both.

"And I," he said.

And with an oath shared, all three companions gazed ahead at the storm clouds that were gathering purple and bruised on the horizon.

35

A Drifter's Calling

They did everything they could to prepare. The sails and lanterns were lowered so they wouldn't be torn down by violent winds. The crew wrapped extra sailcloth round their furs and wore their warmest cloaks. They even constructed a windbreak out of wooden planks to help shelter the bridge. Anyone who wasn't expressly needed for the upcoming endeavor took cover belowdecks.

The wind was picking up. The surrounding landscape was rugged and craggy, like some great god had chipped away at the land with a giant chisel. But as jagged as their surroundings were, there was no mistaking the Two Brothers. They rose high above the world, dark and imposing, stripped of all vegetation by the roaring gales that tore at them relentlessly. The crew had a perfect view of the raging storm beyond, framed by the two mountains like a gateway for giants.

And what a sight it was.

There was no difference between the earth and sky. No visible terrain. Ash gasped as he looked up at what could only be described as a world of roiling, furious gray-white, an impenetrable wall of howling frost that stretched up to the stars.

The Everstorm.

Ash, Lunah, Tobu, and Nuk hunkered down on the bridge, rope tied round their waists and fastening them all to the side rail. Lunah gripped on to her star chart and navigational equipment like her life depended on it. Which it did. She stared at the oncoming maelstrom with wide, fretful eyes.

Kailen, Kob, Twinge, and Teya were down on the main deck, prepared for any task they might be needed for. Yallah stood stoically at the sunstone enjin, now the only thing driving the sleigh forward. It was hard to recognize any of them, they were so heavily clad in furs. Rook's crows took flight, sensing the impassable storm, calling out in anguish as their friend was carried away from them to a place they couldn't follow. Ash's heart hurt for them.

"I'm sorry," Ash said. It somehow felt right, knowing Rook couldn't do it herself.

"GET READY!" Nuk declared in her booming voice, and then she stroked the tiller with motherly tenderness. "Carry us true, pup."

Ash took a deep breath to steady his nerves.

Tobu placed his hands on both Ash's and Lunah's shoulders. "This is what you've both been striving for. The end of the riddle, and the end of your Proving. All that's left is to do it."

"Simple as that," Lunah said quietly.

The *Frostheart* passed through the shadows of the Two Brothers and into the storm.

And it hit them like a charging Gargant.

Furious, screaming winds ravaged the sleigh, tearing painful snowballs and hailstones across its deck. It stung Ash's eyes, the only part of him exposed to the raging elements. Every plank of wood trembled and shook, and the *Frostheart* rocked as if afloat on a thrashing sea. Bracing himself, Ash lowered the scarf covering his mouth and began to Sing his lullaby. He couldn't hear himself over the cacophony, but he knew the Song well enough now that he could've Sung it in his sleep. He formed a fragile link with the stars high above, a tether that felt like it might snap at any moment.

He pointed toward the North Star like they'd re-hearsed, struggling to keep his hand still amid the blast-ing gale. Lunah snuggled up as close as possible into the corner of the windbreak so that she could read her star chart, which was doing its very best to escape her tight grip. Tobu tried to use his considerable size to help shield her, his thick fur coated in frost. Using Ash as her com-pass, Lunah worked out the angle toward where the next star would be, the next point they had to head toward.

Lunah shouted to Nuk, but all voices were lost in the roaring wind, so instead Lunah pointed the way. Nuk wrestled with the shuddering tiller and managed to alter the *Frostheart*'s direction.

They couldn't see anything in the ever-moving haze of the blizzard. It was hard to know which way was up or down. Ash could just about make out the crew taking cover, little more than dark smudges against the gray-white canvas of the world.

How will we know if our plan's working, or if we're just getting lost, Ash fretted, *or when it's time to change di-rection toward the next point?* The frost-heart gave him a reassuring chime, somehow breaking through the noise.

After what felt like a seething eternity, Ash got his answer.

Something loomed out of the white. Something large.

As the *Frostheart* passed it, Ash saw that it was a gigantic monolith, standing alone in the blizzard like a stone
fang. Something huge had been painted on its surface.
Squinting through the chaos, Ash recognized it as the
star symbol Shaard had once shown him—the symbol of
Solstice itself. His belly did a flip. *It's a marker! The stars
in the sky represent the markers in the storm. It really is a
map! We're doing it—we're going the right way!* Ash tried
to say as much to the others, and although they couldn't
hear him, they seemed to have come to the same conclusion. With renewed energy, Ash Sang again, pointing in
the direction of the North Star. Lunah made her calcu-
lations, working out the angle they had to head toward
to reach the next marker. Nuk drove the sleigh in the
direction Lunah pointed. After some time they made it
to another monolith, with Solstice's star emblazoned on
its weathered surface. Even Nuk seemed to gain extra
determination, gripping the tiller harder. They repeated
the process, though it was impossible to tell how much
time passed between each monument. The sight of them
emerging from the snowstorm never got old; Ash's heart
rang with joy each and every time.

The next monolith materialized out of the squall.

Then the next.

But it was tough going. A plank of wood tore from

somewhere on the sleigh, and the crew on the deck scrabbled about trying to catch it, but they only succeeded in getting blown off their feet too, catching on to anything they could to stop themselves from being ripped overboard.

Ash's jaw was going numb from the cold. He was finding it hard to Sing. The rudimentary windbreak that shielded them from the worst of the storm was coming apart from the constant barrage. As Ash pointed north the sailcloth wrappings were torn from his arm. Dagger-sharp wind cut deep into his skin despite his furs.

Another monolith marked their progress.

The noise of the storm was almost unbearable. Ash worried he would never hear anything but the terrible howling of the wind ever again. He scrunched himself into a tight ball, Singing as best he could. Captain Nuk was now becoming visibly exhausted, almost leaning on the tiller she was struggling to guide. *Five clues in the lullaby, five stars shining bright in the sky,* Ash thought, gritting his teeth. *That means there should be five rock markers to point our way.* He'd tried his best to keep track of them, but the storm had frozen his mind as well as his bones, and he'd lost count of how many they'd passed.

It has to be over soon; it has to! Ash screamed into his own head, barely able to hear his own thoughts.

Without warning the wind shelter burst apart around them. The force of the tempest nearly plucked them all off the deck, but Tobu managed to hold Ash and Lunah down, Nuk clinging to the tiller for dear life. Lunah was shouting something, and Ash had to read her lips to see what it was. "I've lost my chart! The star chart!"

Ash gritted his teeth as they passed another stone marker. He knew it was his turn to Sing again, but his mind was being battered by the raging storm. He could barely cling on to the sleigh, let alone Sing a lullaby.

We've come so far! It can't end here!

Nuk was shouting something, asking Lunah for the direction they should head in. Lunah was frantically working something out, the strands of her dreadlocks whipping about her face, free of the hat that had been torn from her head by the wind. She was stretching her arm out, figuring out the directions they'd come from, backtracking the route they'd taken, trying to remember the map, and using all that information to work out where they had to go.

"LUNAH!" came Nuk's bellow, sounding distant and muffled.

Lunah looked unsure of herself, then let out a scream of frustration, defying the storm around her. "THAT WAY!" She pointed starboard, her other arm clinging on to the side rail with all the strength she had.

With a massive push Captain Nuk turned the sleigh.

The entire world seemed to be clawing at the poor vessel and its crew, trying to drag them from the earth and toss them about up in the sky.

Please let Lunah be right, please, please, please, Ash prayed.

He felt so helpless. It wasn't as if he could Sing to calm the storm, or Tobu could fight it, or Captain Nuk outrun it.

The *Frostheart* struggled forward.

On they pushed, on and on.

White and gray. Gray and white.

That was all there was, everywhere and all around.

That, and the constant wind. The ceaseless roaring.

And then suddenly all went quiet.

All was still.

It was almost deafening.

Have we died? Ash wondered. If they had, it was all very serene. *Not so bad,* Ash thought.

He managed to prize open his frozen eyelids.

He could see clear blue skies above. Looking out over the edge, he saw a peaceful landscape of steep, craggy cliffs and bouncy, lush mosses that broke free from the snow-covered ground. The Everstorm still surrounded everything in a colossal, spinning ring, but it now seemed a world away.

"We . . . we've done it . . ." Ash dared to say as the others rose around him, disheveled and shaky. "LUNAH, YOU DID IT!" Ash yelled, grabbing his friend by the arms and jumping her up and down. "You did it, you did it!"

"I . . . *did*?" she said in a tiny voice.

"Aye, my child. As if there was ever any doubt," Captain Nuk said with a big smile, clapping her hard on the back.

The crew on the deck below began to cheer. Even Tobu gave her a nod. Lunah allowed herself a smile, which turned into a joyous laugh of pure relief.

"We did it!"

They'd followed the clues of the lullaby and the map of stars that had been set out for them. They'd made it into the eye of the storm.

36
Strangers in a Strange Land

The world within the Everstorm was a strange one. A beam of light rose up into the sky from a hiding place among a cluster of rugged cliffs, splaying out into multiple strands, which canvased across the sky, raining down into the whirling storm that encircled everything. Ash couldn't take his eyes off the passing scenery as the *Frostheart* wound its way through the terrain, all his senses alert for the slightest sign of a Stronghold or settlement. His fingers trembled and his belly churned. He couldn't see any.

But it wasn't long before that changed. While the crew were shoveling the large drifts of snow that had built up on the decking over the sides, they noticed figures darting among the lichen-dotted boulders and snow-covered trees around them.

"We're not alone," Tobu said.

Captain Nuk signaled to Yallah to slow the sleigh's enjins down. "Let's allow our new friends to catch up, shall we?" she said in a jaunty tone, but Ash noticed how all the crew's hands hovered by their bows.

Eventually they came across a lone man, standing bold as brass upon the snow in a narrow valley. His face was dark and grim, partially hidden by a deep hood. He was dressed in a long, ragged white cloak, its tattered strands billowing with an almost ethereal nature. He stood before the encroaching giant sleigh as though he'd been expecting them, hand held out. The *Frostheart* slowed to a stop.

"He miss the message about the Leviathans or somethin'?" Kailen said as the crew rushed to the side to get a good view of the stranger.

"Careful of the snows, friend!" Captain Nuk yelled down. "Danger lurks beneath."

"You are not welcome,"

the man declared in reply. "Turn back. Only death awaits you here."

"Charmin'," Lunah said. Suddenly a Lurker clawed its way out of the snow beside the stranger, and to the crew's amazement it curled its tail round him, almost protectively. It growled at the intruders. Dozens of camouflaged hunters emerged from hiding places along the steep sides of the valley, bows trained at the *Frostheart*'s crew.

"We will allow you this one chance to leave," the stranger said, petting the Lurker on the head. "Leave and forget what you saw here."

"Easy, friend!" Nuk said, raising her hands along with the rest of the crew. "We're not your enemies. We bring you something important— something I think you're going to want to take a look at . . ."

The ambushers shifted at this, looking to the man before the sleigh, who was clearly their leader. The man seemed as unsure as the others.

"Uninvited strangers intrude into our hidden lands, unannounced and unwelcome. How can we trust you?"

The Lurker growled, baring its fangs.

Eager to defuse the situation, and not liking arrows pointed at his face at the best of times, Ash stepped forward, and began to Song Weave. His Song-aura swirled and danced around him. Songs could only tell the truth, and so Ash told the truth. He Sang of his journey to find his parents, the Song of the *Frostheart* and its crew, of their determination to see the frost-heart delivered to safety. The hunters looked from one to the other, and slowly, to Ash's enormous relief, they lowered their bows, before they too began to Song Weave.

Their auras joined with Ash's, knitting and spiraling into the most intricate, beautiful pattern. Ash's heart surged with joy. He'd never Sung with so many Song Weavers before, and the feeling was unlike anything he'd ever experienced. He felt as though these strangers were all long-lost friends, greeting each other after spending years apart. Though the *Frostheart* crew could not see the beautiful shapes that were being weaved in the air, they could hear, *feel*, the serene, peaceful message that the Songs carried, and smiles broke out all round.

When the Weaving was over the man before the *Frostheart* nodded. "Pathfinders. Let us talk."

Everyone gathered on the snow in front of the *Frostheart*. The Pathfinders were a tad wary of the Lurker that prowled about them, so close they could see the mottled, spotted pattern on its tough hide. None could quite believe their eyes at seeing the beast prowl in front of the Song Weaver hunters so protectively.

Tobu and Twinge carried Rook down the gangplank on a litter. The hunter leader, who had introduced himself as Ottro, got on his knees so his face was level with the Lurker's and Sang quietly. An agreeable rumble issued from the Lurker's throat. Petting the beast's head, Ottro rose and said, "Spots says he will carry your injured."

The *Frostheart* crew shared a glance.

"*Spots?*" Kob asked.

Ottro looked a bit embarrassed. "Yes, well, the, um, the children named him."

"Is it . . . safe?" Ash asked.

Spots gave an indignant grunt, blinking his six eyes as though offended.

"We share a true connection with the Leviathans of this land. As it was before, when we lived in peace with the Leviathans in ancient times. Before we Song Weavers went astray, and human-kin fell in love with war. Leviathans are the guardians of this world. When we need to take something from the land we ask for their blessing."

"And they listen to you?" Nuk asked.

"Sometimes. They are no different from human-kin in that regard. Some are respectful; others can be more . . . difficult."

"And then what?"

"We find a way round them. Or become lunch."

Rather apprehensively Tobu and Twinge placed Rook on Spots's back in between two of his spine ridges so that she was secure.

Rook was right . . . the Leviathans really aren't *mindless monsters . . .* Ash thought in wonder.

Rook was still Singing under her breath, the black

stains around her eyes in stark contrast to her pale white skin, looking even darker out here in the sunlight.

"We have seen this curse before," Ottro said, eyes narrowing. "It is a darkness upon the soul."

"Do you know how to help her?" Ash asked.

"Our healers might. We must get her to them right away, if she's to be saved."

Ash nodded eagerly.

"But first—where is the heart?" a female hunter insisted. "The one from your Song? It is why you've come here, is it not?"

"I have it," Ash said, touching the archeomek casing out of habit. The frost-heart chimed, and the familiarity of its Song-aura gave Ash the bravery he needed to go on.

The Song Weavers shifted, their eyes widening.

"The actual *heart-shard*? We *must* get it to the Elders as soon as possible. Ferno warned us all how important it is!"

"Ferno?" Ash squeaked. "He's my dad! Where is he?!"

"We'll ask the questions!" Ottro snapped. "Show the heart to us."

"I-I'll only give it to you if you promise to take me to my parents!"

Ottro's head tilted with curiosity. "So many demands for one so small."

"We've traveled too far and have gone through too much to be turned away now," Ash said, the *Frostheart* crew growling their agreement.

Ottro thought on this before gesturing toward a group of hunters who waited upon the steep slopes of the valley. "My hunters will take you to them."

At last, Ash thought, digging his boots into the scree, thin ice cracking around his feet as he pushed himself forward, more determined than ever. Every long step on this epic journey had all been leading to this moment. He couldn't tell if his roiling belly and sparking nerves were because of fear or excitement. He was about to meet his parents! He'd done it. He'd found them, and everything was going to be okay.

It was then that he noticed there were no sounds of following footfalls behind him. He was about to turn and see why when he froze in place.

Suddenly he couldn't bear to look back.

As long as he didn't, the awful truth that was dawning on him wouldn't be made real. But what was he going to do, stand on the slope forever? Closing his eyes, he mustered all the courage he could before turning round. There stood the crew of the *Frostheart*, huddled together before their sleigh, feet planted firmly in the ground. They looked unhappy—*angry*, even. The Song Weaver hunters blocked their path. Lunah was wearing her most defiant face, while Kailen and Teya snarled at their captors. Even Master Podd's fur bristled. Tobu's brow was furrowed, but he had a look of reluctant acceptance. He'd been expecting this moment for some time, Ash realized, and had been trying to prepare Ash for it.

"G-guys?" Ash managed to say, though he knew well what was happening.

"Only Song Weavers may walk these lands," Ottro answered. "Solstice has been a safe haven for Song Weavers for centuries and has remained so because of its secrecy. We cannot allow outsiders to see it, no matter how honorable they appear."

"But . . . but that's . . ." Ash felt like he'd misplaced his foot and was plummeting into darkness. He closed his eyes and took a long, steadying breath, but it came out a ragged shudder.

"N-no."

"No?" Ottro repeated.

"NO! They're coming with me, or you won't get the frost-heart!"

"You are one of us, and so we've been generous. But don't think you're so important we won't just take the heart from you." The hunters raised their bows, and Spots's tail flickered with hostility. Ash looked to the

crew, at a loss as to what to do. Captain Nuk smiled with the same warmth that had always made Ash feel so safe, and extended her hand.

"You don't have to go with them, Ash. Leave the heart here, and we can all depart together." The crew looked at him hopefully, Lunah almost pleading.

For the first time Ash saw how the crew really felt about him. They loved him. They loved him even though he'd brought them nothing but danger and trouble, even though he was a Song Weaver. And, by the spirits, Ash loved them too. They'd saved him when all had seemed lost, and they'd treated him like a friend when no one else had wanted him. They didn't want him to go, and Ash didn't want to leave them.

"You are one of us, lad, and you always will be," Nuk said.

Ash looked at her outstretched hand. Half of him wanted nothing more than to take it.

But the whole reason he'd joined the crew in the first place was to find his parents. Every single day, without fail, he'd wondered why they had never come back for him, and at last his parents were mere steps away, after a lifetime of being unreachable. Ash's heart and soul burned to see them.

"You guys will always be my family, but . . . but I have family here too. This"—it took all Ash's strength to get the words out—"this is where I'm supposed to be." Ash could no longer hold his tears back. Nuk pushed past the hunters, ignoring their threatening motions, and drew Ash up into a big, suffocating hug.

"We had quite the adventure together, didn't we? One we will never forget. But this is what you set out to do, Ash, and by the Valkyries' hammer, you've done it!" Nuk's embrace had only succeeded in making Ash's tears fall faster. He hugged her so tightly his arms were almost lost in her blubber. He didn't want to let go. Then an idea dawned on him.

"My—my parents will fix this," Ash managed to choke out through his tears. "I'm sure it's just a mis-understanding. If you'll wait, I'll tell my parents what you guys did for me and they'll make this right—they'll make sure you're all let in!"

Nuk straightened him up and lifted his chin, wiping his tears away as her eyes disappeared into a wide smile. "For you, Ash, we have all the time in the world!"

The *Frostheart* crew approached Ash, their faces twisted with sorrow, ready to say their farewells.

"Don't!" Ash insisted, cuffing away his tears and trying to look confident and strong. "Not yet. This isn't goodbye!" The Song Weavers shifted, but Ash caught the eyes of his friends with a heartfelt intensity. *"Not yet."*

"You'd best hurry back then, I've still got more stories to tell you!" Twinge said. "Like the time I cut that onion!"

The crew laughed, and it sounded like music to Ash's ears.

"Go and find your parents," Teya urged. "They owe you, what, ten years' worth of birthday gifts?"

"Wait here. I'll be right back!" Ash smiled, but it was wobbly. Then, before he could go, Tobu grasped his shoulder. Ash remembered the first time he'd seen Tobu, how terrified he'd been of the menacing yeti. How funny that he now felt safest around him, as though nothing in the world could harm him as long as his faithful guardian was there to protect him.

"I swore an oath to look after you, to keep you safe," Tobu said. "I would follow you to the ends of the earth to honor this promise, if you asked me to." He looked about at the Song Weaver hunters. "But I can think of no safer place for you than here."

"Just wait for me. I-I'll be right back, I promise." Ash grabbed Tobu's arm, tears worrying the corners of his eyes again.

The yeti nodded, then handed him a small pouch. "Take this. Just in case."

Ash did, but refused to look inside. He'd be seeing Tobu again in a few hours tops.

Ottro left strict orders with some hunters to keep watch over the Pathfinders, then led Ash up the craggy

slope after the others. Ash took one last look behind him at the crew who had become his friends, his family. He looked at the sleigh that had been his home. The *Frostheart*. The best sleigh in all the Snow Sea.

"I'll come back for you!" Ash shouted.

The crew raised their fists as one.

"There's always a deck for you to swab, Pathfinder!" Nuk yelled back.

Ash laughed. This *was* a happy moment. He'd found Solstice at long last. He was about to meet his parents for the first time since he was a baby. He'd done the impossible.

So why did he feel so hollow?

37
Eye of the Storm

The hunters led Ash over steep, rugged rocks, while Spots traversed the jagged stone as though it were just a mild inconvenience, Rook lolling on his back. Shriekers flew overhead, nestling among the snow-covered crags, paying the travelers no mind. Except, that is, for one, who eyed them all curiously. One with a slight wobble in its glide . . .

Ash held on to a moss-covered rock that was wet with slushy snow and took a moment to take in the view of the winding river that cut through the valley, a mighty waterfall crashing down at the valley's head. It was stunning, but Ash had no eyes for it. Every part of him just wanted to find his parents now. He'd waited a lifetime, and that felt like quite long enough, to be honest.

"It is not always easy to say goodbye to the world

outside," Ottro said to him, sensing his agitation. "But outsiders cannot be trusted. You'd have learned this the hard way, sooner or later."

"You don't know them like I do," Ash said quietly.

"You're wrong. They're all the same. You made the right choice coming with us. I believe you'll be happy to call this place home soon enough." The man smiled at Ash, who gave a weak smile in return.

Get to my parents and it'll be all right, Ash chanted in his head.

After more scrambling over rocks, they reached the waterfall, and with it a dead end. The hunters began to Song Weave, and to Ash's amazement the deep river bubbled and churned, and from it emerged a massive Gargant. Up and up, like some pale purple-gray hill it rose beneath the waterfall, which cascaded off its back in tumbling rivulets. As the waterfall was parted by the Leviathan, a weathered gateway was revealed behind it, an entranceway to a carved passage that cut through the cliffs. The Gargant let out a bone-rumbling thrum, and the hunters bowed low in response. Ash did his best to copy, still unable to get used to being so close to a Leviathan without needing to fear being swallowed whole.

Taking a breath, Ash followed the hunters under the roaring waterfall, and entered the tunnel beyond, looking up in frightened wonder at the Gargant who watched them pass with cold white eyes.

Ash found his mood lifting despite himself. Everything, his entire journey, the lullaby, the star map—it had all been leading to this moment and what lay beyond these gates.

Get to my parents and it'll be all right . . .

Cold water dripped onto Ash's neck from the cavernous ceiling, startling him. The tunnel was wide enough to fit an entire Pathfinder sleigh. It was lined with statues of roaring Leviathans, the weathered stone doing nothing to lessen their imposing image. But it was what lay beyond the statues that truly took Ash's breath away. A Stronghold of gleaming magnificence. It was circular, an open plaza surrounded by moss-covered towers and buildings with lush vegetation growing vivid and green amid the white stone. All were clearly from the World Before, but unlike the ruins Ash had seen, these buildings looked as though they hadn't aged a winter since the collapse. And in the center of it all, floating above an imposing conical tower, was a gigantic sphere. A sunstone the size of which Ash had never imagined possible glowed deep within the stone globe, its light streaming out of apertures that cut through the orb's surface, and into the sky in cords of brilliant light. It was the source of the strange beams they'd seen as they entered these lands. A design of a big, bold white star was painted upon the sphere's surface.

"It is with great pleasure, Ash," Ottro said with a dramatic flourish, "that we welcome you to Solstice."

As the hunters walked Ash into the plaza, the residents of Solstice paused what they were doing to watch him pass, curious about the newcomer. It was rare indeed that they saw strangers, and it was clearly quite shocking. The hunters Sang brief explanations to the onlookers, only making them stare more intently.

Ash pulled inward. He was a stranger here, an outsider. He studied the faces he dared look up at, hoping to spot his father among the crowd, desperate for a familiar face. The sooner his parents could open the gates to the *Frostheart* crew, the better. And then, finally, at long, long last, Ash, Ferno, and Ember could be a family again.

Get to my parents and it'll be all right, get to my parents and it'll be all right . . .

A large crowd of bystanders had gathered now, parting down the middle to allow Ash and the hunters past.

Just as Ash felt he could take no more scrutinizing, someone began to Sing. Their voice was joined

by another, and then another, and before long to Ash's utter amazement the entire plaza was Singing, a Song of greeting and welcome. Their Song-auras weaved from the plaza, from buildings and avenues, spiraling round Ash and painting the Stronghold with dancing turquoise light. And the Song was beautiful. It saw Ash's anxiety and reassured him that he was now safe, that everything would be all right. Ash lifted his eyes from his boots, and even allowed the edges of his mouth to twist up into a smile. He felt a sudden gratitude to these people he didn't know, *his* people.

They weren't his friends, not yet, but they would be.

Much like the hunters, the residents wore long flowing white robes, bandoliers draped over their shoulders from which bells hung, chiming with each movement. Many had what looked like blue tattoos running along their bare arms, until Ash realized with wonder that they were actually wisps of Song-aura coiling down their arms decoratively as they Sang under their breath. People Sang openly on the sunstone-lit streets as they went about their business, as they worked, living their lives, unafraid. It felt too easy almost, like it was too good to be true, like Stormbreaker's followers would burst through the gates at any minute and capture them all.

But no. The place was happy and alive with energy and music.

It was truly wondrous, and Ash wished his friends were there to see it too.

"So—where are my parents?" Ash asked Ottro as they walked through the crowds, unable to keep quiet any longer.

"All will be revealed in the Storm Tower," Ottro said, indicating the huge central tower they were heading toward. Spots made to carry Rook off to what Ash assumed was the house of healing, accompanied by a hunter.

"Wait!" Ash cried, reluctant to leave her. She was the only friend from the outside he had here, after all. He held her limp hand, still cold and clammy as she muttered sinister nothings under her breath.

Get to my parents and it'll be all right . . .

"She needs healing," the hunter said. "And you need to see the Elders. It's the deal we made."

Ash ground his teeth and let her go. "Please make her better. *Please.*"

"We'll do all we can," the hunter replied. "She's one of us now."

Ash watched helplessly as Rook was carried away past a group playing a lively tune on wind instruments. Ottro laid his hands on Ash's shoulders, comforting at first, but then, with a bit more force, turned him to face the Storm Tower.

He guided him through its mighty entranceway.

Ash could never quite believe the amazing feats the World Before had been capable of, even though he'd already seen some rather extraordinary examples. It turned out that the Everstorm was one of these wonders, somehow stirred into being by the orb above Solstice's

central tower. "It needs a particular Song to work, and so Solstice has a dedicated order of Weavers, *the Choir*, who ensure the Song never comes to an end," Ottro explained as the Choir themselves came into view. Robed Song Weavers sat in a large circle round a glowing sunstone in a large chamber at the base of the tower, chanting a powerful, rhythmic Song in perfect unison. They had their eyes closed, lost in concentration. "A Weaver will often Sing for hours on end, another ready to replace them as soon as they collapse from exhaustion. It's a grueling task, but they do it selflessly to keep Solstice safe and hidden."

Ottro led Ash up a staircase that circled round the tower up to the higher levels. Ash didn't take his eyes off the Choir below as he climbed, astounded by the lengths to which the Song Weavers had to go to keep secret and safe.

No wonder they wouldn't let the crew in, Ash thought, though he knew they'd been wrong to not trust his friends.

A few floors up, the stirring chant of the Choir still echoing off the circular tower walls from below, they came to a huge stone doorway.

"The Chamber of the Elders," Ottro explained as the hunters pushed open the heavy doors, the sound of grinding rock competing with the Choir's Song, "where you shall receive your answers."

38
Alone

A great hall lay beyond the doors. Stone archeomek spheres orbited its vast upper space, smaller than the great orb above the tower, but no less mind-boggling in their flight. Tall windows circled the room, allowing cold light to wash in, the odd snowflake glinting as it drifted in on the gentle breeze from outside. And there, seated on the floor of a crescent-shaped dais at the back of the hall, were the three Elders. They very much lived up to their name, all three of them incredibly old and wrinkly. Each wore the same flowing robes that the Choir had been dressed in. They greeted the newcomers with warm smiles.

"Welcome, welcome!" the tallest of them announced, his voice croaky and broken.

"We beg you excuse our voices," the smallest one said

to Ash, voice just as cracked as the first, "the result of a lifetime serving the Choir, I'm afraid."

"An outsider, Ottro?" said the third in a throaty rasp. "This is rare indeed. Please, do introduce us . . ."

"This is Ash, my elders. He was found seeking sanctuary at our borders. Our Songs have Woven, and I know he is true."

Ash studied the hall as Ottro spoke. With a dragging disappointment, he saw that they were the only ones in the room. His parents were still nowhere to be seen. *Yet.*

"You are welcome in Solstice, young Ash," said the smallest Elder, smiling. "My name is Arrus."

"I am Loda," said the tallest.

"And I am Nell," said the roundest. "But tell us, how did you come to our Stronghold? It is no easy feat."

"He was brought to us aboard a Pathfinder sleigh we caught trespassing upon our lands, though how they managed to navigate the Everstorm we do not know," Ottro said, the Elders' smiles faltering at the mention of Pathfinders. "My hunters have them under guard," Ottro assured them. Ash flinched, disliking his choice of words. "More importantly, Ash comes bearing something very significant." Ottro nudged Ash forward, and the Elders leaned in.

"I—" Ash felt very exposed, and very out of his depth. Thankfully, the frost-heart Sang encouragingly at his side.

"You're almost there. You've nearly done it; you're so close! Just a few more steps . . ."

Hearing the familiar, friendly voice gave Ash the courage he needed. "I've b-brought you something . . . something very precious that needs to be kept safe."

The Elders watched as Ash untied the frost-heart's archeomek casing from his belt and held it up for them to see.

"We . . . the, erm, the Pathfinders who had it called it the frost-heart."

The Elders' tired eyes widened, and they shared a glance with each other.

"We have heard of the Ancient's Heart . . ." Arrus said. "It's . . . it's been lost for centuries—but how on earth did it end up in the hands of *Pathfinders*?"

"You have done well to bring this to us, dear boy. You have just made the world a much safer place." Loda reached out to take the frost-heart from Ash, but Ash hesitated. It sounded strange, but he'd come to see the frost-heart as a friend of sorts. It raised him up when he needed to feel brave and consoled him when his heart was angry. He'd been saying goodbye to too many friends lately and he couldn't bear to part with another.

"Not . . . not until you let my friends into Solstice."

Loda looked surprised. "We cannot do that, Ash. We have a duty to keep our Stronghold safe."

"It will be safe! The Pathfinders are my friends—they're the best, most trustworthy people you'll ever meet!"

"*Child* . . ." Ottro warned, stepping toward Ash, who backed away.

"They saved me! They took me in when no one else would, knowing I was a Song Weaver." Ash's heart was thumping. "Look—where—where are my parents? Ferno and Ember, where are they? They'll back me up!"

"You're Ferno's child?" Nell asked, his eyes narrowing.

"I am! Ask him to come here. Once he finds out what the *Frostheart* crew did for me, he'll tell you to let them in!"

The Elders shared a concerned look.

"Solstice hasn't remained safe and hidden for centuries by opening its gates to the outside," Loda said, sterner this time. "The fate of the world is carried in your hand, Ash, and you would be wise to hand it over to those who know what to do with it."

Ash clutched the frost-heart tight to his chest. "We can't just *hide* here forever!" Something cold was piercing his belly, the biting anger that he'd tried so hard to smother. "I know the truth about the Leviathans—that they're not evil, that they can't control our minds. We need to tell the world! We need to show the Strongholds that we're harmless and make it safe for Song Weavers across the world, not just here. The Pathfinders could help us do that if you'd just—"

"Don't be so *childish*!" Arrus snapped. "Who would listen? This is no fireplace story; this is our survival! We're not a part of the outside world. *They* forced us into hiding in the first place. *They* fear us. *They hate us!*"

"It can't always be like this! Groups of people fearing each other—it'll never end," Ash pleaded. "We can't leave the other Song Weavers to face the Strongholders alone. They're being gathered into an army against their will, being forced to fight the Leviathans—" Ash stopped as he realized he wasn't helping his case; the Elders were snorting in horror at the news. "Where—where are my parents? I want to see them!"

"Give us the frost-heart," Loda said, holding out his skeletal hand.

"No!"

"Boy!" Ottro chided, reaching for the frost-heart, only for Ash to clutch it to his chest tighter.

"I won't!" he cried, his limbs trembling with fear, with anger. His insides were cold, his vision growing hazy and red.

"Stop this foolish game!" Loda yelled, his voice breaking. "You are a Song Weaver, and it is time you started to act like one!"

"WHERE ARE MY PARENTS?!" Ash roared. Silence punched through the chamber, save for the chant of the Choir outside, ululating and calm, a world away from the tension inside the hall. The Elders blinked, and Ottro didn't seem to know what to do, his face red with embarrassment at not being able to control this angry child.

"Your father is not here," Loda said at last.

Ash's muscles went slack. His shoulders fell forward. His arms, before so tense and strained, fell at his sides, as limp as his jaw, which drooped open. His body felt too heavy to keep upright, as though a great mocking weight were forcing him down to the ground, where he would curl up and remain forever.

"*P-pardon?*" Ash managed to choke out, though it sounded to him like the voice came from someone else a million leagues away.

"Ferno left us years ago. We do not know where he is."

Ash's heartbeat was in his ears, thrumming in his head—*buh-bump, buh-bump, buh-bump*—shaking his vision as though counting down to some terrible conclusion.

"B-but—how can that be? He led me here! He's supposed to be here!"

"He led you here for your own safety, that was his main concern. That, and the frost-heart," Arrus said.

"What—what about my mum? Ember?"

"Ferno never brought your mother here. She has never set foot within Solstice. How could she? She was not a Song Weaver."

Ash opened and closed his mouth like a fish, unable to find words. He felt nothing; he had gone entirely numb. The cold frightful anger, the fear, the confusion, it had all left him in an instant, and in its place was emptiness, a void in his mind and soul.

"They're not here? I—I—" Tears splashed onto the backs of his hands, which lay flat on the cold stone floor, as Ash only just realized he'd fallen to his knees. "The—the lullaby's over, though . . . This is meant to be the end. Did my dad leave any message for me, a verse to a Song?"

The Elders shook their heads, their faces softening at Ash's pain.

There must be a mistake, Ash thought. *They wouldn't do this to me. They—they . . . wouldn't abandon me, not again!*

"We are very sorry to be the bearers of such sad news," Nell said. "But you must know: Ferno was always speaking of you and your mother, and he only ever wanted you both to be safe. Your father loved you both very much."

This statement, a sentence that should've been so comforting, finally cracked through the shell Ash had built up over the years. The shell that had kept him believing that he would find his parents, that they would one day be a family again, that had convinced him he wasn't unwanted, that his parents loved him and had a good reason for leaving him. The shell that had kept him going through this whole journey. This stupid, ridiculous, pointless journey his father had sent him on to clear up *his* mess.

Now Ash felt something.

Sensation surged back into his body, a cold so frigid and furious it burned his nerves and seared his muscles, which were shaking at its terrible force.

"YOU'RE WRONG!" he cried, startling the Elders. "If he loved me, he would *be* here! They were never there for me. They were never there to help!" Hot tears burned his eyes, almost unbearable. "I've trekked across the Snow Sea, I've faced awful dangers, I've lost friends, all to find my parents, and they're not even here to greet me at the end of it?!"

The frost-heart reached out and tried to soothe him, but Ash was beyond soothing.

"THIS IS ALL THEIR FAULT!" Ash screamed, his Song-aura erupting out of him in tar-black tendrils, serpentine heads snapping and biting at the others in the room. He poured every bit of his anger, agony, and hate into that scream, hoping to tear the world down for its unfairness.

Ottro dodged out of the way just in time, while the Elders shot up from their seats, faces contorted with horror.

Good, Ash thought, *let them feel how I feel!*

"*Resist!*" the frost-heart pleaded desperately. "*Fight!*"

"*I HATE THEM! I HATE THEM SO MUCH!*" Ash's Song screamed, a cry so extreme his throat went raw. Ottro rushed his own Song-aura at Ash, trying to stop his frenzy, but Ash's shadow-tendrils wrapped themselves round his aura and began to squeeze the life from it. Ash could sense Ottro's panic, and the cold fury within Ash's body swelled with power at Ottro's fear. Ash wailed his hurt, screamed out all his frustration and pain, the bellow sounding more beast than human. The Elders shielded their grimacing faces as they were pushed back by the force, their cloaks billowing in an invisible storm.

The frost-heart begged Ash to remember who he

was, what his father had hoped he would be. Brave. Compassionate. Kind.

"WHO CARES WHAT MY FATHER SAID? HE'S A LIAR! HE LEFT ME ALONE!"

It urged him to think of Rook. Of the *Frostheart* crew—of Tobu and Lunah. How it would break their hearts to seem him like this. Ash's rage lessened for a heartbeat at the mention of his friends, the only ones who actually cared about him. The ones he'd been forced to leave behind.

"SHUT UP! GET OUT OF MY HEAD!"

Ash threw off the frost-heart's embrace, focusing on strangling Ottro's Song-aura, but before he could choke the life from it, Ash felt himself go weightless. He then hit the ground with considerable force, the wind knocked out of him, his aura evaporating like smoke. The three Elders surrounded him, their combined Songs more than powerful enough to extinguish his own.

"ENOUGH!" Loda demanded, his bright aura fading into thin air. "How dare you taint this place with that Song! People have been exiled for less!"

Ash writhed on the floor, gasping for air. He was still furious, but the fall had shaken him back to his senses. His limbs trembled and tears stung his eyes, or was it cold sweat that trickled down his forehead?

"Your father had good reason to flee! He had powerful enemies," Loda said, his voice almost lost.

"The frost-heart is the key to the Devourer's prison," Arrus explained, the heart still Singing in its beautiful, distant voice, trying to comfort Ash and heal his broken heart. "The Devourer is a Leviathan beyond imagining. It was created by hatred and war millennia ago and is only good at one thing: consuming all it touches and leaving barren, lifeless ruin in its wake. You cannot kill it. You cannot even harm it, for violence only fuels its power."

Ash was cowed by Arrus's grim explanation, his anger slowly subsiding, replaced by heaving breaths and shivering limbs. His body was warming now, but he could still feel the chill touch in his soul. He remembered the dark thing he'd seen in Rook's mind.

"I am awake. And I will be free . . ." Its voice seemed to echo round his head, as though it had been seeing through Ash's eyes. Ash struggled to get off the floor, but he felt too weak to lift his own weight.

"It wiped the World Before from existence," Loda continued. "It was only stopped by the combined efforts of the surviving Song Weavers and the last Leviathan Ancients, who managed to seal it away with a Song so powerful it could never be repeated. Not now. Not with our small numbers. Leviathan Ancients were the most powerful of their kind, and even they only *barely* managed to imprison it. It cost them their *lives*." Loda pointed to the frost-heart in Ash's hand for emphasis. "This is a shard of the heart of the most powerful Ancient to have ever lived, a mere memory of what it once was. But the Ancient's Song lives on within it. And it has the power to undo the Song that keeps the Devourer imprisoned, if it is corrupted and reversed. If the Devourer was ever released upon the world again, there would be no stopping it this time. Your father's actions have saved the world. The frost-heart is now where it should be, safe and hidden." Loda reached out his hand once more, his eyes imploring Ash to pass over the heart. "Or at least— it could be, if you do the right thing." Ash sniffed at the snot dribbling from his nose and cuffed the tears drying on his cheeks. He shuddered, still clinging to the frost-heart, the only friend he had left. It Sang to him. It assured him that it was okay, that he was doing the right thing. The distant, friendly voice assured him that he was strong enough to do this, that he was strong enough to live without it.

With no small amount of reluctance Ash handed the frost-heart to the Elder.

Loda nodded. "You have our eternal gratitude. But

never forget who it was that set you on your path. Your father did the right thing."

Ash swallowed, feeling ashamed. He'd let the Devourer in again, and if he wasn't careful, he'd end up cursed like Rook. Or worse—like Shaard. He looked at the floor, not daring to meet the eyes of the Elders.

"Understand, Ash," Nell said in a much softer, kinder voice, "that even in its imprisoned, weakened state, the Devourer's Song is far-reaching. The Devourer sensed your father trying to act against it and did everything in its power to stop him. Your father had to flee. He had no other choice."

Ash remained quiet, trying to process everything he'd just heard. His chest was still heaving with short, heavy breaths.

"I-I'm sorry," Ash said in a quiet voice before scrambling up and running out of the hall. He sprinted down the stairs, taking them three at a time. He passed the Choir and their echoing, sonorous hymn.

He didn't know where he was going.

He just knew he had to go.

39
Choices

The healers weaved Songs of recovery and mending. Their bright blue Song-auras caressed Rook, siphoning the poisonous shadow that had taken control of her. Ash sat hugging his knees beside Rook's bed, watching the healers at work. It was dark and pungent inside the healing house, the smells of various healing herbs, salves, and burning incense cloying together within Ash's nostrils. It reminded him of Arla's tent, though much bigger.

"Is she going to be okay?" Ash had asked when he'd arrived earlier. After his meeting with the Elders, he'd wanted to rush back to the *Frostheart*, but he couldn't just abandon Rook. She'd been unconscious for days; she wouldn't even know where she was!

"It's hard to say," one of the healers had said, a jolly woman who hummed while she worked. "We're doing all we can, but the curse is powerful." She saw the look on Ash's face, and offered him a candied root, trying to cheer him up. "But she's a strong one, and she's fighting with all she has, giving it what-for, I don't doubt!"

Ash took the sweet with a nod, though he wasn't hungry. "I think she'll be okay," Ash had said. Hoped. Prayed. "I think—she managed to keep this shadow, this *thing*, locked away once before. She'll do it again . . ."

The healer smiled. "I believe good ol'-fashioned love an' care can heal just about anything . . ." She'd given Ash a wink before she'd resumed her Song of healing.

As Ash watched the healers, he remembered the bag Tobu had given him before he'd left. Eager for any connection to the *Frostheart*, Ash reached into the satchel and pulled out its contents. Dried salted meat and edible roots. A whetstone. And a pack of arrows. Ash touched the flint point of one. He drew his finger away in pain. Sticking the finger into his mouth to suck at the blood, he smiled. He should've known better than to doubt Tobu's craftsmanship. His heart ached at the thought of his guardian, who'd been so reluctant to see him go.

There was one more thing in the bag. Ash pulled it out and took a sharp intake of breath. It was a small wooden sculpture. It might have had hints of a blobby nature, but Ash could tell what it was meant to be. A yeti. A large warrior yeti. Fierce and strong, yes, but more than that. The face looked sad—almost worried. It was the face of someone who was concerned, and cared deeply. It was the face of Tobu.

Ash clutched the sculpture tightly, warm tears falling down his cheeks.

I've gotten the frost-heart to safety, Ash thought, *and*

my parents aren't here. Why should I stay? I have to get back to the Frostheart. *My real home.*

"Are you so sure you want to leave Solstice?" came an elderly voice, startling Ash. It was Nell, the short, squat elder. He shuffled toward Ash with a big smile, his bald head shining in the candlelight. Ash wondered if everyone had the ability to read his thoughts, or whether he was just saying them out loud without realizing. Nell sat beside Ash with a groan. "Not that I'd blame you, after that little show back at the tower. Goodness, that really was a lot of heavy stuff you had dropped on you, eh? I truly am sorry for that."

"No, I just—" Ash began.

But perhaps Nell was right. In Solstice Ash had seen happiness on the people's faces. They were free to be what they truly were. The Leviathans rarely attacked, were not blinded by hate. There was no ridicule, no fearful gazes and suspicious, whispered rumors from others. There were no armies. No Wraiths. Just Song Weavers and peace.

It was a good place to live.

Perhaps the best.

But Ash hadn't felt this alone since he'd been with the Fira. He thought he'd left this loneliness behind for good, and he wasn't sure he could face it again.

"They won't let you go, you know," Nell said, his face turning serious.

"What?"

"Loda and Arrus. Ottro and the hunters. If you leave, you'd be able to guide your Pathfinder friends back through the Everstorm anytime you liked, and they can't allow that. The Pathfinders know too much."

"They'll . . . *kill* them?" Ash asked, horrified.

Nell chuckled, and Ash breathed a sigh of relief.

"No, no, they'll let the Everstorm do that."

Ash jumped out of his seat. "Then I *have* to get back to them—I have to help!"

Nell grabbed Ash's wrist and pulled him back down. The healers were finishing up with Rook, and Nell waited for them to move to their next patient before speaking in a lowered voice.

"The guards won't let you out. But I can help. They'll listen to me." Ash's eyes widened, and he nodded eagerly. "But you must promise to take me with you."

Ash pulled his head back. A leader of Solstice, wanting to leave? *"Why?"*

"Solstice is about as good as it gets, that's true enough," Nell whispered, eyeing the healers at work. "But we're still bound by the Everstorm. I have spent the entirety of my considerable winters here, seeing no farther than that impenetrable white wall. I am old, but my mind feels young, and curious, and desperate. Even paradise can feel like a prison when you're not able to leave it." Ash glanced at the old man, who was staring off into dreams Ash could not see. "To be able to run the paths between forests and mountains, to be able to point to a spot on a map and know there was nothing blocking your way . . ." Ash had sympathy for Nell. All this time Ash had pinned his hopes on Solstice, thinking the Song Weavers would be honorable heroes, that his parents would lead them to bring peace back to the Strongholds. But it was just another cage for frightened people to hide in. Well, Ash was sick of hiding because of what he was, and he was certainly not about to try to change Nell's mind.

"I'm sure the *Frostheart* would be glad to have you aboard," Ash said.

Nell barked out a laugh and clapped Ash's knee, his eyes twinkling. "Then we have no time to lose, my boy!"

"What about Rook? I can't just leave her here!"

Nell turned to her unconscious body, her grimacing face, her darkened eye sockets, vivid and poisonous. "Your friend needs care, the kind she'll only find here."

Ash took one of Rook's hands, watching as her eyes flickered underneath her closed eyelids, lost to the terrible malice of the Devourer. Surely, he couldn't just abandon her here. But if he took her from Solstice, would she ever recover?

"Taking her with us may seem like the right thing to do, but it would actually be unspeakably cruel. She can be saved here. She can make a home, surrounded by people who will care for her," Nell said gently.

Ash squeezed Rook's hand. It seemed that no matter what path he took, he'd have to leave friends behind. He shut his eyes tight and ground his teeth, not wanting to let go of Rook, his strange, frightening, wonderful friend.

Nell went on, shaking his head. "She'd have to be one of the most powerful Song Weavers who ever lived to get out of this on her own—"

At that very moment, Rook shot up from the bed.

"AAAAAAAARGH!" she screamed, like one who had just woken from a nightmare.

"AAAAAAAARGH!" Ash and Nell screamed, jumping into each other's arms.

Rook coughed and spluttered. Her glossy black eyes were open, her bright white pupils darting about the room in wild panic.

"Where am I?!"

"Don't worry!" Ash reassured her, his heart racing

with shock, but singing to see his friend awake. "You're safe. You're in Solstice—you're being looked after!"

But his words only seemed to alarm her more.

"Where's frost-heart?!"

"It's here, with the Elders. It's safe, don't worry!"

"*No. No. No. NO!*" she screamed, startling Ash. The healers hurried over. *"Shouldn't be here. I shouldn't be here! I told you to leave me. You should have listened!"* She leaped out of bed, but her weakened legs caused her to tumble over onto the floor. Ash, Nell, and the healers rushed to her aid, but she was still trying to crawl forward. *"Where Elders? Take me to them!"*

"You need rest!" a healer said. "You're in no condition to—"

Rook tore her arm from the healer's grasp. "*Release me!*" she hissed. "They *will have heard me.* They *will have followed!*"

"Who are *they*?!" Ash asked, his heart thumping faster.

The deep bellow of the Gargant that guarded the Stronghold entrance rumbled through the cliffs. Rook's unnerving black-and-white eyes widened in horror.

"*They're here.*"

40

Not Alone

Solstice looked as peaceful as ever. Song Weavers were happily going about their lives. A couple were even in the middle of courting, one playing the flute to another who listened with googly eyes and a gooey smile. It was noticeable, then, when a wild-eyed Rook forced her way in between the couple, giving the flute player a hard shove and causing her to play a note that sounded like a mursu burp.

"Out of the way!" Rook rasped, scurrying past on all fours, Ash and Nell chasing as best they could, winding their way through the startled crowd.

"Sorry!" Ash yelled as he passed the disgruntled lovers. "She hasn't slept very well!"

"You two, with me!" Nell ordered two passing hunters, just in case Rook's strange panic proved justified.

Rook tore into the Storm Tower, passed the Choir without a glance, and clambered up the stairs to the tower's heights as Ash took the stairs two at a time to keep up. She burst into the Elders' chamber in a rush of black rags. Arrus and Loda spun round at the sudden commotion.

"*Where's heart?*" Rook asked.

"Who on earth are you?!"

"*HEART?!*" she shrieked.

"It's here; it's safe!" a startled

Arrus said, revealing the frost-heart's casing. "We were just discussing the best, most secure vault to keep it safe in . . ."

Ash looked around the chamber as Nell and the hunters arrived behind him, panting and gasping for breath. Everything seemed fine and just as he'd left it. The storm-Song of the Choir resonated throughout the tower, giving it a serene, sacred atmosphere.

"*Not too late . . . ?*" Rook Sang.

Ash breathed a sigh of relief. Maybe Rook's hysteria had just been a side effect of the Devourer's curse?

"Everything all right?" Arrus asked, confused.

"*Help bar doors,*" Rook hissed, pulling the heavy doors together. Ash, Nell, and the two hunters shared a glance, before rushing to her aid. The stone doors ground along the floor. Just before they sealed shut, they came to a stop, inches apart. *Strange,* thought Ash, joining the others as they pushed harder, but the door wouldn't budge. Confused, they all looked down, and to their surprise saw the butt of a spear sticking through the gap, preventing the doors from closing. They paused, trying to figure out why a spear would be there of all places when a heavy weight pushed back against them, forcing the doors back open.

"*NO!*" Rook screamed. "*PUSH!*"

"Spirits—" Nell gasped as they pushed back with all their might.

Ash gritted his teeth with the effort, his boots losing purchase on the floor. But it was no use. The doors slammed open with a *boom* that resounded throughout the tower, forcing the others to stagger back.

Ash's blood went cold as he witnessed the scene before him. Wraiths poured into the room like black mist. There must've been twenty of them at least, their hideous forms armed with wicked spears and bows. But it was the twisted, misshapen horns of the Great Horned One who strode among them that really made his heart skip a beat.

How did they find us? How did they get in?!

The Solstice hunters rushed at them, but were immediately cut down by the Wraiths' blades before they could even raise their own.

"Fiends!" Loda spat, covering Arrus as he made a run for a side door in the hall, the frost-heart clutched under his arm. A Wraith fired its bow, sending Arrus crashing to the floor, an arrow sticking from his leg. The frost-heart skidded out of his hands to the center of the chamber.

"ARRUS!" Nell cried, rushing to help him.

"We've come much too far," the Great Horned One

said, and Ash was shocked to hear that its voice was calm and smooth and nothing like the rasping hisses he had heard from others of its kind. It sounded almost . . . *human*. "And been through far too much to have the frost-heart taken from us now."

Rook let out an animalistic cry and slashed at the Great Horned One with her dagger, but the Wraiths quickly overwhelmed her and threw her to the ground. Ash backed away toward one of the far windows, but there was nowhere to run. The Wraiths advanced, eerily keeping step in perfect unison to a rhythm only they could hear. They were Singing, if it could be called that. It was more like a growl, coming from deep within their chests. It corrupted the air, rolling out like a storm cloud, beckoning the people of Solstice to gather in front of the tower.

Wraiths forced Ash to his knees as the Great Horned One picked the frost-heart from off the floor. The frost-heart Sang out in distress, its Song full of anguish at being in the hands of its enemy. Rook struggled and screamed like a cornered animal as the Wraiths held her down.

"GET OFF IT, YOU MONSTER!" Ash found himself shouting.

The Great Horned One turned to look at him with its soulless pitch-black eyes.

"Careful what you say, Ash."

Ash recoiled at the mention of his name. "We all know how dangerous it is to judge something we do not understand, don't we, now?" The creature strode before him. "I am simply taking back what you stole from *me*."

The Wraiths circled Ash and the Great Horned One, and Ash watched in utter horror as they reached for their faces and began to *pull them off*. Then it clicked. Their grotesque, monstrous faces were not faces at all, but masks. The Wraiths were not demons from the underworld or the lost souls of the dead at all. No, they were something much worse, much more unnerving and terrifying.

"You're . . . *people* . . ." Ash said, his belly racked by cold. They looked wild and frightening, harsh and cruel, but they were human-kin nonetheless. Black veins leaked from their eyes, eyes that stared at Ash with heated malice. *The same eyes as Rook . . .*

"Not just people—*Song Weavers*," the Great Horned One said, slowly removing its own mask. "Just. Like. *You*."

Ash gasped as the Great Horned One's true face was revealed.

Those bright, turquoise eyes. Those scars. That grin, like a wolver, flashing its fangs before it bit down upon its prey.

It was Shaard, and he held the frost-heart in his grasp.

41

Something to Fear

"You . . ." Ash whispered.

"Me," Shaard replied, amused.

"*TOUCH HIM, I KILL YOU!*" Rook howled.

Shaard chuckled. "It's good to see you again too, Rook! Even though you *betrayed* us, your very own *family*, you've still gone out of your way to help us out in the end. I should be thanking you, really." Shaard saw the look of shocked confusion in Ash's eyes. "You didn't know? She's very secretive, our Rook, isn't she? I suppose we all have to be to survive in this world. Rook is one of us, you see. My most promising Weaver, in fact! As was your father. Both Wraiths, who, up until their ill-judged desertion, helped us in our noble fight against the Strongholders."

"*Liar . . .*" Ash growled, but only because he didn't want to believe it. Rook had fallen to the Devourer before, that much Ash knew. She'd known how to use Shaard's Song—no, the *Devourer's* Song. Rook herself had said the Wraiths were the Devourer's servants. What Shaard said made horrific sense. Ash looked to Rook for reassurance, for her to insist it was another of Shaard's lies. But all he saw was shame scrawled across her face, his belly sinking as the awful truth came to light.

"Rook, *no . . .*"

Ash felt like he was going to be sick. The Strongholders were right. Song Weavers were monsters after all. *They'd* been the scourge upon the land all along, not Leviathans. And Ash had been tricked again. He was so *stupid*!

Rook was shaking her head frantically, moaning with sorrow.

"The Song she Sang that allowed you to escape back at the forest was the Song *I* taught her," Shaard boasted. "I taught you *both*, in fact, and I don't remember you complaining when it helped you save your friends in Shade's Chasm, Ash. Dear Rook may have been whispering the Song under her breath, quiet as a squink, but her aura shone bright as a beacon for the Devourer—and us—to follow." Ash could only listen in horror, his body trembling. "But she wouldn't have led us anywhere worthwhile, Ash, were it not for you," Shaard continued. "You solved the riddle. You pieced together the map. *You* led us through the Everstorm, right to Solstice's front gates. You truly lived up to the title of *Pathfinder*, and for that you have our thanks."

"*Should've left me*," Rook wept. "*Told you to leave me!*"

"I *should've* left you!" Ash snapped, desperate for someone other than himself to blame. "You're just as bad as him!"

Anguish wracked Rook's face and Ash was glad. But his own actions whirred around his head like a storm.

What have I done? he kept repeating to himself. *What have I done?*

"But enough of our little catch-up," Shaard

said, striding toward the seething Elders. "How do I un-cover the Devourer's hidden prison?"

"Ferno warned us about you," Loda said. "Lost to the Devourer's corruption and lies. I see that all he said is true. You *have* lost your mind."

"Ferno was my friend," Shaard said. "He saw the sense in my plan. He helped me put it into motion!"

Another stab into Ash's heart.

"Yet he still had enough sense to escape your clutches," Loda said.

"Don't you see?" Shaard laughed, holding his arms up high. "It doesn't matter—there is no escape! Now, tell me how the prison is hidden. Together *we* could control the Devourer. *We* could use its power to return Song Weavers to our proper place as rulers of this land! I'm trying to fight for Song Weavers everywhere."

"The Devourer's Song fills those who Sing and hear it with hate. Look at your warriors. Look how it consumes them!" Arrus gestured at the Wraiths, who

twitched and spasmed, grunted and hissed, as though it took every bit of their strength to stop themselves from launching into a violent attack. Their sun-flare pupils burned with an insatiable anger, their mouths curling up into frothing snarls as they growled their dreadful chant. "They lose a piece of their humanity every time they Sing it!"

"Not if we stand together!" Shaard insisted. "I've been there from the beginning, and look at me! I've not lost myself. It's made me more powerful than ever!"

"Only for as long as the Devourer has a use for you," Loda warned, and Ash heard the frost-heart Singing of the power Shaard was planning to meddle with, power far beyond his control. "Your actions do nothing but put everyone, Song Weaver or not, at risk. You are a poor excuse for a Song Weaver." Loda spat these last words.

Shaard's smile did not leave his face, but his eye twitched.

"Save me your lectures. I have spent a lifetime researching the Devourer, and I don't need a history lesson from some bumbling old dodderer."

"And yet you have failed to learn from history's lessons."

"I learned enough to know that you Solstice natives are the descendants of the Song Weavers who ruled the

World Before. I know your bloodlines were trusted with the knowledge of how the Devourer was hidden." He pulled Arrus's head up by his hair, holding a blade to his exposed neck. "And you will tell me how to uncover it."

"We have sworn our lives to keeping the prison's whereabouts a secret. You'll never find it!"

"I already have." The shock on the Elders' faces was clear to see, despite how hard they tried to hide it, and Shaard relished the minor victory. "You think the Devourer's Song wouldn't lead me to it? A lifetime of searching? I know where it is, but I don't know how to get in. Some kind of archeomek hides the entrance, and you *will* tell me how to pass it."

"Kill us, if you must," Arrus said, teeth clenching with pain. "The secret will die with us."

Shaard massaged his temple with frustration, then made to draw his blade along Arrus's throat.

"WAIT!" Nell shouted. Shaard raised an expectant eyebrow. "I know how to reveal the Devourer's prison. I'll tell you want you want to know! Just—just don't hurt anyone!"

"Nell, what are you *doing*?!" Arrus hissed.

"He's right," Nell said, voice quivering. "I've been thinking it for many years now, since I first heard about the Wraiths from Ferno. I'm sick of hiding. I'm sick of

Song Weavers being kicked around by Pathfinders and Strongholders. I want to see the world outside. I want to be *free*. And if it means I save your lives in the process, then all the better."

"*Our lives?* You do this, Nell, and you will doom us all!"

"I—I don't believe you. I have seen what we are capable of. Look at us, we even control the *weather* with our Song! What if . . . we *can* use the Devourer to fight back against our oppressors? Isn't that a chance we should take?"

Loda and Arrus were aghast, unable to believe that one of their own could be so easily swayed.

"At last, someone is seeing sense." Shaard placed an arm over Nell's shoulder and walked him to a large balcony that overlooked Solstice. The Wraiths stopped their Song, allowing Shaard's words to be heard. "Fellow Song Weavers!" he said, addressing the crowd who had gathered below, all looking baffled and frightened at this strange Song that had invaded their home, this strange shift in the usual peace of their Stronghold.

"Do not listen to this untrustworthy worm!" Loda shouted, and the Wraiths grabbed him and covered his mouth before he could say any more.

"Please, do not be afraid!" Shaard announced. "We come to you not as enemies, but as friends, as *liberators*!" He held up his gnarled white mask. "We wear these masks

to strike fear into the hearts of our enemies, but to you,
fellow Song Weavers, let them be a symbol to rally behind,
an emblem of your freedom that is being fought for! My
name is Shaard, and I am the leader of the Wraiths." The
crowd rumbled with unease, some even crying out in fear.
"Forget what you have heard about us! It is all lies. We
are on your side, and always will be. We scour the lands
beyond these walls, looking for Song Weavers who suffer
under the cruel rule of the Strongholds. We free them. We

give them a home, where they've always had none. Where they've felt alone, we give them a family. We gather them to our cause, to fight for Song Weaver rights and freedom!"

The Wraiths raised their spears and let out a cheer that sounded more like a war cry.

"You are nothing but murderous pirates!" someone shouted.

"Well, what choice do we have?" Shaard asked honestly. "We have to take what we can to survive, for the Strongholds give us nothing. Aurora helps all those in the Snow Sea, except for people like *us*. As long as Aurora is in control we will be treated as their lessers."

Shouts of agreement came from the crowd, nods of support. Ash hated himself for recognizing the things Shaard spoke of. It all sounded so convincing, but Ash had seen that it was more complicated than that. He'd seen great Pathfinders and caring Strongholders too.

"Even now," Shaard continued, "the Pathfinder Council has given the command of the entire Pathfinder fleet to one bloodthirsty warrior, Commander Stormbreaker. She is hunting Song Weavers, forcing them against their will to be used as weapons in a war against the Leviathans. This Commander Stormbreaker will be sending these Song Weavers to their needless deaths!"

There were gasps of shock and shrieks of panic. "The

Leviathans are not our enemies," an old man pointed out. "We have proven we can live together in peace—war will only enrage them, as it has in the past!"

"Wise words!" Shaard nodded. "We must end her war before it begins! And even if Stormbreaker could win against such a foe, do you believe the Pathfinders will free the Song Weavers afterward? Live alongside us in peace? They have seen the power we wield. They have seen the weapons from the World Before that we can control. Look at your Storm Tower! What they wouldn't give for such power! No, they will never live peacefully alongside us. We will always live under their boots and tyranny, unless we do something about it!"

"But we're safe here—the storm hides us!"

"For now, maybe. But if the Pathfinders manage to drive the Leviathans from these lands, how long before they find a way through your defenses? They'll be free to roam the Snow Sea, safe from attack." Shaard had the crowd's full attention now. "Well, perhaps it's time we truly gave them something to fear."

Shaard nodded to the Wraiths that stood behind him, and they began to chant their terrible Song, the droning chant that had tormented Ash for so long. The crowd grasped their heads in their hands, grimacing at the terrible din. Then another sound filled the air.

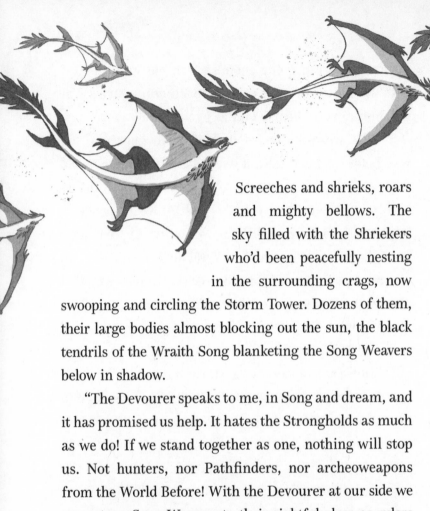

Screeches and shrieks, roars and mighty bellows. The sky filled with the Shriekers who'd been peacefully nesting in the surrounding crags, now swooping and circling the Storm Tower. Dozens of them, their large bodies almost blocking out the sun, the black tendrils of the Wraith Song blanketing the Song Weavers below in shadow.

"The Devourer speaks to me, in Song and dream, and it has promised us help. It hates the Strongholds as much as we do! If we stand together as one, nothing will stop us. Not hunters, nor Pathfinders, nor archeoweapons from the World Before! With the Devourer at our side we can return Song Weavers to their rightful place as rulers of this world!" The Wraiths let out another roar, bloodcurdling and brutal. "So, who will join us?" Shaard asked the crowd, raising his arms grandly. "Who will join in our fight against the Strongholds, to take back what is rightfully ours?"

Some in the crowd cheered. But most remained silent. The Wraiths continued their chant, the Shriekers whirling above menacingly.

"You'll get us all killed!" someone shouted, and cries of agreement rang out from the crowd.

"We don't want your war!"

"Where are the Elders? What do they have to say about this?"

Shaard gripped the balcony railing in surprise. Ash could see he had not been expecting this.

"Get out of our Stronghold! Leave us in peace!" the crowd shouted, surging forward toward the tower entrance. An arrow clacked off the balcony, inches away from Shaard, who stumbled back. Ash squirmed under the Wraiths to see through a gap in the balcony's stone guardrail and saw that it was Ottro who had

fired the shot from the plaza, his hunters at his back, Spots growling up at the intruders.

"A pity," Shaard said. "Perhaps I didn't make myself clear." He began to bark out his Song, his shadow-aura surging toward Spots at the hunters' side. Ash quickly tried to block Shaard's Song with his own, but he was still being pinned by a Wraith, who pushed down and choked Ash's Song from his throat. Ash could only listen in horror as Shaard forced Spots to attack the hunters. He closed his eyes tight, trying his hardest to block out the screams. Finally, after what felt like an age, Shaard released the Leviathan, and the sobbing, frightened wails of the Song Weavers outside replaced his Song.

There were more cries of alarm as Wraiths appeared from the cliffs that encircled the Stronghold, from the tunnel entrance, from between buildings and out of shadows, joining their ghastly voices to the endless chanting. There were hundreds of them, and they had the Song Weavers trapped and surrounded, the air thick with terror. *So many . . .* Ash fretted, before panic clutched at his insides. *The* Frostheart! *Did the Wraiths get them too?*

"Those *true* Song Weavers among you will join our ranks and defend our kind as any loyal Song Weaver is honor bound to do," Shaard said. "Anyone who refuses is a traitor to our cause and will be dealt with as such." Children were crying, parents were holding them, doing what little they could to protect them. "Remember what you are! Remember that victory does not come without sacrifice!"

With that Shaard swept round, his black cloak flowing behind him. "Gather them into the sleighs. We'll need them all for what's to come. Kill any who resist."

The Wraiths made guttural sounds in response. Ash wasn't sure they could even form words anymore in their haze of rage; he'd not heard one of them speak a word. Rook screamed unintelligible curses at Shaard as she was lifted roughly to her feet.

Ash only shook in horror as they lifted him too. "You . . . you killed those hunters!" Ash stammered as Shaard approached. "They were innocent—they were Song Weavers!"

"It's a terrible waste," Shaard admitted. "But they were traitors. Just like you two."

He nodded at the Wraiths who held Rook, and they dragged her kicking and screaming to a window. Ash's scream caught in his throat as without hesitation they threw her out of it.

The world froze. All sound disappeared; all movement stilled. He was dimly aware of Shaard saying something to him, but all Ash could see was the image of Rook falling into thin air.

"Ash? Are you there, Ash?" Shaard said, grabbing his face and shaking it to catch his attention. "I was saying I should do the same to you. But despite the fact that you tricked me back at the Isolai, despite the fact that you've made my life . . . *difficult*, that I've had to chase you halfway across the Snow Sea, I still like you. Call me crazy, but I think I'm just a sentimental fool at heart. Here, up you get," he said, offering Ash his hand. Ash didn't take it, and shakily got to his feet by himself. "This is your last chance," Shaard said. "Join us. Follow in your father's footsteps, as you have been this whole time. Join us to finish what he helped me start. Without us, no matter what you do, wherever you go, you will be hated. Why be hated, when you can be *feared*?"

Ash's mind raced. He didn't know how he'd lost everything so quickly, how it had all gone so terribly wrong. *Maybe I'll never belong in the Strongholds, maybe I don't know what I'm doing, or where I belong. But I do know one thing for certain . . .*

He knew it so clear and true; he did all he could to hold on to it.

"So you can use me?" Ash said in a small voice. "Like you use people to get what you want? Like you use the Leviathans? No. I will not join you."

Shaard's smile left his face. He sighed, genuinely disappointed.

"I expected as much. I even respect it, really. Your father was much easier to convince."

"Perhaps Tobu was a better teacher than you gave him credit for."

Shaard chuckled. "Yes. Perhaps that's it. But I'm afraid I can't have you scampering about ruining my plans any longer. Off you pop, Ash." And with that Shaard picked Ash up and threw him out the window too, the very same one his friend had been thrown from moments before.

42

Sole Purpose

The ground below rushed toward Ash with horrifying speed, and then, with a sudden stomach-wrenching jerk, the world shuddered. It took moments for Ash to realize he'd been snatched right out of the air. His vision spun as he clung to Rook's hand for dear life, vertigo pulling at his innards. He supposed he should've been thankful that he hadn't plummeted to his death, but Ash was starting to think this was almost as bad. Rook carefully hoisted him up onto the narrow ledge that she'd miraculously managed to catch hold of and was now perched upon.

Ash shuffled his back against the tower's wall, trying to get as far from the edge as he could, his hands slick with sweat, the wind snatching at his furs. He could see Wraiths far below marching the Song Weavers out of Solstice, Nell at the forefront of the crowd, off to awaken the Devourer from its prison. Nell truly must've felt oppressively confined by Solstice to act this way. He shared Shaard's view that Aurora and the Strongholds of the outside world were to blame for his confinement, for his lack of freedom, but little did he know that life out there was truly no different. Ash failed to see how unleashing untold destruction upon the Strongholds would help anything get better. But the wheels had been put in motion, and chaos was coming, starting with Nell's home itself. The Song Weavers tried to huddle together, but families were being torn apart, friends and lovers too. Many had their hands tied with thick rope. Their peaceful lives had been shattered. *Ruined.* Ash saw Loda and Arrus among them, quiet and ashamed at their failure to keep the Devourer's prison a secret, to keep the people of Solstice safe.

A circle of Wraiths were chanting their Song, forcing the spiraling Shriekers above to keep watch. For the first time in a thousand years the Everstorm had stopped raging. The Wraiths had torn the Choir from their sworn duty and marched them out of the Stronghold too. Ash saw Spots hiding in a corner, mewling with anguish and sorrow at what he'd been forced to do.

"*Have to stop him,*" Rook Sang, shuffling beside Ash. "*Need to find way off tower.*"

"Don't talk to me."

"*Reclaiming frost-heart is everything.*"

"I'm not doing *anything* with you! You're one of them! You lied to me, just like Shaard!"

Rook winced. "

Ash—I explain . . ."

"NO! How can I ever trust you again?"

Rook began to Sing, her Song-aura reaching out for Ash, but he didn't Sing back.

"*Ash, please . . .*" Tears ran down her black-streaked cheeks. "*I never would betray you! I made promise. Promise to your father.*"

Ash turned his head from her. Part of him wanted to reject her—to see Rook get her comeuppance for what she'd done. For betraying him, despite all the faith he'd put in her. But another part of him, a bigger part, knew that it was wrong. That more hate was the last thing that was needed now. And despite himself, Ash was still curious about what she might be able to tell him. *She knows more about the Wraiths than any of us. And she's the best link I have to my dad. Maybe . . . maybe she could still help?*

"*Song cannot lie,*" Rook Sang. "*Please . . . listen!*"

And so Ash did.

The anger in Ash was immediately washed away by a

tide of deep regret and desperate sorrow. He was startled by the raw honesty in Rook's Song, her relief in being able to finally reveal the truth. Though the Devourer had torn through the barrier in her mind in the cruelest way, it had also allowed her to reach her deepest memories, ones that had been deliberately hidden for so long.

Ash saw a young girl, perhaps only eight winters old. Silver hair, large bright eyes. The little girl was an ulk rider, traveling across the hills where she lived with her parents, hills that the Pathfinder sleighs couldn't reach. It didn't matter. Her parents acted like Pathfinders instead, delivering supplies and messages between the hill Strongholds. It was dangerous work, as the hills were still infested with Leviathans, but they were determined to do their part, to do what others could not. For the girl and her parents had a secret. They were Song Weavers. They used their gift to make peace with the Leviathans, with all the creatures that lived on the highlands.

Life was hard. It was grueling, and unforgiving. But the girl was happy.

Then everything changed.

The girl was older. Almost full-grown. She never found out how they were discovered, who started the rumor. But the Strongholds had uncovered their secret. They knew they were Song Weavers, and they feared them for it.

Hated them. They refused the family refuge behind their walls. Without shelter from the elements, without being able to share in the Stronghold provisions, the wilds slowly took its toll on the family. The girl was frightened. Her parents were growing weaker by the day, insisting that what small amounts of food they could muster went to her, to keep her strong. The girl hated it. She would've gladly given up her share. But they wouldn't have it. Tears froze at the young woman's eyes every night. She felt so helpless. So *useless*. She couldn't protect those she loved.

The day came when the wilds stole her parents from her.

The young woman was left alone. Abandoned by the Strongholds, unloved, *cursed*. But day in and day out, she endured, always without a shoulder to cry on. She only survived because of her curse. The thing they had hated her for had been the very thing that had saved her.

Many times she came close to giving up, to leaving herself at the mercy of the spirits. But before she could, one of the hill Strongholds was attacked. Spearwurms, Hurtlers, Lurkers—they tore it down in a night of bloody carnage.

Figures had stepped out of the fire and smoke. The ones who had brought the Leviathans and attacked the Stronghold. Others, like her. A man offered her his hand. Offered her a family, a *home*.

Ash's belly turned as he recognized a younger Shaard, smiling that terrible smile of his.

The young woman was no longer alone. She had a family that cared for her, and they took revenge for the terrible things the Strongholds had done to them. It was a fight against the strong, protecting the weak and helpless. What they were doing was right and just. But in truth they did unforgivable things too. Ash saw the young woman with silver hair standing beside others, screaming with hatred. Leviathans forced to tear down Stronghold walls, to rip Pathfinder sleighs to pieces. The Song Weavers relished the power the Devourer gave them, mocking how pathetic those without it were. Ash's heart clenched at what he saw. It was awful, and the unyielding belief these Song Weavers had that they were doing the right thing made it even harder to stomach. Rook trembled with remorse and horror at the memories, barely able to recognize herself. Her parents would've been heartbroken. But back then she'd felt powerful for the first time in her whole life. She felt like the Strongholders deserved no less.

The visions shimmered and warped to show an Auroran dock. Rook met with Ferno there, deep in the shadows. Ferno had acted as a spy for the Wraiths, learning the secrets of the Council and Pathfinders before passing them on to Rook, who passed them on to Shaard. But this was not a normal meeting. They were both very afraid.

An unnatural Song was eating them from the inside, tearing bits from their soul every time they Sang it, every time they forced a Leviathan to hurt others. They were frightened of what they'd become and ached with regret. Many others in their group were already lost, or well on their way, blinded by hate and corrupted by the Devourer. They had become monsters, and if Rook and Ferno didn't stop soon, they would be lost forever too.

But Rook was strong. She fought with everything she had to reclaim her humanity. Her parents had given their lives to help others, after all. She began to wall away the darkness within her, to shield herself from its wrath. But her friend, Ferno, was losing the battle for his soul. The Devourer had its claws in him, and it wasn't going to let go. Ferno had to flee, far, far away, where even the Devourer's Song couldn't reach. Rook was devastated. Ferno was her only friend in the whole world. She'd lost everything once more. The thought of being alone again was almost too much to bear.

"Not everything," Ferno had assured her before he left. "You can still correct our mistakes; you can still stop this madness. The frost-heart is safe for now. Shaard will do everything he can to find it, but I have put a plan in motion that will lead my son to it first. He will find you, and when he does, I need you to help him. Promise me! Protect him and the heart. Get them to Solstice. Get them to safety."

Rook's heart swelled at being given a purpose again. She could still do some good in the world. Although she would never forgive herself for the things she'd done, perhaps saving this boy would ease her wounded conscience.

"I promise," Rook swore to Ferno. "I swear I will."

Ash could sense the Devourer now, walled away again in Rook's Song, but straining against the new barrier she'd managed to create. It bellowed in fury, clawing and reaching. Sensing the danger, Rook dissolved her Song-vision.

Ash fell out of the Song-trance and back into his own body. He felt like he'd just winessed echoes of his own memories, of how he could've ended up, had he met Shaard before Tobu.

"Rook . . ." He placed a hand on her trembling shoulder.

"*Understand if you hate me,*" she whispered.

"We were both tricked by Shaard and his lies."

Rook nodded regretfully. *"Wraiths meant to be freedom fighters. Have all fallen to darkness now."*

"And all this time Shaard has been their leader . . . behind all the awful things they've done . . ."

"Took years to discover key to Devourer's prison was aboard Frostheart. Did not know what it was, back then. Afterward, Captain Nuk always escaped Shaard's grasp, always one step ahead of Wraiths. After years of failure, Shaard tried something new. Slunk onto Frostheart not with force, but like shadow, using trickery to act like friend. Fira kept you hidden for years. When you climbed aboard Frostheart, Shaard couldn't believe luck. He couldn't have known Ferno was trying to bring you and the frost-heart together. Ferno planned quest for you, but doing so made everything easier for Shaard too. The two of you brought to same sleigh at same time. World Weave behaves in strange ways, sometimes . . ."

"But what about Shade's Chasm? The Wraiths nearly killed us all!"

"Temptation too great for Shaard to steal you and heart from Frostheart using his black fleet. Thought to corrupt you with Devourer's Song. Bring you to his side. He cares not for his warriors. No cost too great for him."

Ash watched the Wraiths disappear into Solstice's entrance-tunnel, leaving the fabled Stronghold behind. He wasn't sure whether he should curse them or feel sorry for them. "Why . . ." Ash began, hugging his knees to his chest, "why didn't you come for me, after you'd made your promise to my dad?"

Rook looked into Ash's eyes. *"Didn't know where you were. Ember and Ferno kept secret. Escaping Shaard left me wounded and broken. Took refuge in Skybridge, where Ferno said I would meet you. Waited. Many years, trying to hear you."* She dragged her hands through her scruffy hair. *"Trusted World Weave. It shifted, finally, on day you solved first lullaby riddle. Sent my crows to find you right away."* She took a shuddering breath. *"Poor crows. Sensed evil in me. Scared them away, just like you."*

"They would be here if they could." Ash smiled weakly, trying to reassure her.

The two Song Weavers perched side by side in a shaken silence, brooding over all the terrible things that had happened to them.

Solstice was empty. All the Song Weavers had been taken, and Shaard had set off with Nell and the frost-heart, on his way to bring total carnage to the world. Ash gazed out at the desolate Stronghold, a place he'd once dreamed he would call home. But now . . . now he realized there were bigger things at stake. Things that *really* mattered. He thought of Lnah, Tobu, Captain Nuk, and all the others he loved out there being hurt because of this endless cycle of mistrust and vengeance.

Well, the world might keep throwing trials his way, but perhaps it was time he fought back. Perhaps it was time he did something instead of hiding. Adrenaline surged through his veins, warming and uplifting, a far cry from the biting cold of the Devourer's hate. He didn't know where he could go now, or exactly what he could do. But he did know that the Strongholders, the Pathfinders, the Song Weavers and Wraiths, they were all hiding from the same simple truth. That they were all exactly the same as each other. And something had to change.

On quaking legs Ash rose to his full height, back firmly against the stone. "Well, we're not much use sitting up here, are we? We need to get the frost-heart back—you have a promise to keep, after all!"

Rook looked up at Ash, hope returning to her strange eyes. But the hope quickly turned to alarm as her eyes darted past him and up to the sky.

Ash followed her gaze and saw with horror what had alarmed her.

The swarm of Shriekers that had been circling the Stronghold were diving down toward them.

The Wraiths had left, and their hold over the Leviathans with them. The Shriekers were furious—and hungry for revenge.

43

Connections

"*HUMANS! ENEMY. HATE. DESTROY!*" the Shriekers screamed as they crashed down onto the tower's columns like a monstrous hailstorm.

Ash and Rook immediately Sang together, trying to still the Shriekers' rage. Ash prayed that Rook would be able to sway the Leviathans like she had back in the forest, but her Song felt delicate and frail, like it might burn away in the sun.

"*Too weak. Devourer took toll. Can't . . . focus!*" She grimaced, eyes shut tight. "*You. It has to be you!*"

The Shriekers scrambled toward the ledge Ash and Rook were stranded on, their claws sinking into the stone columns like they were made of mud. Ash tried not to panic. He took deep breaths and Sang even harder. Ash's aura flowed around the Shriekers', trying to persuade them to stand down.

"We're on your side! Please, be calm! We're peaceful—we're friends!"

"HUMANS. USE. FORCE. CONTROL." The Leviathans clambered over each other in their rush to snap the Song Weavers up in their jaws. "STEAL ANCIENT HEART. DOOM US ALL."

"We don't want to control you! We want to help! We want to get the Ancient's heart back too!"

A Shrieker leaped forward and caught the edge of the ledge, and Ash's stomach rose into his throat. The beast was so large that most of its body hung off the precipice, clawing and scraping at the stone to keep itself upright. It stared at Ash with hungry white eyes.

"CANNOT TRUST HUMAN. THEY LIE. THEY CHEAT!"

"LIE! CHEAT! LIE! CHEAT!" the others cried.

It reared back its head, opening its jaws wide, thick saliva dripping from its daggerlike fangs. It snapped toward Ash, who closed his eyes in fright.

But instead of the painful clamping of jaws, Ash felt the ledge give another crashing shudder. Daring to look, he saw that another Shrieker had landed on top of the first, and with a jolt Ash recognized it. It was the wounded Shrieker that had been following him since they'd left Aurora.

Had it come to Ash's rescue?

"MY *HUMAN. IF ANY EATS HIM, SHOULD BE* ME!"

Oh, maybe not.

The two Leviathans wrestled for space, the wounded one coming up on top, forcing the other to leap to another column.

"*You know that I'm not like those others!*" Ash pleaded. "*I saved you! I stopped the guards from killing you!*" The fury in the Shrieker's eyes lessened, and it looked unsure, or as possible as it was for a massive, salivating monster to look unsure.

"*BLAMED ME,*" it roared at Ash. "*ACCUSED ME. TURNED ME AWAY.*"

"I was scared!"

"*SCARED?*"

"*Scared, like you, like all of us! Scared of what I didn't understand. But I know now. We all need to stop Shaard. The one who uses the Devourer's Song. We need to stop him from releasing it, otherwise there won't be a world left to fight over!*"

A long, deep rumble came from the Shrieker's throat as it studied Ash, adjusting its weight, its large head drawing closer and closer, until Ash could've reached out and touched its snout.

"*EAT HIM! EAT THEM! EAT THE HUMANS!*" the other Shriekers screamed.

But instead the one before Ash probed at him with its Song-aura. Ash let the Shrieker delve deep into his emotions and desires. He shivered, as though standing naked on an ice plain. And even though he wasn't searching for it, Ash felt the Shrieker's inner self too, how scared and upset it was at the wounded, unbalanced world around it. Ash's fears of Leviathans were revealed, but so too were his connections with them and his desire to understand them better. Its Song encircled Ash's core, the very center of all he was. Ash instinctually formed a barrier, just as Rook had. There were some things one couldn't share with others, fragile, precious things that belonged to no one else. It was his *soul*. The Shrieker's aura recoiled at being rejected for a second time.

It was then Ash knew what he had to do.

Ash quashed his instincts to block the Shrieker, remembering what Rook had taught him, and all the distrust and misguided accusations that had been thrown his way during his life. Leviathans had suffered the same. He had to trust the creature; otherwise, how could it ever trust him?

Falling to his knees, Ash bowed his head. Despite the protests of his mind that were begging him to reconsider his plan, Ash dropped his barrier. "*There*," Ash Sang in a small frightened voice. "*This . . . this is who I am.*" Ash was laid bare. *"We need your help to stop Shaard. If we don't, the whole world will be in danger, every single one of us. So I'm asking you . . . No, I'm begging you, to see past your hate, and to help me stop him."* Ash clenched his eyes shut, his Song juddering as he resisted holding his breath.

The Leviathan searched his soul with surprising delicacy and respect. To Ash's amazement, instead of some terrible intrusion, it felt like he was being pulled into an embrace, as though he were being let in on some great secret, strengthening his connection with the Shrieker, his bond to nature, to the entire world. He'd never felt such a part of something, such belonging. Their Songs leaped and danced round each other, these two entirely different creatures, these enemies, weaving an intricate pattern of understanding and kinship. They were both of the same world, and that made them one. Ash felt breathless, elated, as though he could suddenly achieve anything.

Opening his eyes, he found the Shrieker staring back at him, its strange, alien mind racing behind its white eyes. After what felt like an age, the Shrieker reared back its head and let out a scream.

Its Song echoed throughout the plaza, over the Storm Tower and around all of Solstice. Its Song told the other Shriekers of what it had seen in Ash and the truths it had discovered. Ash couldn't understand the words in its Song, but he knew that the emotions, the ideas, they all sounded good.

Ash let out a heavy breath, his limbs feeling like they barely had the strength to move.

"BOY IS TRUE. BOY IS HONEST!"

The other Shriekers let out their ear-piercing screeches, as Rook came up behind Ash.

"You did it!"

Ash smiled at her, but the Shrieker wasn't done with him yet.

"HATEFUL ONE. ANCIENT HEART. MUST STOP!"

"Yes, we need to stop Shaard. I—I need you to get a message to my friends."

Ash still had hope that the *Frostheart* had escaped the Wraiths' wrath, only because Shaard hadn't gloated over the fact that he'd caught them. It wasn't much reassurance, but it was all he had. "They're on a sleigh with red sails, with the sign of a—" Rook shook his shoulder vigorously as the Leviathan cocked its head in confusion.

"Won't understand. Crew won't understand Leviathan flying toward them bearing message."

"I . . . er . . . yeah. I didn't really think that through, I guess . . ."

The Shrieker pulled a strange face, then lifted itself awkwardly onto the ledge, dropping low and flexing as though ready to pounce.

"What . . . ?" Ash began.

The Shrieker bent its legs, lowering its belly close to the rock. It straightened its tail to act as a ramp up onto its back. Ash hesitated. The Shrieker turned its head and snorted with impatience, rocking its back to and fro as if to encourage him.

"No . . ." Ash said. "Absolutely not! You can't be serious!"

"Is *serious*," Rook Sang, pushing Ash forward. "*Leviathans not known to joke around.*"

44
Chase

The world below—far, *far* below—sent Ash's vision spinning. He was drenched in a cold sweat and had the overwhelming desire to barf. He decided that wouldn't be the most sensible idea, however, considering that he was riding on the back of an unpredictable Shrieker, so instead he shut his eyes tight and gripped even tighter on to the creature's sides.

The Shrieker had made short work of the climb to the top of the Storm Tower, the giant sphere casting a shadow over them as it rotated above like a moon.

Rook let out a sound Ash had never heard her make before. It was a squeal . . . of *joy?* She pointed up, trembling with excitement, as there, cresting over the cliffs, was a flurry of black feathers. *"My friends!"* she Sang with delight. *"Came back! Found me!"* She held out her

arms as though they were wings, tears streaming down her cheeks as her dear crows darted and swooshed about her, sharing in her joy.

Ash could only gulp, holding back another urge to puke. The Shrieker adjusted its weight for takeoff, rolling its shoulders and rocking its passengers side to side.

It took a run-up.

"Oh spirits, noooooooooooooooooo!" Ash screamed as the Leviathan leaped from the tower's edge and soared through the air. Ash's stomach fell behind, the speed of their descent so great it knocked the scream from his throat and brought tears streaming from his eyes.

I'm doing this to save the world, I'm doing this to save the world, he chanted in his head, hunkering down as close to the Shrieker as he could. The Shrieker opened its wings, catching an air current and lifting even higher into the sky, over the cliffs that encircled Solstice.

"I HATE THIS!" Ash cried out, burying his head in the Shrieker's rough skin as Rook laughed. The sound of her laughter made Ash untense his muscles just a bit. He actually dared peek over the Shrieker's back.

Okay, that was a mistake. He winced, pulling back fast. The craggy, rocky world was rushing past below them at a tremendous speed. Ash could feel the Shrieker's muscles moving beneath him, expertly shifting depending on the air currents. In the near distance they could see a fleet of black Wraith sleighs, heading straight for a titanic cloud of mist and snow that circled the land, all that remained of the Everstorm and the centuries of churned, blasted ice being buffeted through the air.

Options played out in Ash's head, or at least their worrying lack of them.

There was no way he could take on all of the Wraith fleet, even if he had the help of Rook and a Leviathan. The Wraiths would take control of the Shrieker and make short work of Ash and Rook before they could even get close to the frost-heart.

"The other Song Weavers that Shaard forced onto his sleigh, maybe they'll help us?"

"*Would have to get to them secretly,*" Rook Sang. The Shrieker rumbled its agreement. "*Look there!*" Rook pointed.

Below and farther to the south, streaking toward Solstice, Ash could see the red sails of the *Frostheart*. His heart soared at the welcome sight. They were okay! They'd managed to avoid the Wraiths. Atop the maze of crags the sleigh passed through nestled dozens of Shriekers, stirring and growing agitated. But it wasn't the *Frostheart* they were reacting to. Ash could hear a cry for help, a desperate plea for aid.

It's the frost-heart, Ash realized with shock, *it's calling to them!*

"BROTHERS. SISTERS," the Shrieker they rode Sang to its brethren as they passed overhead. "*AID US. STOP DARK ONE!*"

There were certainly enough Shriekers to tear Shaard's sleighs to shreds, but Ash realized why the Leviathans were hesitating. The Wraiths would use their dark Song to control them and turn them against one another. *Unless we can protect them with the Song Weavers . . .* Ash thought, a plan forming.

The Shrieker whined, alerting Ash to hold on even tighter. They were among the crags now, the tall, rocky spires racing past them as they swerved and shifted in the air to avoid them. *"Please,"* Ash Sang to the Leviathan. *"Land on that sleigh!"*

It screeched its reply, and folded its wings, darting down like an arrow.

It was then that Ash silently swore to never ride a Shrieker again.

The *Frostheart* crew and others Ash did not recognize darted about the main deck in shock, pulling out their bows and preparing for what they believed was an attack. At the last moment the Shrieker opened up its wings, killing its momentum, allowing it to drop gracefully onto the sleigh's main deck.

"Don't shoot, don't shoot!" Ash cried out, trying to

roll off the Shrieker and getting a leg stuck, forcing him to hop around like a lunatic. Rook leaped off with dextrous grace. The Shrieker hissed and bared its fangs at the Pathfinders' weapons.

"ASH?!" the crew said as one. The strangers Ash had spotted were the group of hunters Ottro had left to guard the *Frostheart*, who now gawked at Ash with bewilderment.

"You do realize that's a *Shrieker* you were jus' ridin', right?" Lunah said.

"How in blazes did you *do* that?!" Kob asked.

"Shaard and the Wraiths have the frost-heart!" Ash blurted, wasting no time explaining.

"Shaard made you give it to them?" Tobu growled.

"No, he's the leader of the Wraiths!"

"The Shrieker is the leader of the *Wraiths*?" Lunah asked.

"No! Shaard is the leader of the Wraiths, who are actually evil Song Weavers in masks, and they came to Solstice and stole the frost-heart!" Ash said, exasperated.

The *Frostheart* crew glanced at each other.

"Well, I feel like if you just said that from the beginnin', it woulda saved a whole lotta time," Lunah said.

Ash groaned. He was so happy to be back with these nitwits.

"We saw the black fleet approaching and were forced to hide," Kob explained. "There were just too many of them. But we knew we had to check for survivors and try to find you—to do anything we could to help."

"What of our people?" one of the hunters asked, fear worrying their voice.

"The Wraiths took them all," Ash said, clenching his fists. "He plans to release the Devourer and use it to attack the Strongholds—the whole world! We have to stop him before it's too late, and I think I have a plan!" Most Pathfinder crews would've paled at these words, or just outright disbelieved them. But luckily this was not most Pathfinder crews.

"I say, sounds like we'd better catch up to him, then, eh?" Nuk bellowed from the bridge. "Can't be having an apocalypse now, can we? It's bad for business! We were wondering why the Everstorm chose today to end after a thousand years. Where's that slimy wart headed, Ash?"

"South of here!" Ash pointed in the direction he'd seen the Wraith fleet heading.

"All hands on deck! We have some thieves to catch!" Nuk ordered, heaving hard on the tiller, the *Frostheart* groaning as it changed direction. "Good to have you back, Ash! Life was beginning to feel a tad too quiet without you."

The crew rushed into action, keeping a healthy distance from the Shrieker who eyed them all suspiciously from the middle of the deck. Ash ran to his tent on the upper deck; Lunah punched him in the arm as he passed, a massive grin on her face. Ash grinned back, then bustled into his tent—his wonderful, tiny, stale-smelling tent—and grabbed his bow and quiver, heart racing with fear, but excitement too. Something caused him to freeze, however.

Tobu had arranged his carved sculptures in a line beside his bedding. There was an older female yeti, whom Ash assumed was his life-mate. Next to her, a young yeti cub. *His son*. And beside him, to Ash's surprise, was a figure that looked almost human-kin. A young boy, with messy hair.

Ash let out a shuddering breath and backed out of the tent. He came face-to-face with his guardian himself. Tobu placed a hand on his shoulder.

"Did you find what you sought? The place where you belong?"

"I think so," Ash said with a smile.

He dived forward and buried his head into Tobu's thick, scratchy fur. His face was hot with tears. And then, to Ash's amazement, Tobu hugged him back. It was subtle. It was just an adjustment of his mighty arms, a slight tensing that could've been mistaken for a flinch. Anyone else would've missed it, but Ash knew better.

45

Stronger Together

The black sleighs passed into the giant, swirling clouds of frozen mist that had once been the Everstorm. You could still barely see a few feet in front of your eyes, but it beat rushing through a raging blizzard, that was for sure.

A dark shape swooped across the Wraith sleigh's deck, though it was hard to make out what it was through the thick fog. A Wraith rushed to investigate, huffing shallow, frantic breaths. It snarled as it uncovered nothing in the gloom. Another Wraith joined him at his back, although this one was large. Far larger, in fact, than he ever remembered there being among their crew. He turned just in time to see a black-clad yeti throw him over the side of the sleigh.

Tobu kept low, creeping over to the cages where

the Song Weavers were being held, with Lunah, Rook, and a few of the hunters joining him. The Shrieker who dropped them off rose higher into the mist, Ash clinging to its back, the others soon lost to his sight.

I hope this works . . . Ash prayed.

To create the Wraith costumes, they'd had to use some fine silks that Nuk had picked up in Aurora, and, much to her utter dismay, dip them in tar so that they looked black and aged.

"Do you know how much trade I would've gotten for those?" Nuk had complained.

"We shall reap the profits of a world unended, captain," Master Podd had said.

Nuk had sighed. "As always, you are correct, Master Podd."

It wasn't much of a disguise, but they were hoping that, combined with the thick mist, it would be enough for teams of the crew to sneak aboard two of the black sleighs and release as many Song Weavers as they could, taking out any Wraiths before they could raise the alarm. Then the Song Weavers could be told of the plan to get them out of there. The *Frostheart* was somewhere behind the black sleighs, driven by Nuk, Master Podd, Arla, and Kob, closing in and waiting to come to their aid. Everything was ready. The rest was up to Ash.

"Let's go," Ash whispered to the Shrieker as they hovered above the sleighs below. It growled low in its throat. *Just need to find Shaard in this misty gloop so that we can dive for the frost-heart when the others give the signal . . .*

Ash listened carefully, hoping to use Shaard's own trick against him and hear the cries for help from the frost-heart, using its Song as a beacon just as Shaard had used Rook's. The silence was almost oppressive. The mist dampened the sound further still, making Ash feel closed in and trapped.

Suddenly—

There.

He'd found it: the frost-heart's familiar distant Song.

His heart hurt to hear his friend—as he'd come to think of it—crying out for help.

Strange . . . Ash thought, his nerves tingling. *It doesn't sound like it's coming from any of the sleighs . . . It's . . . it's coming from . . . in front?*

"*DUCK!*" Ash Sang, as the Shrieker dived just in time to escape the slashing claws of another Shrieker that tore through the mist, disappearing again into the endless white. But not before Ash saw the smokelike darkness that gripped its neck and the black-clad figure who rode on its back.

"Shaard!"

Ash tried to hear him, to pinpoint his location, but he couldn't react fast enough. Shaard struck down their side like a spear, his Shrieker rending its talons through Ash's mount, the creature letting out a wailing scream.

"*Still so much to learn,*" Shaard's Song mocked.

Ash pulled his bow from over his shoulder, nocking an arrow while desperately casting his eyes about the mist. Shapes shifted, and the world seemed to roil and sway.

Another crashing, thunderous strike.

Then another, this one nearly ripping the bow from Ash's hand.

Shaard disappeared as fast as he reappeared, hiding

in the mist and leaving no sign or trace as to where he could've gone. Ash's Shrieker whined in pain, adjusting its wings below him, trying to stay airborne despite its wounds. *"I'm sorry! I'm so sorry!"* Ash tried to soothe it. *"He's moving so fast!"*

"NOT ATTACK BROTHER," the Shrieker Sang, despite the fact that their lives could very well depend on doing so.

Ash strained his ears, listening as hard as he could. *Where* was *he?*

The next attack came from directly ahead. Ash loosed his arrow, and Shaard was forced to swerve, his blade missing Ash by a hairsbreadth.

Ash was down to his last arrow.

Ash took a deep breath, trying his best to slow down his racing heart. He focused on his surroundings. The howling of the wind, still strong despite the storm's disappearance. The labored breaths of the wounded Shrieker below him. He could hear the sound of snow shifting under the black fleets' runners, the roar of their enjins, the creak of their rotten timbers.

And he heard the frost-heart's Song coming from above.

Ash fired his bow, and the arrow took Shaard in the arm just as he appeared out of the mist. Shaard roared in pain, his Song's grip over his Shrieker momentarily lost. The Shrieker, regaining its senses, twisted and writhed, trying to throw Shaard from its back. Ash's Shrieker keened in delight, barking out support for its brethren. But before Shaard was thrown, the bitter chant of the Wraiths pierced the mist from the sleighs below, taking control of the Shrieker once again and allowing Shaard to keep his hold on it.

"So close!" Shaard congratulated Ash, tearing the arrow from his shoulder and clutching at his wound as they glided side by side. Despite being shot, Shaard's smile remained as always. "But you forget! We Wraiths stand together as one! Together we are *strong*! What are you? You don't know where you belong! You have no loyalty. You can't even pick a side, and that makes you *weak*!"

But the Wraith Song was not the only Song that could now be heard. Another broke through the mist, this one natural and strong. Ash emerged from the cloud at that very moment into the clear, welcome light of day.

He yelped with joy when he saw that his friends had managed to free the Song Weavers on the two sleighs, and many of their previous Wraith captors lay unconscious on the deck. A battle now raged for control of the Wraith sleighs; Lunah, Tobu, and Rook were fighting through the last Wraith defenders on one, while Kailen led a charge with Twinge, Yallah, and Teya on the other, with freed captives and hunters joining them. The Song Weavers Sang a Song of protection, their combined Song-auras forming a barrier that shielded the dozens of Shriekers that emerged from the mist-clouds, with the *Frostheart* roaring up behind it all.

Shaard's face fell at the sight. The Wraiths across the fleet sent their Song-auras toward the encroaching

Shrieker swarm, but their voices were almost drowned out by the shouts and cheers of their Song Weaver prisoners, who, gaining courage from the events around them, began to add their defiant Songs to the protective weave, guarding the Shriekers who had come to their rescue. The Wraiths couldn't break through the barrier made by the Song Weavers and Leviathans Singing together.

"We're stronger than you think!" Ash cried as he dived down toward Shaard, his Shrieker's talons ready to tear him from its brother's back.

But in a flash of screaming, blinding light, Ash found Shaard torn away from his grasp, the entire world spinning and echoing with the deafening sound of an explosion.

46

Weaker Apart

It happened just off to their left side. The Shrieker cried out in surprise, steadying its wings and catching an up-draft, pulling up to avoid falling. A wall of white snow cascaded over the liberated Wraith sleigh below in a blossom of blinding light. Ash's ears rang and his heart pounded through his chest. Then another explosion, the force of it rattling through his bones.

"What the—" Ash looked back with wide, fearful eyes and saw the unbelievable.

Smudges of darkness stretched from the horizon and poured over the land like a dark flowing scar.

Leviathans.

Hundreds upon hundreds of them, of all shapes and sizes, emerging from the snow and ice and racing toward the Wraith sleighs. It was like a great migration. Ash had never heard of anything like it, let alone seen it.

"*HEAR CALL. PROTECT HEART,*" the Shrieker he rode Sang.

But that was not all that headed their way. Close by, Pathfinder sleighs were following the Leviathans from the west, a small fleet of them. Flowers of fire and light erupted among the Leviathan swarms, flinging giants into the air like leaves in a breeze.

"*Archeoweapons!* It's Commander Stormbreaker!" Ash gasped. "She's followed the Leviathans here!"

"Ah, your beloved Pathfinders, just in time!" Shaard laughed from below. Another explosion boomed, this one blasting a hole right through a liberated sleigh. It swerved and skidded through the snow, nearly capsizing from the force of the impact. He saw his friends clinging on for dear life, the Song Weavers thrown about, the protective barrier dissolving with their concentration.

"NO!" Ash cried.

The Shrieker swarm dived toward the Wraiths, but they were vulnerable without the barrier, and the Wraiths' snaking aura rushed toward them like poison.

Ash could only watch in horror as the Wraiths forced them to turn upon each other, claws and teeth tearing through thick hides.

Ash's Shrieker wailed in pain. *"BROTHERS! SISTERS!"*

Commander Stormbreaker's fleet drew close behind, firing their terrible archeoweapons at the Wraith sleighs and Leviathans both. The *Frostheart* was forced to pull away, the blasts too close for comfort.

We don't have much time; she thinks we're all Wraiths! Ash thought in panic.

"Charge the sleigh toward the Pathfinders!" Shaard commanded the Wraith who still steered the sleigh Tobu's team were on. *"Lead them away from us. Nothing is more important than getting away with the heart, do you understand? For the cause!"*

The Wraith obeyed without question, turning the sleigh in a wide loop before charging through the oncoming archeomek fire, straight toward the swarming Leviathans and oncoming Pathfinder fleet. The *Frostheart* zoomed past it, probably wondering where on earth it was going.

"Seems you have a choice to make, Ash," Shaard shouted, gliding down toward the Wraith fleet. "Do you try to take the frost-heart from me, or do you save your friends? You can't do both!"

He was right.

The sleighs his friends were on were being torn to shreds by Stormbreaker's weapons.

"Perhaps, if you hurry, you could make it in time to persuade Stormbreaker to hold fire. Decisions, decisions . . ."

"How could you do this?!" Ash shouted back. "The sleighs carry Wraiths and Song Weavers too—they'll all die!"

"And they'll sacrifice themselves for a cause greater than themselves! Than all of us! But do you have what it takes, Ash? Can *you* make such a sacrifice to get what you want?"

Ash gritted his teeth. He knew taking back the frost-heart was the most important thing to do. If the Devourer was released, it'd be a great deal more people than one sleigh whose lives would be in danger.

But the Song Weavers were innocent in all this. They'd been forced onto that sleigh. *And . . . and my friends.*

Could he leave them to die? He would never be able to live with himself. He would go back to being all alone . . .

"It's not your fault," the frost-heart Sang to Ash. Its voice cut through the chaos and destruction, still eager to help Ash despite the danger it was in. Despite the fact that Ash had failed it. Its Song lent Ash strength, and saved him from despair, from feeling like everything was crashing around him. *"None of this is your fault."*

With a cry of frustration Ash Sang to the Shrieker,

asking it to head for Stormbreaker's sleigh. It resisted, determined to get the frost-heart.

"*Please!*" Ash pleaded. "*We can't leave them all to die! My friends, the Leviathans, they'll all be killed!*"

"*HEART. HEART. HEART.*"

"*NO!*" Ash Sang more forcefully than he'd intended. "*We have to save them first, and then we'll get back the heart. I promise!*"

The Shrieker wasn't happy about it—Ash could feel its hesitation, the same as his—but it opened its wings, caught a gust, and flew higher into the air, just as Shaard landed safely aboard one of his sleighs.

"*I thought as much!*" Shaard mocked, his Song filling Ash's head as they went in opposite directions. "*You will help the Song Weaver cause, Ash, even if I have to make you.*"

Ash's Shrieker raced past the charging black sleigh, the battle for its control still raging below. Snow erupted round it, shards of the hull exploding into the air.

"*Faster, we have to go faster!*"

The Shrieker screamed with effort.

They stormed past the Leviathan swarm. There were Lurkers, Hurtlers, Spearwurms, and even the hulking forms of Gargants, all with a single-minded determination to catch Shaard's sleigh. The Shrieker cried out as

it saw the frozen bodies of dead Leviathans killed by the archeoweapons. Ash could feel intense sorrow bubbling up inside it.

"*Brothers . . . Sisters . . .*" it howled, before its Song grew red with growing rage. "*HUMANS. KILL.*"

"*I'm going to do everything I can to stop them!*" Ash assured it, but he could feel he was losing the creature's allegiance.

We were so close! We nearly had Shaard; we nearly stopped him!

The Pathfinder sleighs now opened fire upon them, on the only Leviathan actually charging toward them. The Shrieker twisted and twirled through the air, winding through the balls of deathly light, speeding forth with tremendous speed, determined to catch those responsible for this heinous attack.

"*ATTACK. HATE. KILL!*" the Shrieker screamed.

"*DON'T!*" Ash Sang back. "*PLEASE DON'T!*"

But the Shrieker wouldn't listen. It went into a dive, Ash only just managing to stear it toward the Stormbreaker's sleigh, the *Kinspear,* singling it out by the icon emblazoned on its sails of a Leviathan being pierced by an arrow. He could see Song Weavers aboard, Singing to power the strange deadly weapons.

"*HUMANS! KILL! DESTROY!*"

"*STOP IT!*" Ash screamed, forcing his Song-aura to restrain the Shrieker's. He pierced through a crack in its Song and forced his thoughts into its head. The Shrieker flinched as though it had been struck, and they plummeted right down onto the main deck of Stormbreaker's sleigh. Ash's world spun, finally coming to a stop in a wave of pain. His vision was black for a moment, then flared back with red spots. Ash was aware of the Pathfinders surrounding them, firing their bows at the screeching Shrieker.

"Stop it," Ash mumbled, barely able to find his voice. "Please, stop fighting . . ." He pulled himself up, eyes focusing just in time to see the Shrieker slash at a Pathfinder with its claws. A red mist sprayed into the air. The Shrieker was full of arrows, its blue blood leaking from its sides, but it did not still its fury. "STOP IT!" Ash managed to cry.

The Pathfinders ignored him, stabbing at the Shrieker with their spears.

"*GO! LEAVE! SAVE YOURSELF!*" Ash tried Singing at the Leviathan, but it too wouldn't listen.

"*KILL. KILL. KILL!*" it shrieked, and many Pathfinders clutched at their ears in agony.

Ash built a Song up within him. He didn't want to do

this, but he had no choice. He didn't want the Shrieker to get hurt. He wouldn't let anyone else die!

"*GO! LEAVE THIS PLACE!*" Ash screamed, his aura turning dark, almost black, serpentine tendrils wrapping themselves round the Shrieker's aura and forcing it to listen. With a terrible, anguished roar, the Shrieker bounced away off the sleigh. It hit the ground hard, snow spraying as it rolled and somersaulted, before it finally came to a stop, limbs splayed and tail crooked.

Ash was racked with guilt. He watched as the Shrieker struggled to pick itself up, keening out with distress.

I had to do it, Ash tried to assure himself, panting and weak even from a few seconds using the Devourer's Song. *They would've killed each other . . .*

The Pathfinder fleet soared away from the Shrieker's crumpled body, and it was soon lost to Ash's sight.

"Who are *you*?!" came a commanding husky voice. Ash was forced round and found himself face-to-face with Commander Stormbreaker herself. "Explain yourself! What do you think you're *doing*?!"

"Song Weaver traitor!" the Pathfinders growled, and one jabbed his spear toward Ash.

"Please . . ." Ash managed to say, "stop shooting the archeoweapons—you're making things worse!"

"Watch your tongue, boy! Do you know who you're speaking to?" said a crewman.

"The Leviathans must be destroyed, and their Wraith allies with them," Stormbreaker said, a large blade ready in her hand.

"The Leviathans are trying to help!" Ash cried out.

"Pah, the boy's lost his mind to their Song!" another Pathfinder said, seizing Ash with his big arms.

"That Wraith sleigh is not what you think it is, it's full of innocents!" Every muscle in Ash's body cried out in pain.

"*Innocents?*" Stormbreaker asked.

"Song Weavers, *Pathfinders* . . ."

Concern flickered across Stormbreaker's face at this, her eye locking on Ash's as her thoughts raced. Still the archeoweapons fired at the Leviathan swarm, at the Wraith sleigh that had tried to charge them, but now sat broken and still upon the ravaged snow, too damaged to move. Smoke poured from between its timbers, the amber flicker of fires reflecting off the black wood. Could his friends possibly still be alive after all this?

"Why should I trust *you*? You attacked us, mounted on a bloodthirsty Leviathan!"

"*Please* . . ." Ash pleaded, desperate. "There's no time for this! I'm not your enemy. Everyone over there—

they're friends—they're trying to stop the Wraiths from releasing the Devourer!"

At this the Commander's eye widened.

"CEASE FIRE!" she ordered.

Her crew were clearly shocked, but signal flags were raised for all the other sleighs to see. The Song Weavers who were controlling the archeoweapons stopped their Singing. In a few moments the Pathfinder sleighs went quiet.

The silence was almost deafening after all that chaos and noise.

And to Ash, that seemed about as good a time as any to fall back down onto the deck, unconscious.

47

One Step Behind

Being the closest to the *Frostheart*'s warming sunstone enjin, Arla's healing tent was always nice, cozy, and soft. All the herbs that dangled from its scaffolding gave it a natural smell. A smell of earth and wet leaves, of exotic plants that once rubbed would leave a pleasant smell on the fingers.

Ash sighed, wrapping himself tightly within his bed furs. He didn't want to ask why he was there, or for how long, but he supposed he should. Opening an eye, he nearly jumped out of his skin. Lunah's face was an inch away, her bright brown eyes studying his face.

"Oh good, you're awake." She had a deep cut on her forehead.

"You're gonna give me a heart attack one day!" Ash wheezed.

"*Please*, you've been through worse 'n that." Ash supposed she was right, as the memories of the chase flooded back into his brain. "Remember when I hid in that barrel for a whole hour in the hold an' jumped out an' made you scream like a baby? THAT was something worth havin' a heart attack over."

"When you put it that way . . ." Ash groaned. He sat up in his bed, wincing at the aches that still burned in his muscles. "How is everyone, did they all—"

"They're all fine," Tobu said; he had been sitting behind Lunah. "Go easy, boy, you took quite the fall."

"That was pretty awesome what you did back there, Ash!" Lunah said, making a bird shape with her hand and waving it through the air. "I saw you soarin' through the sky on that Shrieker! Maaaaaaan! What I wouldn't give! Ash, *Monster Rider and Deck Diver*. And yet you still can't make 'em do a backflip . . ."

"We gained control of the two sleighs we attacked and have taken the Wraiths prisoner," Tobu continued.

So the Wraiths' secret must be out, Ash thought. *They're not demons or ghosts. They're Song Weavers, but no less vengeful than a monster from the underworld. Will that make the Strongholders hate Song Weavers even more?*

"Most of the Song Weavers we freed have been

taken aboard Commander Stormbreaker's sleighs. The
ones who survived."

Ash pulled a face. "Better than being in Shaard's
evil-doomsday-death army, I suppose."

"That could be applied to many things in life," Lunah
said wisely.

"What about . . . what about Shaard?" Ash was almost too afraid to hear the answer. Both Tobu's and Lunah's faces darkened.

"He got away," Tobu said. "With the frost-heart, and
many more Song Weaver prisoners."

Ash's insides twisted. He clenched his eyes shut. "He has everything he needs. The frost-heart . . . Elder Nell to show him how to open the Devourer's prison . . . I've—I've failed. Everyone was counting on me, and I've failed them all . . ."

"We'll stop him. This is not over," Tobu said.

"Yeah, not by a long shot!" Lunah said, flexing her muscles. "We're still hot on his tail, an' now we have Commander Stormbreaker at our back, not to mention the blimmin' horde of Leviathans chasin' after him. He's as good as done, he is. He can't run forever."

"And . . . you'll be coming with us?" Ash asked Lunah hopefully.

"Me? Yeah, course!"

"But . . . your Proving . . . ?"

"The Provin' can wait, I think. There's more important things goin' on—what with this maybe being the end of the world an' all. But *stars above*, I did find Solstice, so anythin' else should be a breeze, right? Guess that means I'm stuck with you losers for a bit longer, though."

Ash laughed, and his ribs hurt.

Captain Nuk poked her head into the tent, investigating the sounds of their voices.

"Ah, the hero awakens!"

She came to Ash's bedside, the gentlest of smiles on

her face, as though she were happy to see him, but worried about something all the same. "How are you feeling, Ash, dear boy?"

"Okay, I think. A bit groggy."

"Aye, well, I'm not surprised. It's a rare day you see a young boy riding on the back of a Shrieker!" She ruffled his hair. "The Commander would like to speak with you, I'm afraid. But if you're not ready, I'll tell her that she can jolly well wait."

"I'll—I'll speak with her," Ash said. She had seemed to recognize the name of the Devourer, and that made Ash curious.

"Only if you're ready. Don't let her boss you around like she does everyone else."

Ash nodded but got out of bed. He had to steady himself as the tent spun, but his head soon cleared, and he was ready to go.

"Thanks for having me back," Ash said quietly.

The others shared a look.

"Ash, it was like you never left," Nuk said.

Ash nodded.

"No, seriously, you were barely gone a day," Lunah added.

"It is important one follows their own path, wherever it may take them," Tobu said.

Ash nodded and took a deep breath, preparing himself for Stormbreaker's questions.

"I'm just glad it brought you back here," Tobu said before leaving the tent himself.

With a smile, Ash followed.

It was early morning outside, the air misty, crisp and cold, not yet touched by Mother Sun's light. The *Frostheart* was in formation with the Pathfinder fleet, with Stormbreaker's large battle-sleigh *Kinspear* running alongside them. It wasn't every sleigh the Pathfinder fleet could muster, but it was an impressive sight nonetheless.

Ash was relieved to see the entire crew there going about their duties. Rook stood at the prow, her crows perched at her side, hood back up to disguise her Wraith features. Commander Stormbreaker stood in the center of the *Frostheart*'s deck, flanked by four Pathfinders, her large cloak flowing in the wind. She wore a strange expression as Ash approached, her one eye burrowing into him as she studied him intently. It was like being examined by the Shrieker's Song all over again. Her mind was clearly racing behind that sharp eye, usually so cool and calm, but now edged with intrigue. Ash swallowed hard. He had a strange sensation when he saw her, but he suspected it was because he was being stared at by the most powerful person in all the Snow Sea.

"Thank you for coming to speak with me." Storm-breaker greeted him with a smile. Her voice was gentle and kind now, and seemed out of place coming from such a vicious warrior.

"Mm," Ash mumbled, not out of rudeness, but from nerves.

"Seems you were trustworthy after all, though I might have some suggestions for your entrances in the future. Still, I thank you for your warning. I would never have forgiven myself had I killed any of our own." Ash stared at his feet. He felt vulnerable, despite Nuk, Lunah, and Tobu standing just behind him. "It was an incredibly brave thing you did, charging headlong into the fire like that."

Ash nodded. A silence drew out for a time.

"Tell me, boy, what do you know about the Devourer? The few that know of it believe it to be just a legend. But you seem convinced it is real."

Ash took a deep breath. "I've—I've heard it's a powerful Leviathan, the strongest one that's ever lived. The ancient Leviathans and Song Weavers from the World Before sealed it away with a powerful Song, but—but if Shaard releases it, it will destroy everything . . . Oh! A man named Shaard is the leader of the Wraiths." Ash realized she probably had no idea who he was.

But he was wrong. "Unfortunately I've crossed paths with Shaard before," Stormbreaker spat with distaste. "So he has everything he needs to release this monster?"

Ash nodded.

"Then the situation is far worse than I thought. We must do all we can to stop him, or else every single Stronghold will be in danger."

"You . . . you believe in the Devourer too? I—I only ask in case you know how we can stop it."

Stormbreaker looked to the brightening horizon, flakes of snow shining in her hair.

"The Devourer is what set me on my crusade against the Leviathans. The Devourer stole everything from me. My life-mate. My *child* . . ." She dropped her guard then and looked so terribly sad that Ash had the urge to hug her. She composed herself, her emotional, broken expression replaced by her usual stoic, implacable face of a fierce warrior. "*Ferno, what have you got us into now . . . ?*" she muttered under her breath with a bleak little laugh.

Ash went cold as ice. His senses burned, his head spun, his knees trembled.

Tobu's eyes narrowed. "Ferno . . . ?"

Stormbreaker nodded. "He was my life-mate."

"Did you ever go by the name Ember, commander?"

Nuk asked, side-eyeing Ash, whose thoughts were churning faster than he could make sense of them.

The commander blinked, surprised. "That—that was the name I used to be known by . . . back at the Fira Stronghold, where I come from. How do you know that?"

Ash tried to speak, but his voice caught in his throat. He swallowed and managed to get out his burning question.

The most important question he'd ever asked in his whole life.

"*Mum . . . ?*"